MW01242562

# Whispers

# in the

# Tropics

A Novel

Glenda Potts

Contact the author:

https://www.facebook.com/GlendaPottsAuthor

*Valerie,*
*May we hear divine*
*whispers to bless*
*our lives!*
*Brenda Potts*

This book is dedicated with love to my husband and family. And with humble appreciation to friends who encouraged me in my writing or offered valued expertise during production.

# CHAPTER 1

A bolt of anxiety zigzagged through Tiffany Birdwell the moment she stepped onto the swinging bridge stretching high above a rainforest in Costa Rica. Gasping, she flung her arms up in the air and straddled the bridge as it swayed sharply from side to side. "What's happening?" she cried.

"Excuse me! You can't loiter in the middle of this skinny bridge," bellowed a short stocky woman behind her. "You're blocking the way for the rest of us."

Tiffany lowered her head and lunged for the guardrail. "Sorry. I'm so sorry." Clutching the rail with both hands, her knuckles turned whiter than the clouds above.

The huffy woman, a member of the tour group Tiffany joined for a morning hike in the Monteverde Cloud Forest Reserve, tapped her on the shoulder. "I mean, the bridge may be about a football field in length but it's only a yardstick wide. And surely you knew it would move. After all it *is* a swinging bridge."

Cold-blooded fear clung to Tiffany like a leech,

sucking away her logic and self-control. Fueled with images of disaster, she whispered, "I ... I know, but I—"

"You shouldn't have signed up if heights send you into orbit." The woman scowled and cut loose with a few steps from an Irish Jig. "See—it doesn't take much to make the bridge move."

Closing her eyes, Tiffany pictured the thick support cables of the suspension bridge snapping loose to dangle like snakes from a tree limb. In her mind's eye the collapsing footbridge sent her tumbling through space toward the thriving terrarium far below.

When she managed to open her eyes Zachary, the tall handsome guide with piercing blue eyes stood before her. "What happened?" he asked, ruffling his thick blond hair. "Are you okay? Trust me; the bridges are designed to sway. Besides, they are inspected frequently."

"That's good to know," she said, longing to disappear into thin air.

"So, will you be all right?"

"I ... I ..." Tiffany shook her head. "Yes, I'll be fine." But she couldn't stop thinking about the earthquake that hit Costa Rica along the Pacific coast the previous year. Though half-expecting tremors to rattle the rainforest at any moment and send her flying, she lifted her chin and loosened her grip on the side of the bridge. Flipping a hand through the air, she motioned for him to leave. "Don't mind me; just go on. You've got a job to do."

Tiffany wanted to trust the guide. She wanted to believe the bridge would not collapse out from under her, but she had a habit of expecting the worst in scary or unfamiliar situations that nearly drove her nuts.

Zachary spoke briefly to the group about the safety of the swinging bridges, and reminded them they were designed to move. "However, I'll ask you to please refrain from running or jumping—anything that would create unnecessary movement."

Embarrassed, Tiffany ducked her head and inched along the side of the bridge as though delicate jewels dotted the walkway. She caught up with the group in time to hear Zachary describe a few of the plants and trees indigenous to the rainforest. And for a few moments the new information and Zachary's long, muscular brown legs distracted her. But then she made the mistake of glancing down.

The view through the bridge's steel mesh floor gave the illusion of walking on top of the jungle, as well as in it, causing angst and exhilaration to spar within her. It reminded her of the time she rode a Ferris wheel that stopped when her seat reached the top. It had rocked precariously in mid-air for what seemed like forever.

Tiffany was far more than a thrill-seeking tourist trying to escape life's mundane moments in an exotic rainforest. She had come to Costa Rica to study tropical biology. And after completing a couple of semesters, she planned to return to the University of San Diego in California to finish her studies. Eventually, she hoped to teach high school biology in her home state of Kansas. This was her dream, but she doubted it would happen since the mere thought of speaking publicly made her heart pound. The contradiction between what she wanted to do and what she believed herself capable of doing kept her on edge.

She couldn't credit bravery for finally making the decision to study so far from home. She had wavered for weeks, but Margaret, her college roommate had insisted, and even offered to accompany her. "I'll spend the summer helping you adjust to living in a foreign country,"

Margaret had said. But on their first full day in the tropics Margaret refused to leave the hotel room.

Tiffany wanted to believe the courage to travel all the way to Central America to study was evidence fearfulness had begun to fleck away from her soul—perhaps in little bits, like well-hung wallpaper painstakingly removed. If so, maybe crossing the swinging bridges would remove another piece.

The rude woman, who earlier taunted Tiffany, jerked a list from her blue nylon fanny pack that had the name Lucy plastered across it. "Will we see a toucan today?" she asked. "And by the way, how do they differ from a scarlet macaw? Are they the same size? Sound alike? Look alike?"

Zachary raised his eyebrows. "To answer your first question—"

"And what can you tell us about a quetzal? When do you think we'll see one?" Lucy asked as she pulled a well-worn guidebook on Central American birds from her backpack.

"I can't promise we'll see a toucan or a scarlet macaw, let alone a—"

"And why is that?" asked Lucy.

Rubbing his hand hard over the back of his neck, Zachary explained it was rare to spot a quetzal. "They're wary birds that sit high in the trees, sometimes motionless for hours. They're widely revered, and lots of tourists come here for the sole purpose of seeing a quetzal, but few actually get to see one."

Lucy grunted and shook her guidebook in the air. "That's disappointing. This book indicates the quetzal is the greatest find in the rainforest, so I hope you can scare one up this morning."

Tiffany had not given much thought to tropical birds

since observing a few as a young girl in the aviary at the San Diego Zoo, but her recent commitment to study plants and animals of the rainforest had sparked a special interest in the exotic creatures. "Will you please tell us about the toucan?" she asked.

Smiling, Zachary described the keel-billed toucan as one of six different species of toucans common to the Monteverde area of Costa Rica. "It's often referred to as rainbow-billed because it has a colorful beak of yellow, lime, orange, pale blue, and crimson."

Lucy riffled the pages of her guidebook. "So what about the scarlet macaws? What do you know about them?"

Tapping his fingers on the guardrail, Zachary told the group the scarlet macaws were about thirty-four inches in length and capable of making ear-piercing noises with a proud air of authority while moving from branch to branch.

"What do they look like?" asked Lucy. "Can you tell us?"

Zachary tightened his jaw muscles. "The scarlet macaws are magnificent birds with colorful feathers of yellow, green, and blue. But I'm sorry to say they are now an endangered species. In fact, they're seldom spotted here in the reserve."

"And what do they eat?" Lucy persisted.

"Nuts and fruits in the canopy of trees."

Tiffany knit her eyebrows together. "So what has endangered the scarlet macaws?" she asked, admiring Zachary's patience with the overbearing woman, whose rapid-fire approach to asking questions made her insides squirm.

"When developers clear forests located near human settlements for building projects their natural habitat is disturbed. Plus, I'm sorry to say that many people trap them to sell as pets."

Tiffany flinched at her dismal images of felled trees and caged birds. "Can anything be done to stop this injustice?" she asked. "It makes me sad that the greed of man often trumps the needs of wildlife."

Zachary's eyes brightened as he explained several conservation groups had made plans to reestablish the scarlet macaw population through a number of breeding programs.

When he continued to lead the group over the first bridge, Tiffany hovered at the side for a moment to stare at the jaw-dropping view. The mass of trees looked like they had been painted from a palette of pale to bright green. Sighing deeply, she gazed at the soft blue sky that met the top of the sprawling green canvas, hoping the beauty of the compelling rainforest would override her feeling of impending doom.

As Tiffany left the side of the bridge to rejoin the group, a slender young woman wearing a black T-shirt, black denim shorts, and black heavy-duty hiking boots fell into line beside her. Covered with copper-colored freckles, the woman of average height appeared to be in her early thirties. "Hi, I'm Katy Kelly from Chicago. I'm backpacking through Costa Rica this summer," she said, offering Tiffany her hand.

Tiffany stated her full name, Tiffany Faith Birdwell, and explained why she had come. Then she fanned out her arm. "Can you believe all of this? The bridge reminds me of a magic carpet the way it stretches out over the trees and funnels us into this intriguing place."

"I'd say that's overstating it," Katy said.

"And to think we might actually see wildlife! This is all so unbelievable that I wonder if I'm dreaming."

Katy's eyes widened. "Dreaming? My goodness, you really are invested in the spirit of this place, aren't you?"

"And you're not? Even though I only arrived yesterday, I'm already in love with the tropics."

"Yes, the rainforest is nice," said Katy.

Tiffany shot her a shocked look. "*Nice? Only nice?* It's such an amazing panorama that it exceeds all of my expectations. And it's hard to believe my roommate Margaret slept in this morning and missed all of this." Margaret's blasé attitude toward the lush beauty of the tropics baffled Tiffany so much that she questioned her sanity.

"And you signed up to come without her?"

Tiffany sighed. "And I probably shouldn't have, since I'm afraid of heights. I don't know how I missed hearing that the tour included walking across a series of swinging bridges."

Katy tucked a strand of russet-red hair behind her ear. "Yes, I noticed you were intimidated right from the start, but I'm sure the bridges are safe."

"I suppose, but I have a tendency to fret about everything."

"So you're a worrier?"

Tiffany frowned. "I'm afraid so. I worry whenever I have to travel by plane, and every time a cloud comes up, I start to fret that it means a tornado is in the forecast. And I could go on, but I'll spare you."

"But a lot of people are afraid to travel by plane. And a healthy respect for a tornado is wise."

"But my reaction is excessive. And I'm even more afraid of the things I cannot touch or see."

"Like what?"

"Like the fear of failure or rejection."

"So you're insecure?"

Disgusted over behaving like a nervous turtle bobbing its head in and out of its protective shell, curious one minute and scared the next, Tiffany's laugh came out as a grunt. "You nailed it. And it keeps me from doing things I want to do."

*What is it about this Katy woman that makes me spill my guts? Thank goodness I won't see her again after this morning.*

"So you're afraid of what *might* happen or of things that exist mostly in your mind?" asked Katy.

"Exactly! I want to teach high school biology, but it chills me to the core just to think about speaking to a group of people, even teenagers," Tiffany said, feeling her face burn. "Maybe I should say, especially teenagers— most of them are such hard critics."

"If you want to teach school, then you'll have to find a way to overcome your phobia about talking in front of others."

"But how? Are you implying it's a choice I can just decide to make?" Tiffany wished she could push a button to erase her last several remarks. She wanted to appear brave and in control like everyone else, but when anxiety struck, she usually talked too much, often making ill-timed remarks.

"Yes, I believe you do have a choice. You have to stop assuming dreams can't come true. Just make up your mind you can and will become a teacher. Just do it."

Tiffany touched the small gold cross hanging from her neck and gently rubbed the dove of peace nestled in the center. She disagreed that conquering fear was a matter of choice. It could not be as simple as making up your mind—at least not for her. She needed help to make such a turnaround. And right now it seemed impossible to think she ever could.

Seconds later, Lucy slowed her pace to stroll alongside Tiffany and Katy, who brought up the rear. "Say, I read in my travel guidebook that several of these swinging bridges are suspended somewhere around two hundred feet above the earth. That's really high, you know; it kind of gives me the shivers."

Tiffany squeezed her sweaty palms into fists.

Lucy stared at Tiffany. "In fact, I've noticed you poking behind, and behaving as though you think we're all about to swing into oblivion. It makes me wonder why you came." She laughed and walked away.

Katy shook her head. "Let's catch up with the rest of the group. We don't want to miss any more of Zachary's good information about this place."

"Go on ahead. I'll just be a second." Tiffany nodded to her left. "I'm going to take a couple of pictures of these epiphytes."

Katy waited, looking puzzled. "Epiphytes?"

"Epiphytes are plants that grow on trees."

"That's right, you said you're a biology student."

Focusing her camera lens on a tangled mass of tropical vegetation in the center of a tree trunk, Tiffany honed in on a specific exquisite white orchid with deep lavender edges, snapping until satisfied she had a perfect shot of the beautiful flower. "The bromeliads and orchids make the trees look like mini flower gardens," she said, "and I love how the thick, gnarled vines cling to the trees as they weave upward toward the light."

Katy shrugged. "I hadn't noticed."

"Hmmm … Do you suppose we're like plants?" Tiffany asked as she studied a few epiphytes through her binoculars.

"What do you mean?" Katy scrunched up her face.

"I'm not sure. There's such a mystery about creation

that it makes me wonder about a lot of things."

"For instance?"

"Like whether the Creator wants us to lean on Him for nourishment and support instead of trying to go through life alone?"

"What are you talking about?" Katy asked, raising her voice.

"Maybe the way epiphytes grow on the trees for nourishment or the way vines climb to the top to reach the light is how we should rely on the Lord." At Katy's strange expression, Tiffany added, "You know, maybe we are meant to rely on Jesus for a healthier way of life? And maybe He'll open our eyes to see the light or truth of our situations as we cling to Him?"

Frowning, Katy darted her eyes between Tiffany and the epiphytes. "I'm not sure where you're going with this. Are you suggesting we should gravitate toward some divine light in search of protection and guidance for our lives?"

"Maybe …" Tiffany wanted to take back her reference to Jesus as soon as it left her mouth. Katy would think her nuts for certain.

Scowling at Tiffany, Katy slowly shook her head back and forth. "No. I'd say comparing us to plants is absurd. You've gotten too philosophical for me."

"I didn't mean to sound ridiculous. And I admit it's a new wrinkle for me." Tiffany regretted she had spoken her mind over something so abstract.

With a lop-sided smile, Katy said, "I'm so sorry I can't stick around this wonderful rainforest much longer to try to wrap my head around your far-fetched ideas."

Katy's sarcasm did not bother Tiffany, for although her courage rushed in and out like sea waves teasing the shoreline, overall, the charm and mystery of the rainforest emitted a special peace that fed her with the hope she could some day metamorphose into someone confident and brave.

Suddenly, Tiffany staggered and grabbed the guardrail. "What was that?" she asked as the bridge swayed back and forth. Shaking like a puppy during a spring storm, the familiar inner battle between awe and apprehension made her weary. Why did she think she could do this? Was she crazy?

But this time, Tiffany refused to linger by the side. She let go of the rail and turned to catch Katy's eye. Determined to continue hiking across the bridge, she lifted her chin and tucked her bright yellow T-shirt into her faded blue jeans. "Let's go. My apprehension is wearing me out."

Could Tiffany, if given enough time, become the victor in the age-old conflict between fear and faith? It was a major question that often plagued her.

## CHAPTER 2

"This is such a rare and beautiful place. I find it ironic that an insecure farm girl from Kansas is walking in an exotic jungle. I love all of the stimulating sights and exciting sounds." Tiffany said, as she and Katy hurried to catch up with the group at the mid-way point of the first swinging bridge.

"Did you hear Zachary say the mist-filled clouds blow in from the coast and provide the rainforest with the important nutrients and moisture it needs to thrive and grow?" Katy gave her head a good shake. "And right now, the heavy mist has made my hair damp."

"But the mist that borders on rain shouldn't surprise us. After all, it's called a rainforest with good reason."

Katy raised an eyebrow. "Well it has certainly done a number on your hair."

"No doubt. Sometimes I'd like to trade hair with my friend Margaret. She has blonde hair that's pencil-straight, while mine is creepy black and ridiculously frizzy, especially in humid weather."

"Talk about blond hair—have you noticed Zachary's

hair?" asked Katy.

"Come on now, anxiety may have kept me from appreciating the full joy and wonder of the tropics, but I'm not blind." Tiffany let a plucky smile tease her face at the thought of Zachary's thick golden curls.

"I've seen Zachary glancing at you with a quizzical expression as though he doubted you were listening."

"No, I haven't heard his every word, but enough to recognize he knows a lot about the rainforest."

"And his charm makes learning all the more fun, doesn't it?" Katy arched her eyebrows. "Lucy seems to enjoy him. She always works her way in to stand as close to him as possible."

"Don't mention her name. That obnoxious woman makes me want to scream."

"I've noticed. And so has she, which is why she keeps after you. You need to work on that."

Tiffany rolled her eyes. "So did you spot Zachary's tattoo? It's a tiny frog on his left arm. It's the Blue-jeans frog—named that because its purplish-black back legs contrast with its orange body, which gives it the appearance of wearing a pair of blue jeans."

"Are they common to Costa Rica?"

"Yes, but beware—even though the Blue-jeans frog is cute and innocent looking, it's poisonous," Tiffany said.

"What's the matter? Did you think I planned to pick one up?"

"How would I know what you might do? We're total strangers."

Katy hooted. "You're absolutely right. But strangers or not, I'm going to share a secret with you. I have a small tattoo of a blue butterfly on my left shoulder."

Tiffany clamped a hand over her mouth. "I can't imagine having a tattoo. But I do like Zachary's little frog—the way it's poised on his arm as though ready to jump off to parts unknown."

Katy smiled. "I wonder if he views the little guy as a symbol of freedom and courage. That's what my butterfly tattoo meant to me when I got it several years ago."

An animal barked in the distance just as Tiffany and Katy rejoined the group. "What was that?" cried Lucy, who was underfoot again.

"The cry of a howler monkey," Zachary answered. "They're black and—"

"What? Cry of what?" Lucy asked.

"A howler monkey," Zachary repeated. "Howlers are common to the rainforests of Central America and—"

"A monkey? And I thought it sounded like a dog." Lucy cackled as though someone had delivered the punch line of an award-winning joke.

"Lots of people think it sounds like a dog barking," Zachary said. "The howlers are among the loudest of all the animals in Central and South America."

"Oh right, I forgot. I've actually read about them," Lucy said. Then she informed anyone within earshot that her guidebook stated the male howler monkey was about the size of a small dog and could be heard up to two miles away in the jungle and as far away as three miles across a lake. "Oh, and the book also says the males make a loud guttural howl, while the females only wail and groan."

"Correct, and you've just finished my spiel about the howlers," Zachary said, looking at Lucy. Then he turned to the group and announced that since they were at the end of the first bridge, they would take a ten minute break. "It will give everybody an opportunity to take photographs and make individual observations."

After the group scattered along the bridge, Tiffany

focused her camera on a small, brightly colored bird perched on a wide frond of a nearby fern. "Zachary handled Lucy with the patience and grace any mother would surely praise," she told Katy. Then she glanced at Zachary in time to see him dig through his backpack, jerk out a bottle of water, uncap it, and gulp greedily. While she pondered the likely source of Zachary's apparent frustration, a shrill, rhythmic sound resonated throughout the forest.

"I wonder if that's the elusive quetzal," Lucy said, appearing from nowhere. "Or if they're even in this part of the world."

Katy lifted her binoculars to search for the screeching bird. "From what I understand, they're worth the wait."

Tiffany didn't want anything or anyone to spoil her high from making it across the first bridge, so she turned her back to Lucy. Taking a deep breath of the moist morning air, she began to recall some of Zachary's information about the tropical birds of the Monteverde rainforest.

Then she turned to Katy, and expressed her desire to learn all about the big exotic birds. "I'd like to be able to identify them by sound, as well as by sight."

Katy smiled. "I've read very little about the birds. They're interesting and beautiful, but I'll leave the studying to you."

"What makes you think there's room for another expert on tropical birds?" asked Lucy.

Tiffany frowned. "I haven't a doubt." But in truth, she did doubt. She doubted everything, but Lucy's attitude fed her stubborn streak.

Katy winked at Tiffany as Lucy sauntered off.

Tiffany muttered through clenched teeth, "She makes my stomach feel like a swarm of ants has invaded it. It's all I can do not to slap her."

"She bugs me, too. But we should try to ignore her."

Tiffany shuddered. "I'm already uptight about the height of these bridges, so I don't need her ridiculous sarcasm making matters worse."

"She's after attention—always heckling somebody. And it's for sure she has you figured out," Katy said, as Zachary announced they would begin hiking over the second bridge.

"Yeah, and all of my ambivalence makes it easy for her, doesn't it? One minute I'm scared, and the next minute I'm entertaining some grandiose idea of staying on to work as a naturalist. Maybe I'm nuts," Tiffany said as they followed the group.

"Or just confused. I think using the rainforest as a classroom sounds like fun."

"Yes, it sounds intriguing all right, but what am I saying? I couldn't do it—speak in front of others as if I had all the answers. And there would always be someone like Lucy to intimidate me."

The bridge jerked and swayed. Tiffany lurched. She stumbled. She grabbed the guardrail, ducking her head as though a bee had buzzed her ear.

"What's wrong?" asked Katy. "A little boy just rushed past, causing the bridge to rock more than usual. I have a fair imagination myself, but I believe the bridges are safe. They probably undergo annual inspections. Maybe this is a time to trust. Maybe it's a time for blind faith."

Frowning, Tiffany said, "Whatever that is."

Katy shook her head. "Yeah, whatever that is."

Forcing a laugh that came out as a cackle, Tiffany turned to walk alongside Katy. "I'd love to have your logic. I always presume the worst."

Katy gave Tiffany a pensive look. "It isn't always easy

to trust, is it?"

"Not for me. I have a habit of conjuring up unrealistic situations. Only moments ago, I imagined a jaguar waiting for me with open jaws—somewhere down there." Tiffany shuddered as she peeked over the side of the bridge.

"I've read there aren't many jaguars around these days and that they don't often bite, unless they're frightened."

After catching up with the rest of the group, they heard Zachary say jaguars were an endangered species. "They rarely attack people unless provoked," he said.

"I told you so," Katy mouthed to Tiffany.

After Zachary invited the group to move on, he remained behind a few seconds. "I noticed your reaction when that kid flew by a while ago. Are you okay?" he asked Tiffany. "Are you dizzy? I *promise* the bridges are safe."

"That's what I hear." Tiffany faked a smile as embarrassment heated her from head to toe.

"You made it through the first bridge, and we're almost over the second one. When we're back on firm ground again, we'll break for a few minutes before crossing the third and final bridge. And by the way, it's a short one, so hang in there. Of course, we have to backtrack, but you'll be used to the bridges by then. You'll be fine."

Katy moseyed with Zachary to the front of the group, while Tiffany lingered to admire the massive ferns and showy flowers clinging to the trees. The bridges held an aura of power that intimidated her into believing they would collapse and leave her grappling for a swinging vine.

In the middle of a new adventure, and on the verge of embarking upon many others, she wanted to remain calm and clear-headed. She wanted to loosen up. So she planted her feet firmly along the side of the bridge, held on to the rail, and looked out over the rainforest to focus on the divine assistance she had heard others talk about. She did not often pray. And when she did, she never knew where to direct her needs or how to connect to a supreme being on a personal level.

Without looking up or bowing her head, she took several deep breaths and fixed her eyes just above the rippling treetops, hoping her thoughts and concerns would somehow drift heavenward.

*Help me ... Please? Help me trust—not just on this bridge today, but in other places and other times.*

Like a fine tropical mist, the unspoken words sprinkled her soul with a smattering of peace. And as she continued to admire the beauty stretching before her, an image of herself walking tall and brave flashed before her. She liked the confident girl she saw so much that she lifted her shoulders and smiled. And in that euphoric moment, the sky opened and waters parted, giving her something important to savor and build on.

"Thank you," she whispered as the bridge continued to sway. But this time it seemed to move with pride and durability, as though begging for appreciation. She even had a flicker of respect for the workmen involved in the amazing engineering feat of the bridge.

This current wave of encouragement brought about an unfamiliar cockiness. In awe of her mini-miracle, she stepped forward with growing confidence and a breath of courage to cross the remaining bridges.

## CHAPTER 3

"It's about time you returned. Where have you been?" Margaret asked, as Tiffany rushed into their hotel room.

"Where have I been?" Tiffany dropped her hiking gear to the floor. "I can't believe you'd ask that after refusing to go with me."

"I refused to go? No, you slipped off without me."

Tiffany walked to the window and plopped onto a chair. She pulled off her hiking boots, letting them plunk onto the floor. "Yesterday evening you said the rainforest could wait and that you intended to sleep in today. Remember?"

Margaret jammed her hands into the pockets of the lime green cotton T-shirt she wore over her bright orange bikini. "But I didn't know you planned to dump me at this dinky hotel all day long."

"Dinky? Well aren't we in some kind of a mood," Tiffany said. She considered the hotel at the edge of Santa Elena small and rustic, but nice. "I made it clear I wanted you to go. I hated the idea of going alone with strangers."

"Then you should have stayed here and sunbathed by

the pool with me. So why did you decide to go alone?"

"I'd read about this area for weeks and didn't want to wait another day to take a first-hand look."

"So what happened?"

Irritated at Margaret, Tiffany decided to collect her thoughts before answering. She stood and looked out the window at a row of hydrangea bushes lining the fence. Then she lifted her gaze from the beautiful blue blossoms to the dense, green terrain just beyond the hotel property that swelled and dipped with character.

Lured by the mystic rainforest, Tiffany had tiptoed out of the room as Margaret slept. And even though she believed Margaret could sleep through a monkey jumping through the window and swinging on the overhead light fixture, she had carefully turned the knob and inched the door shut so she wouldn't awaken her.

Margaret stamped her foot. "Listen here, I'm not going to let your silent treatment guilt me into apologizing for not going with you. I plan to nurse my jetlag for days—whatever it takes to get back to normal."

Tiffany suddenly felt a little smug that Margaret had missed out on the adventure. She turned to look at her. "You asked how it went—I'll start at the beginning and be brief. Early this morning, while you slept like the dead, I joined a group of tourists in the hotel lobby for a tour in the rainforest. The guide, Zachary Caldwell briefed us on what to expect. Then we rode in vans to the top of the mountain to begin the two hour hike. Zachary pointed out a number of interesting plants, animals, and birds as we hiked over a series of swinging bridges."

"Swinging bridges? I thought you were afraid of heights."

"I am. But I signed up in such a hurry that I didn't notice the details."

"So were you scared?"

"Yes, off and on. I had an anxiety attack, in fact, as I entered the first bridge, and a few more times along the way. But I met a nice lady who distracted me part of the time. Plus, Zachary's charm and confidence helped me stay grounded—at least enough to forge ahead and finish the hike."

"So you had a good guide?" asked Margaret.

"The best! And the rainforest was beautiful and interesting. I guess it was one of those love-hate situations because I certainly enjoyed the hike even though I had crazy thoughts about the bridges collapsing right out from under me."

In bed, later that night, Tiffany's head filled with a kaleidoscope of colorful jewels—intriguing sounds, glorious smells, and unique images—from the hike in the rainforest. The outing had whetted her appetite for studying tropical biology, but she did not take lightly the huge task of learning about the complex environment of the Central American rainforests and the animals, birds, and plants common to them.

Answering the call to leave her homeland for a new adventure of this magnitude had stretched her to the point of discomfort, but she had come. Although the morning hike had made her quite anxious at times, she had mustered the courage to push on. But would her courage last?

Gradually, Tiffany's thoughts began to whir more in rhythm with the slow moving ceiling fan. After covering herself with a sheet to block the cool night air drifting through the open window, she stared at the soft moonlight bathing the room, and asked, "Margaret, are you awake?"

"Huh?"

"Are you awake?"

"Am now—what do you want?"

"Have you ever seen snow?"

"Only a little, once."

"Only once?"

"I grew up in the south. Remember? It seldom snows in Alabama."

"Oh my, you've missed out. A big snowfall is so magical," Tiffany said, visualizing the drama of pristine white snow turning gray leafless trees and evergreen shrubs into beautiful sculptures. "With every good snowfall, the lawn quickly disappears under a massive, white blanket."

"Whatever."

"The mild tropical weather here is quite a contrast to the Kansas prairie where I come from. Some winters the snow drifts higher than the corn plants grow in the summer."

"… can't imagine."

"Snowflakes remind me of sugar—they're so pure and white."

"Sounds like the beaches of Alabama and Florida along the gulf."

"I hope you see a real snowfall someday."

"Me too. Now for goodness' sake, can I go to sleep?"

Tiffany wanted to tell Margaret that with every snowfall she and her sister Karla caught snowflakes with their tongue or sculpted angel wings in the snow blanketing the yard. And that they always built the perfect snowman, complete with a stocking hat and scarf, but Margaret's breathing indicated she would not have heard.

Did she mean it when she told Katy she might stay

here? And live this far from her family? Could she learn to call Central America home? Or for that matter, find happiness here? Was she at some preordained crossroads in her life? Or was she simply on a high due to the charm of Costa Rica?

Though answers would not come tonight, she believed whether she chose to live in the city or the country, or North America or Central America, she would continue to spend as much time as possible outdoors, studying plants and respecting animals. And though her greatest dream was to teach school, she sensed the courage to speak publicly would not come from her strength alone. Standing before others with all eyes fixed upon her as she spoke would necessitate a magical act of courage from a realm beyond her.

She turned her thoughts back to the hike, especially as it ended at the hotel. Although she never expected to see Katy again, they exchanged cell phone numbers before parting. She had enjoyed their chance encounter and hated to say goodbye, but heaved a huge sigh of relief when Lucy rushed to her rental jeep without looking back.

When one of the tourists engaged Zachary in a lengthy conversation, Tiffany missed the opportunity to thank him for the wonderful adventure. She hoped to meet up with him again. Maybe she would sign up for another one of his tours, since any further knowledge from him might be helpful in getting off to a good start in her classes this fall. Besides, how could she resist the combination of intelligence, charm, and good looks?

Although the bridges frightened her, on the whole, the rainforest impressed her so much that she had finished the hike with a measure of decorum. If she could just overcome her ridiculous faintheartedness, maybe one day she would know the kind of peace her grandmother often referred to—a peace that passes understanding.

Smiling, Tiffany fluffed her pillow and snuggled into a comfortable position. Then just as her mental screen neared a final blip, something rustled outside the window. As she strained to listen, her mind took flight. Was someone lurking out there? A person? An animal? Had something sinister stolen her air? Or was it only the wind whistling through the trees?

Quaking inside, the eerie silence was the only sound that passed her ears as her wild imagination held her rigid in bed.

A strange sense of foreboding had pushed aside her drowsy thrill over the potential for new and exciting beginnings.

## CHAPTER 4

In his apartment at the edge of Santa Elena, Zachary woke to a vivid image of the gorgeous girl who was part of the small group he escorted through the rainforest only yesterday.

Tall and slender, Tiffany had creamy skin that begged to be touched. And her long curly hair, as black as coal reminded him of the pretty strips of ribbon his mother crinkled with scissors to decorate packages.

Several times on the bridge, Tiffany appeared upset, but her interest in the rainforest seemed genuine. She was a bit more relaxed after meeting another young woman, also alone on the tour, and by the end of the hike she behaved as though she had made a measure of peace with her surroundings.

By the time Zachary slid out of bed and headed for the shower, he was dedicated to the notion of searching for her. He knew only her name but he wanted to know more. Where was she from? Why had she come? Would she stay all summer? She was one good looking girl and he could use a summer fling.

Suddenly, the slick bar of soap shot out of his hands. As the warm water poured over his muscular body he wondered if she could be a tourist who had already moved on. What if he never saw her again? If it were not for the full day already scheduled, beginning with the group he was to meet following breakfast, he would begin the search for her right away.

Several capuchin monkeys frolicking in the nearby trees entertained him as he dressed. Their soft clucking sounds, a sharp contrast to their usual loud morning yelps made him smile. Zachary's deep love affair with the tropics made him feel as though he had lived there in another life.

Of course a black cloud hovered over him sometimes, especially after one of his awful nightmares, but he decided not go there this morning. He preferred to live in the moment. After lacing up his brown hiking boots and glancing in the mirror for a final check, he grabbed the keys to the jeep and raced out the door, eager to greet another day.

Zachary had arranged to meet George Baldwin for breakfast at the Rainforest Hotel where his first tour of the morning would begin. George, a long-time resident of the area had taken him under his wing not long after he moved to Costa Rica.


"Good to see you, Zach. I just got here," said George, who was already settled at a table tucked in the corner of the café.

A warm feeling came over Zachary when he saw George's face light up at the sight of him. He also liked that George had shortened his name to Zach. He viewed it as a liberty a father might take.

"How did your tour go yesterday?" George asked. "Were there any interesting people in your group?"

"Yeah, especially this one girl named Tiffany Birdwell. What I wouldn't give to meet up with her again."

"Was she a tourist? Or maybe she's here to study at the institute?"

"I didn't have a chance to find out."

"Tell me about her."

Zachary gave a brief physical description of Tiffany and mentioned her unusual interest in the plight of the scarlet macaws. "And you know how important the macaws are to me."

After Zachary ordered a literal feast for breakfast, and George had ordered his monthly splurge of Gallo pinto and a fried egg, George said, "If she's here to study awhile, you'll run into her somewhere. This town isn't that big."

"I hope you're right. Besides her good looks, I loved that she seemed to have such a strong interest in learning about the rainforest."

With a straight face, George asked, "What about the others in the group? Or was it a private tour?"

Zachary enjoyed George's sense of humor. "As a matter of fact there were about a dozen tourists all together. And there was this one woman that nearly drove me out of my mind. She wouldn't shut up. She was a trouble-maker."

"Oh, how's that?"

"You know how I like it when the tourists ask questions? Well this one woman broke all of the records. She made me jumpy, asking more questions than the entire group combined. And she didn't wait for an answer to one question before asking another."

"Sounds like a pushy broad."

"Yeah, she pushed all right. She pushed for details before I could give my spiel about the wildlife, plants, or whatever. And she pushed her way through the group to stand as close to me as possible. But her arrogant attitude that I should or could scare up a quetzal is what bugged me the most."

"Oh my, you seldom see one of those rare birds."

"And I'm not a magician. Almost everyone who comes to vacation here wants to see one, but I've lived here two years and haven't seen one yet.

"You will, Zach, you will. I take it you didn't talk to the mystery girl afterwards."

"No, she disappeared right after the tour ended at the hotel when someone from the group asked me about hiking solo in the area, but overall, she was the bright spot of my day. I'll have to admit that between the obnoxious woman and the hot babe, I could hardly keep my mind on what I wanted to tell the group. I tried to keep my wits about me and be professional, but neither of them made it easy."

George smiled. "I'm sure you handled yourself quite well."

"Well I certainly love telling the tourists all I know about the Monteverde rainforest," Zachary said. Then he expounded for the next several minutes on how much he enjoyed his work. "You know how much I dig this wild, remote place. It's a great job."

"Say, I'm scheduled to speak tonight here at the Rainforest about the founding of Monteverde. Do you suppose you could come?"

"Sorry, I'm leading a group in the rainforest tonight. Maybe another time," Zachary said as he checked his watch. "I better run. I'm already a little late meeting my first group."

As Zachary paid his bill at the front cash register, he saw Tiffany rush out the front door of the lobby. "Wait!" he shouted. "Wait, Tiffany. Wait!"

He cursed his rotten luck to barely miss her. It had to be her—not too many girls had long black, curly hair. He wanted to chase after her, but he could see the group of tourists gathered in the designated meeting place near the front desk. He had no choice except to join the tour group in the lobby, but he vowed to find her. She looked like someone he would enjoy larking about with for a few months.

## CHAPTER 5

George pushed back from the dinner table. "I'm excited about speaking tonight. You know what a pleasure it is for me to share stories about moving here."

Nellie looked at him with a sideways smile. "But do you remember the details? We left Alabama such a long time ago."

Leaning back in his chair, he intertwined his fingers behind his head. "Of course, I do. We pulled up roots to come here as newlyweds when we were only in our early twenties." In his mind's eye, George could still see his sweet, innocent bride doing her part to make a success of their new life as pioneers in unsettled territory.

Nellie patted his hand. "I'll say this much for you George, you've held up well through it all. Why look at you, you're still so spry. And your enthusiasm is downright contagious. Most people would never guess you're in your eighties."

"Now don't sidetrack me. I need to stay in a certain frame of mind for my talk tonight," George said, grinning like a lottery winner. "So anyway, I've never regretted our decision to move here, have you?"

Nellie frowned. "Well it's for sure moving to Costa Rica created many hardships for us."

"We had some rough times, all right," George said.

"Rough? That hardly describes the first several years we lived here. We went through a lot of difficult circumstances to get where we are today."

"And it took muscle, plus brains to make it all happen—to found a new settlement in foreign land and make it home."

Nellie narrowed her eyes and pulled her rose-colored sweater close around her. "That's right, but if you ask me, it took more than brains and brawn. It also required heart—a brave heart to trust things would work out when we were often blinded to the way ahead."

George flinched at Nellie's words, for he remembered how much she struggled in the early years to be brave and strong. "You're right. It took a lot of courage to move here. And then to stay."

Nellie began stacking their dinner plates. "But a merciful grace saw us through all the highs and lows. And the same grace will see you through your talk tonight."

"I'm counting on it."

"It's for certain you'll do a great job speaking—you're a born storyteller."

"Well, it's for sure I should have this one down, since I've told it so many times." Chuckling, George scooted his chair back and stood to leave. He leaned over and cupped Nellie's delicate chin to lift her lined face for a goodbye kiss. Then he snatched his old blue windbreaker from the coat rack and hurried out the door.

As George maneuvered his jeep along the narrow, rutted road leading to Santa Elena, the nearby small settlement, he sent up a silent word of thanks for Nellie and the life they had built together in Costa Rica. Basking in contentment, he gave credit to the Lord for his many blessings.


Later, as George scurried along a sidewalk in the heart of town, he ran into the Cortez family. After speaking briefly with Juan and his wife, Maria, George made a point to speak to the children, a boy and a girl, approximately five years of age. Their sweet faces always made him think of his own twins, gone from his life but not from his heart.

He had met the Cortez twins the year before when their father lost his job. A friend of Juan's, he had visited him several times, trying to bolster his spirits with encouraging remarks. *Don't give up hope; you have much to offer. Hang in there, you'll find work.*

A compassionate man with a great deal of interest in others, George seldom passed up an opportunity to stop and talk, but tonight he bustled along, focused on his mission.

He arrived at the hotel several minutes before 7:00, hoping for time to relax and collect his thoughts before his talk. It pained George that his mental acuity had lessened over the years, but he believed that even though he could not stop the clock, he could stay in good physical condition and continue to learn new things. He also believed that to stay young at heart, he needed to remain passionate about a variety of pastimes. And one of his favorites was sharing stories about moving to Costa Rica and helping to establish Monteverde.

George saw several locals in the audience, many he knew quite well. He also noted a number of strangers with backpacks and cameras that he assumed were tourists. A couple of young ladies seated on the front row without the typical tourist gear made him wonder if they were in town to study at the Monteverde Institute.

The girl with the black curly ponytail held a pen poised over a notepad as though planning to take copious notes, and he had not yet spoken a word. Her attentive air indicated an open and fertile mind, and one capable of receiving the seeds of thought he intended to plant about how the Lord helped them settle the area against overwhelming odds.

He hoped many in the audience found his talk interesting, but even if his words about the goodness of God fell on only one set of open ears or into one receptive heart, his time would not be wasted.

Soon thereafter, George Baldwin began his talk: "The Quaker faith believes that an inner light—the light of God shines within everyone. Peace-loving Quakers are unwilling to bear arms against other humans. So my wife and I, along with several fellow Quakers, moved to Costa Rica from Alabama in 1951 in search of a more tranquil way of life. We left everything familiar behind to move to a country dedicated to peace rather than fighting."

When George noticed the young girl writing as though her life depended on it, while her friend whispered in her ear, he decided to deliver the heart of his story about the events leading up to their decision to relocate to Central America.

"In 1948, I was arrested along with a number of other Quakers for refusing to register for the war draft in the United States. We believed that rather than participating in war, we should respond to conflict in a peaceful manner. But holding fast to our convictions resulted in jail time."

George noticed both girls stared wide-eyed at him at the mention of arrest and imprisonment, but he hoped they would hear the bigger message he intended to thread throughout his talk.

"We earned parole after serving four months of our one year and one day prison sentence. Then we started making plans to leave the United States as soon as possible."

George explained that in researching where to move they were pleased to learn Costa Rica had abolished its army following the country's revolution in 1948. The country's political situation, stable government, and sound economy were also quite appealing.

"We found Costa Rica's large middle class population of friendly people to be attractive," George said. "And since most of us were dairy farmers in Alabama, the moderate climate provided an extra incentive to shift our allegiance."

Then George spent the next several minutes painting a picture with words of their harsh journey from the United States to Central America that involved crossing the borders of Mexico, Guatemala, El Salvador, Honduras, and Nicaragua. They encountered legal hurdles and other setbacks during the three months of travel over unpaved, rough, or boggy roads with only a truck, a jeep, and a trailer of supplies to see them through. "Why, sometimes it took four hours to travel less than a mile when we had to carve out a road in raw, untouched land," he said.

George had spoken on this topic many times, but he had never noticed anyone as dedicated to taking notes as the young lady with the curly black hair. Her show of interest encouraged him to continue with his reflections.

"After purchasing land in the verdant mountainous area of the central highlands region, located around 160 kilometers east and a little north of San Jose, we set about the arduous task of forming roots to found this settlement we call Monteverde, which means 'Green Mountain.' And certainly, whether this is your home or you're a visitor, you can easily see it's an appropriate name for this lush green area."

In continuing his talk, George described the monumental task of building roads, creating homes, establishing schools, and constructing a worship site. They had to clear part of the virgin forest for dairy farming in order to meet the expense of food, clothing, and other basic essentials.

"We struggled hard to meet our ordinary needs and survive the living conditions of a remote and largely uninhabited area. Heavy rains often thwarted our efforts. But fortunately, we were blessed to receive help with our projects from a handful of friendly, diligent farm families who had lived in the area since the 1940's."

When George stopped to glance at his notes, the girl with the ponytail wrote so fast her pen nearly blurred across the page. Her steadfast focus inspired his summation remarks: "So the possibility of living a simpler life in Costa Rica held great appeal for us. But unfortunately, although escaping the military draft made life easier in one sense, it didn't make things simpler overall. We avoided the draft and fighting our fellowman, but we fought harsh circumstances and Mother Nature as we sought to establish a new way of life on foreign soil."

After pausing for a sip of water, George delivered his heartfelt conclusion: "We missed our families and friends. We missed home and many of the ways of home. But when we lost strength, God empowered us. When we doubted, He reassured us. When we feared, He encouraged us. And when blinded to the way ahead, He motivated us. The Lord walked with us through the sunshine or rain of our days, whispering hope to our weary hearts."

George paused to clear his throat and make eye contact with a few of the people in the audience, including the two girls in the front row. "In conclusion, I would say that we pushed on through difficult circumstances and a lot of tough years, but in truth the Holy Spirit shepherded us, even nudging us along from time to time when we stumbled and fell short."

By now the young writer had rested her pen. The look of awe etched on her face startled George so much that he made these additional last remarks: "Suffice it to say that we felt led to make the huge decision to relocate to Central America. With the Lord's help, we completed impossible tasks and solved difficult problems to settle here. And for a long time now, we have been privileged to call Costa Rica our home."

After the applause ceased and the crowd thinned, Tiffany mustered the nerve to approach Mr. Baldwin to thank him for sharing his story. "If at all possible, some time I'd love to hear more of your wonderful stories."

"Thanks. That's kind of you, young lady. How did you happen to come to the hotel tonight to hear my talk?"

"I saw a notice about the event posted in the lobby of the hotel where I'm staying. It sounded interesting, so I decided to come over this morning to check out the details."

"Are you new in town?" George asked.

"Yes sir, I arrived last week to attend the Monteverde Institute in the fall. So I'll be here awhile."

"What will you study at the institute?"

"I plan to study tropical biology and the biodiversity of the delicate ecosystem of the rainforests of Costa

Rica."

"Wow, that's a mouthful," George said, impressed by her ambition. "I hope you'll enjoy it here."

"I'm sure I will. I love it already, and can't wait to begin my studies."

"Great!" George beamed. "We need people who are interested in learning about our wonderful environment and are willing to teach others how to appreciate and preserve it." Then he pulled a pen and a scrap of paper from his shirt pocket. "I believe I can speak for my wife when I say we'd love to have you visit us while you're here studying. So if you don't mind giving out your phone number, we'll call to set up a time."

Then George turned toward Margaret. "Now who's this young lady with you?" he asked.

"Oh, I'm sorry." Tiffany motioned for Margaret to step closer. "This is my friend and roommate Margaret Mitchell from Alabama."

"I'm happy to meet you, Mr. Baldwin," Margaret said, dripping with manners and charm.

George pumped Margaret's tiny hand up and down. "Hello, young lady. It's nice to meet you, too. Alabama is it?" he asked.

"Yes sir, I'm from Mobile, Alabama."

"How about that—we're from the same state. I knew we needed to meet. So did your parents name you for the author Margaret Mitchell who wrote the famous book about Atlanta and the Civil War?"

"*Gone With the Wind?* No sir, but I am quite familiar with the book. Scarlet is my all-time favorite character."

He chuckled to himself at the image of her squirming during his talk like the impetuous Scarlet O'Hara probably would have. "So tell me, are you also here to study tropical biology?"

"Oh no, not biology. I'm sure I'll study something, just not in an official way. I've come to vacation and explore."

After only a brief exchange, George appreciated Margaret's obvious southern charm, but Tiffany's tentative manner and genuine interest in his beloved country appealed to him more.

All the way home, he pondered the notion of helping Nellie plan a dinner party. They could invite his young friend Zach and one of the young men from the states that had come for the summer to do volunteer work at the Butterfly Gardens. And of course, they could ask the astute young lady and her charming friend from Mobile that he had just met. Zach would also appreciate Tiffany, and all that lovely, frizzy black hair. Then the light dawned. He laughed out loud thinking about the fun he would have surprising Zach.

He would mention his thoughts to Nellie and offer to help her plan a menu. They could serve a variety of cheeses from the nearby cheese factory as an appetizer. Maybe he would have a chance to share with the young people how the Quakers founded the Monteverde Cheese Factory and how it grew over the years from hard work, but most of all from heavenly grace.

As a rule, George preferred to let his life be a testimony to God's wonder-working powers, but he believed certain situations called for using a few words to plant seeds of thought about the Creator's wondrous love and merciful grace.

## CHAPTER 6

"Hey, I'm Zachary Caldwell from upstate New York," Zachary said, offering his hand to the young man behind him in line as they waited for a table at a local diner in Santa Elena. "Are you vacationing here?"

"I'm Jason Adamson, and no, I'm not just here to sightsee. I'm from Iowa and I've come for the summer to work in the volunteer program at the Monteverde Butterfly Gardens. It's part of my study program as a biology student at the University of Iowa."

Zachary explained he had moved from New York to Costa Rica a couple of years before to work as a naturalist. "The butterflies are one of our more popular tourist attractions. What will you do at the gardens?"

"Conduct tours in the insect and butterfly areas. The volunteer program includes meals, but I wanted to check out the town. And when I saw the flashing neon lights and graveled parking lot here at the diner, I whipped in on a whim. It reminded me of a little country café I ate at with my buddies back home."

"This place is always crawling with tourists, so what

do you say we share a booth?" asked Zachary.

When the waitress announced the featured entrée for the evening was vegetable lasagna, chocked full of goodies—peppers, onions, tomatoes, zucchini, and yellow squash that were sautéed with several Italian seasonings, Jason looked like someone hit him with a blast of cold water. "So no meat? Or cheese? For goodness' sake, I'm not a vegetarian."

"No, there's no meat, but there's a lot of thick, gooey cheese—made at the factory up the mountain," she said.

After they ordered the lasagna, Zachary introduced his favorite subject, and one he believed would interest Jason—the flora and fauna common to the thick forests and misty mountains of Costa Rica. "There are several hundred different kinds of birds in the Monteverde Reserve," he said, "but toucans are the most familiar to tourists."

"But most of the tourists come to see a quetzal, don't they?" asked Jason. "I certainly want to see one."

"As a matter of fact, they do—especially the male quetzal. It has a reputation as the most striking bird in the tropics, what with its bright red breast and shiny green body. And its twin tail feathers that sometimes grow to be about three feet long."

"I take it you've seen one?"

"Nope. Sorry to say, I've yet to spot one. Quetzal sightings are rare. But I will."

"I'd like to at least catch a glimpse of one while I'm here," Jason said. "But in the meantime, what else can I look forward to seeing this summer? Are there many jaguars around this part of Costa Rica?"

Zachary explained that even though over 200 mammalian species rustle through the jungle, many are difficult to spot. And that some, such as the elusive margay and jaguar are endangered.

"But I thought the jaguar was considered by most people to be the symbol of Central American jungles," Jason said.

"They are, but unfortunately, deforestation has caused a decline in their population."

"What can you tell me about the Monteverde Reserve? Like when was it founded? And why?"

"In the early seventies, some twenty years after the Quakers arrived in the area, they established the reserve to protect the rainforest. Ecologists, scientists, bird watchers, and wildlife lovers from all parts of the world visit the reserve for a variety of reasons, but primarily for the purpose of study and research," Zachary said. "The reserve is quite a tourist attraction and a real boon for Santa Elena's economy."

"I plan to take a serious look at the reserve, but there are also several other areas I'd like to explore while I'm here."

"You'll love the climate here in north central Costa Rica. Monteverde is located along the continental divide roughly 1500 meters above sea level, which makes it lush and green all year round."

After polishing off their vegetable lasagna, Zachary suggested they order a piece of peach-mango pie. "It's a great dessert. They top it off with vanilla ice cream and chocolate sauce. Of course, we'll have to do an extra sprint to burn up the added calories, but it'll be worth it."

"Sounds good, but don't count on me for a sprint. I'm not too keen on working out."

Jason wasted no time testing the dessert when it arrived. After the first bite he sighed and licked his lips. "This is great, especially the ice cream. But it doesn't compare with my dad's homemade ice cream. It takes the prize."

"My Granddaddy Bell made a lot of ice cream when I was a kid," Zachary said. "He had one of those old wooden freezers. He let me help pack ice around the container of cream and pour on that special salt that makes the cream harden faster."

Jason leaned his head back against the booth. "Yeah, we made a freezer of ice cream almost every Sunday afternoon during the summer. We had lots of family and friends over to help us eat it. I'm crazy about the stuff."

"Maybe you're crazy about ice cream because you associate it with good times. Or maybe you're just down right addicted to it."

"Hey, what's this about addiction? I hope you're joking, but if that's the case it sure beats some addictions people have these days. I didn't touch alcohol or drugs as a teenager. Somehow, I avoided the lure—thank goodness."

Zachary fidgeted in his chair, wondering why he had opened his yap about addictions. "By the way, did I mention the ice cream is produced at the cheese factory that's on the road leading to the reserve?"

"If they offer tours, I'd like to go, especially if they give out ice cream samples." Jason chuckled.

"We'll make a run up there while you're here. I know one of the founders of the factory; he'd love to tell you how it started, and how it grew and prospered through the years."

Before parting, Zachary offered to stop by the gardens sometime over the weekend to let Jason practice the spiel he would use when leading groups of tourists. Besides, he had a hunch Jason could use some company. Loneliness could drag you down. He had been gone from home around six years, including his college days, and he still struggled with loneliness at times—especially when he dwelt on the past.

# CHAPTER 7

Toward morning, Zachary opened his eyes and sat straight up in bed. Breathing raggedly, he darted his eyes around the room that was still quite dark. But the forbidding cave in the dream that had just awakened him had been even darker.

In the dream, he was lost in a black void, fumbling his hands over the cave's wet, slimy walls as he crept along trying to find his way to the entrance. For a while, his heavy breathing and chirping insects were the only sounds breaking the menacing stillness. Then from nowhere a furious squawking and the ominous sound of beating wings filled the cold damp air. Powerful talons grazed his head and knocked him to his knees. His heart turned over in his chest as salty tears mingled with the blood trickling down his face and across his lips. Nausea gripped him as fear filled his gut.

Unable to make any sense of the awful dream, Zachary shuddered and bolted from bed. He rushed to the shower and turned the water on full blast. As he lathered his body, questions from his mother during the summer he prepared to move to Costa Rica came to mind: *Why are you moving so far away? Are you trying to run from your past? Or hide from painful feelings?*

"Running from my past? Painful feelings? Of course not," he had told her.

Haunted by his mother's voice, and not wanting to spend another minute dwelling on things he could not change—things too sad to think about—he finished in a hurry, turned off the water and grabbed a towel. He stepped into the fresh light of day and took a deep breath.

Just before leaving for his first tour, Zachary gave Jason a quick call. "I don't have much time—headed to work, but I wanted to tell you about a dinner invitation from George and Nellie Baldwin."

"Who?"

"The couple I mentioned last night that came from the United States back in the early fifties and helped found Monteverde. Don't you remember me telling you they were part of a group of Quakers that established the cheese factory where the wonderful ice cream is made?"

"Oh yeah. So are you saying they want me to come to their home for dinner?"

"George called early this morning to invite me to a small dinner party for tomorrow night and wanted to include the newest volunteer at the butterfly gardens. It pleased him we'd already met, and he asked me to bring you along."

"I don't know. I …"

"He has gobs of neat stories—ones that make you know your life's been pretty cushy so far. What's the matter? Got a better offer for Saturday night?"

Jason chuckled. "Maybe. I'll have to check my social calendar."

"Don't you think you should meet a few locals and

immerse yourself in the culture while you're here? Who knows, you might decide to stay."

"I don't know about staying, but maybe you're right I ought to meet some folks while I'm here."

"I take that as a 'yes'. By the way, they're also inviting a couple of girls they want us to meet. Maybe that'll entice you."

"Costa Rican girls?"

"No, they're from the states. George says one's here to study at the institute this fall and the other is her friend who came along on a lark. So what do you say? They might be good looking."

"I don't know. I've never dated much—always had something better to do."

"It's not like a real date or anything."

"I'll think about it. But right now, I've got to go. I'm hoping to spot a calico butterfly today. Did you know they're the only butterfly in the whole world capable of making a noise?"

"But you said nothing compares to the blue morpho, right?"

"Absolutely! In fact, many people consider it to be the most impressive creature in the tropics. But the tarantula in the insect area is also impressive, though for a different reason."

"Most people freak out over tarantulas. But then my mom goes nuts over even a little bitty spider."

"My sister hates spiders worse than anyone." Jason heaved a big sigh. "Talking about family makes me think about home. I haven't been home since Christmas break—came here from college at the end of the spring semester. Bad plan. I should have gone home first."

"But you wouldn't admit to being homesick, would you? If you ask me it's all the more reason why visiting the Baldwins for some home cooking is a good thing."

"I hadn't thought of it that way. It sounds like a plan, man. You've got yourself a deal."

Zachary certainly wouldn't admit to being homesick, but in truth, he missed home. He missed the Adirondacks, and of course, his mom and grandparents, and a few old friends. But most of all, he missed the family life that ended several years before he left home.

## CHAPTER 8

"Eeenie meenie miney moe, catch a monkey by the toe," Margaret chanted as she pointed at the clothes she had spread over her unmade bed. She wanted to choose the perfect sundress for the Baldwins' dinner party.

Looking up from her book, Tiffany pulled herself from a slumped position on her bed and glared at Margaret. "Did you know that old children's nursery rhyme originated somewhere around the 1850's and people used it around the world for a long time?"

Margaret gave her a blank stare. She did not have enough clothing to choose from because her mother insisted she keep her luggage to a bare minimum. And although packing lighter did simplify matters—less to carry and keep up with—her choices for the dinner party tonight were far too limited, leaving her in a quandary.

"I'm sorry to say that the controversial word 'nigger' in the rhyme replaced the original word 'tiger,'" Tiffany said. "It was offensive to our black brothers and sisters and took *faaarrrrr* too long for the word to go out of favor."

Margaret held a bright turquoise sundress close to her body and studied herself in the mirror. "Oh please. We chanted the rhyme often back in Alabama, but we said 'monkey' instead of 'nigger.'"

"I'm relieved to hear that. I seldom heard the rhyme growing up, but I had a very nice and innovative high school Spanish teacher, Mrs. Brown that used it, along with other children's nursery rhymes to help us retain the lessons. She wanted to make learning fun. And it worked. At least it did for me." Tiffany described Mrs. Brown as one of those rare teachers who cared about the student as a whole and tried to touch the soul, as well as teach the mind. "She was my favorite teacher. She inspired me to want to teach, but I doubt I can pull it off."

Margaret tossed the dress onto the bed. "Hmmm… That's nice."

"It's a good thing I took Advanced Spanish in college," Tiffany said. "My Spanish skills will come in handy if I decide to stay. And as more people cross the border back home it will be more important that we're bilingual." Then she began to recite the choosing rhyme in Spanish: *Tin marin de dos pingue—*

"So where was I?" Margaret asked as she kicked a pair of shoes under the edge of the bed. "Oh yes, the turquoise sundress—it makes my blonde hair even blonder. That's what I'll wear tonight. And my multi-strand liquid silver necklace and dangle silver earrings will be the perfect addition to the overall look I want to achieve."

Tiffany screwed up her face. "For goodness' sake, Margaret, the invitation isn't to some important state dinner that requires a perfect ensemble."

"What's that supposed to mean?" Margaret asked.

"So what are you wearing?"

Tiffany flipped her kinky strands out of her face. "I haven't thought about it."

"Surely you jest."

"Nope." Tiffany shot forward and reached across the space between their beds to finger Margaret's showy sundress. "So what shoes does this little number call for?"

Margaret shoved aside a pile of clothing to make room to plop beside her sundress of choice. "My thin-strapped silver sandals with one inch heels, of course. They'll pull everything together and provide the final 'wow' factor, don't you think?"

Tiffany rolled her eyes, grabbed her book, and jumped off the bed. "I'm out of here. I need to find a quiet spot to read."

"Fine with me," Margaret said, as the door clattered shut behind Tiffany.

Socializing with people almost the age of her great grandparents didn't appeal to Margaret, but she was ready to be out and about. Since arriving, she had left the hotel only once and that was to hear Mr. Baldwin's talk. She hoped he had not noticed her restlessness that night, but when it came to talking about 'churchy' matters or having faith in a higher power, she would rather see the subject change direction. Any trace of serious regret that she had not paid much attention to Mr. Baldwin flickered through her mind faster than a firefly shines the light of its tiny tail. She had no time for guilt. Life was too short.

Margaret had graduated from college in the spring with a teaching degree in Elementary Education. But she now questioned the logic of spending all day, day after day, in a classroom with a bunch of over-active kids. She doubted teaching could fulfill her.

The choice to spend the summer in Costa Rica

prolonged her search for a job, but her wealthy daddy had not minded footing the bill for an extended vacation in the tropics. And if someone special happened to come along this summer, she would not have to think about finding a job. She'd rather find someone to take care of her like her daddy always had.

In fact, Margaret, a bit of a daydreamer, easily fancied herself returning to the South to live a life in keeping with the fictitious, pampered heroine of *Gone With the Wind*. Especially the way the lovely, carefree Scarlet O'Hara was before the Civil War when casual hopes and idle dreams filled her head, and many southern gentlemen vied for her attention. Imagine spending lazy afternoons drinking mint juleps in the shade and star-filled nights dancing in a long, bouffant gown, scooped low at the bosom and cinched tight at the waist like Scarlet did.

As Margaret put away the last of her clothing, she grinned at the lazy caramel colored fur ball right outside the window. She hoped the two guys invited to the dinner party would be more entertaining than the little sloth that moved as crazy slow as a battery-operated toy losing power.

Then Margaret giggled as she recalled the word "sloth" meant disinclination to action or labor, and that it certainly defined *her* this summer—lazy to the core.

## CHAPTER 9

Hours later, Tiffany rushed into the cramped hotel room to find Margaret primping in the bathroom. "I'm running late. I need a quick shower."

Margaret pulled away from the mirror and glanced at her watch. "This isn't like you. Will you be ready on time?"

Tiffany grabbed her underwear, black denim jeans, and a short-sleeved coral T-shirt—the neck and bottom edged with lace for a dressy touch—and headed for the bathroom. "No problem. Well that is if you'll finish your makeup in the bedroom."

Margaret tossed her cosmetics in a bag. "There's not much light in there at the mirror over the desk, but you give me no choice. So what happened to you, anyway?"

"I lost track of time reading *Rebecca*."

"Rebecca? Who's she?" asked Margaret as she left the bathroom.

"That's the title of the wonderful book I'm reading. I'd love to write like Daphne du Maurier did. Her description of the story's setting is stellar, and she opens you to the heart and soul of the characters in ways that appear seamless," Tiffany yelled just before she shut the door, but not before she saw Margaret shake her head.

Ten minutes later, when Tiffany emerged from the bathroom dressed for the evening, Margaret still primped with great care, applying beige foundation to her face as thoughtfully as a commissioned artist painting a portrait.

Tiffany puzzled over what took Margaret so long. "You're still at it?" She did not want to arrive late to dinner.

With her chest heaving, Margaret slapped the cap on her bottle of makeup. "The humidity's high this evening and you know it's harder to put on makeup when you're perspiring. By the way, why are you wearing those?"

Tiffany finished buckling her sturdy, dark brown gaucho leather sandals. "In case there's a problem on the rough unpaved road that leads up the mountain to the Baldwins' house. Some of the roads around here aren't the greatest. Many need a lot of work, in fact."

"Well I'd rather look good than practical."

"Maybe you can stay with the jeep if I need to go for help."

"That's not going to happen. You worry too much."

"I'll give you that; I do worry too much. It's a curse," Tiffany said, as she pulled her frizzled hair into a classic ponytail to cool her neck. She longed for just a fraction of Margaret's laid-back style. Did nothing faze her? Or give her pause for thought?

Margaret leaned in close to the mirror, and with great care began applying a soft blue-green eye shadow to her eyelids. At one point she stopped long enough to glance at Tiffany. "What's wrong with you? You're fluttering around like a demon is after you. Do you even look forward to the evening? Aren't you curious about the two guys they invited?"

"Yes to both of your questions, but most of all I'm eager to see Mr. Baldwin again and to meet his wife Nellie," Tiffany said, as she stood by the window looking in to a tiny hand mirror to brush a little blush onto her cheeks. "It wouldn't take a professor of nanotechnology to detect that he's well grounded in his faith, which is something I'd like to know more about."

"What do you mean?"

"I'd like to learn more about a faith journey—how faith grows or how people keep their faith." She picked up her mascara and gave her eyelashes a quick swipe. "I'm hoping to hear more of his wonderful faith stories tonight."

"It was evident the other night that his talk held your attention," Margaret said. "I've never seen anybody take so many notes or hang on to a person's every word the way you did."

"Well I'm sorry, but Mr. Baldwin's tales of traveling for miles and miles through uncharted territory to move from North America to Central America stirred my imagination. I mean, can you even imagine how difficult it must have been to travel over muddy, rutted roads for long periods of time, while trying to find food to supplement your meager supplies?"

Margaret grunted and continued to work on her eye shadow project.

Tiffany slapped her tube of mascara into her makeup bag. *How can she be so nonchalant about everything?* "And Mr. Baldwin's witness of a superior hand leading them through their trials as they settled here also touched me," she added.

Margaret fetched her eyelash curler. "As a kid, I heard

people testify at church revivals about how Jesus took hold of them and changed them to the good, like some unbelievable miracle had taken place. If you ask me, some of their fiery testimonies were far-fetched. They scared me far more than they ever touched me."

Wondering how even the strongest skeptic could remain untouched by Mr. Baldwin's witness to the love and goodness of God, Tiffany refused to give up. "At any rate, I want to know more about Mr. Baldwin's unshakeable faith and how he maintains it. As far as I'm concerned, his stories have great merit. I find them quite believable."

Margaret bugged her eyes and clamped an eyelash curler over her eyelashes. "Well whatever you say," she drawled.

"Weren't you listening to anything he said? He talked about their serious concerns, but testified a powerful faith carried them through their tough situations and harsh circumstances."

During the time Tiffany had known Margaret, she had received numerous clues about her lack of interest in religion. And her disinterest was especially evident the other night during Mr. Baldwin's talk when she fidgeted in her chair, crossing and uncrossing her legs, while sneaking peeks at her watch.

After Margaret had carefully coated her eyelashes with dark brown liquid mascara, she said, "For heavens' sake, aren't you going to wear even a little foundation? I mean, even with your olive complexion you need some color."

"Nah, like you said, it's too humid to apply makeup, and besides I've been in the sun several times since we arrived." Tiffany dabbed on a layer of lipstick, and then tossed the tube and mirror in her makeup bag and zipped the bag shut.

"Well as you very well know, I haven't gone out much. Jet-lag's rough. It takes forever to get your body back in the groove after a long flight."

"For heaven's sake, Margaret, it's only a two hour time change from California to Central America. Besides, we've been here for days."

"Nevertheless, while you've traipsed all over the place, I've been holed up in this hotel room trying to recover from the long, boring flight."

"Your choice," Tiffany said as she put small gold cross earrings into her earlobes and took a last glance in the mirror.

"Don't tell me you're already ready," Margaret roared as she fumbled through her lipstick collection.

Tiffany flipped her wrist to check the time and then reached for her backpack. "Yes, it's time to go."

Margaret jerked the cap from a tube of lipstick. "You're rushing me. All I can say is that this shade better work with my dress."

Tiffany stood with her hand on the doorknob watching Margaret coat her mouth with bold tangerine lipstick. She considered Margaret's blasé attitude toward timeliness as thoughtlessness, but she supposed Margaret viewed her obsession with punctuality as perfectionism.

What do they say? Opposites attract? Yes, sometimes they do and often with good reason, she decided, as they rushed out the door.

# CHAPTER 10

"Time's passing," George said as he assisted Nellie with last minute preparations for the evening meal. "They'll be here in a couple of hours. So how else can I be of help?"

For their dinner party, George and Nellie planned a *casado*, a typical menu that marries various components to form a well-rounded, nutritious meal. George roasted pork over coffee wood to give it a nice smoky flavor, and Nellie prepared *comida tipica*, the traditional beans and rice dish, as well as a carrot, tomato, and cabbage salad.

Nellie gestured toward the cabinet above the oven with a glance and a nod of her head. "Will you reach the wooden tray on the top shelf? I need it for cheese and crackers."

With his feet flat on the floor, George pulled the tray into view. "Oh, I bought this for our twenty-fifth wedding anniversary, didn't I?"

"Yes, a hundred years ago. Isn't it nice?" Nellie asked as she ran her fingers over the satiny Costa Rican guapinol hardwood. "Our nice wooden serving pieces remind me of the fine silver gifts my mother and grandmother used through the years. They always dressed the dining room table with their best silver, linens, china, and crystal for company, and often on Sundays for the family."

"And let me guess—they always put flowers on the table?"

"Oh yes, Mama never failed to arrange a beautiful bouquet of flowers in a low crystal bowl or a silver container, depending on the occasion or her mood."

When Nellie finished rinsing the tray, George patted it dry. "And they never dreamed of doing anything else, right?" he asked.

"Oh no, Mama thought traditions should be carried on, and so did my grandmother. My grandmother used to say with great conviction that traditions help tie your soul to your roots."

"But of course you broke tradition a long time ago when you chose to leave your southern roots to come here with me."

"Yes, I did. And I left many lovely family treasures behind that were symbols of a certain way of life." Nellie remarked that for many years a society of people, including her family, passed down their silver from generation to generation, along with their pride and prejudice."

"Try looking at it this way, Nellie—about the silver— at least you're not forever polishing tarnished silver. It's a big chore, isn't it?"

"Hmmmm … I wonder if perhaps some folks are like tarnished silver."

"What is that supposed to mean?" George threw back his head and laughed.

Nellie grinned. "Now stop laughing, George, and let

me try to explain. Removing tarnish from silver reveals a surprising loveliness underneath, right?"

"Right."

"So maybe there's a correlation—maybe some folks have an unattractive veneer that must be removed before the pretty stuff underneath can show and shine."

"So?"

"So don't you think it's unfortunate some folks live a lifetime without discovering their inner beauty?"

George scratched his head. "Huh? I think it's time I went out back to cut that bouquet of hydrangeas you need for the dinner table."

As George cut blossom after blossom to form a well-rounded bouquet, he thought about Nellie and how she wandered off on tangents. Sometimes she wore him out analyzing thoughts, feelings, and even dreams.

Seconds later, a fat yellow and black bee landed on a nearby blossom, reminding George that people often gravitated toward Nellie for her warm, listening heart and wise counsel. She was a good lady, but like everybody else, she had faults. Nellie could be quite stubborn at times. And yet, her dogged nature and ability to make things happen had helped them tremendously through the years. No wonder he loved her so.

When George returned to the kitchen with the bouquet of hydrangea blossoms, Nellie went to work arranging and rearranging the big floppy mop heads in a low glass container. George watched Nellie fiddle with the flowers until she had created an exquisite arrangement worthy of adorning the dinner table.

After she centered it on her grandmother's beige, tatted lace tablecloth, one of the few family heirlooms for entertaining that she brought from Alabama, she stepped back for a better view. "Are they low enough? Mama always said the flowers must be low enough for guests to see one another while visiting."

"They look fine to me."

Nellie fiddled a couple of more minutes with the flower arrangement, moving it by a fraction of an inch several times before she finally left to change clothes for the evening.

A half hour later, and only moments before the guests were due to arrive, Nellie rushed back to the living room wearing an orange and cream striped cotton shirtdress. She stopped long enough to tune in dinner music and adjust the volume down on their meager little speakers.

George finished buttoning his favorite shirt, a bright navy blue, covered with palm trees that Nellie had given him the previous Christmas after one of their rare shopping trips to San Jose. "Now Nellie, you know that music won't be 'rap' enough for our young guests."

"But Mama always said you need soft music when you're trying to visit. She called it background music." Nellie took a last glance at the dining table and smiled. "I'm ready," she said as she smoothed her hair with the palm of her hands.

Seconds before the doorbell rang, George sent up a quick word of thanks for Nellie's energetic enthusiasm and contagious, spirited ways.

# CHAPTER 11

"I tell you, you don't need to fret. The Baldwins are wonderful, caring people," Zachary said as he and Jason arrived for dinner. "Being around George and Nellie will be a special treat. Trust me, you can't help but like them."

"I hope you're right. Now how long did you say you've known them?" asked Jason.

"A couple of years—the summer I moved here. I met them at the same diner where I ran in to you the other night, and we hit it off right from the start. They're good people—an interesting couple. George tells a great story and Nellie is quite the cook. Plus, they both have big, caring hearts." Zachary brushed a white fleck from his purple button-down shirt just before he pressed the doorbell.

After Zachary and Jason exchanged greetings with George and Nellie, and presented Nellie with a single long-stemmed red rose, the doorbell rang. When Tiffany walked through the door, Zachary's heart pounded like a woodpecker chiseling a hole in a tree. The *ra-ta-ta-*

*tatting* in his heart moved quickly to his head, making it difficult to think.

*Was it Tiffany? Was it the nervous girl on the bridge? Of course! Her curly, black hair was just as beautiful as he remembered.*

Tiffany nodded toward Margaret as she handed Nellie a small box of chocolates. "From both of us," she said.

When Tiffany was introduced to Zachary, she told him she had been in a group he had led a week or so before. "You did a great job of guiding us through the rainforest that morning."

Tiffany's unassuming air and natural beauty, even more evident this evening, stole Zachary's breath away. "I hope you enjoyed the tour. I mean, sometimes you reminded me of a porcupine. You know, a little stiff and prickly?" *Oh groan, how did I come up with that one?* "I mean, were you on a mission or something?"

Tiffany frowned and narrowed her eyes until long, curved black lashes almost touched. "A mission? I hadn't thought of it that way, but maybe so." She laughed. "Anyway, it was a great tour. Thanks for such an informative morning."

"I hope I left you longing for more. Uuuhhh … I mean for more information about the rainforest." He had never made so many stupid remarks. Where was his confidence? He wasn't the least bit subtle or cool. He sounded like an idiot.

Tiffany's eyebrows shot up, revealing soulful eyes the color of fluorescent moss growing on trees and the moist forest floor. "You mean there's more? I thought you covered everything that morning on the hike."

After only a blank look from Zachary, she added, "I'm serious. I learned a lot that day. But I hope to learn more when I study at the institute this fall."

"So you're not just a tourist passing through?" He had never been more disoriented around a girl before. At least she could not read his mind to know what an impact she had on him.

"Yes, I'm more than a tourist. I'm here to learn tropical biology in a classroom setting as well as in the rainforest. And I also hope to learn new things as I explore with Margaret this summer."

Zachary had seen Tiffany's serious side that day on the hike, but tonight a lighter side prevailed. She seemed different—more approachable.

The moment Tiffany turned away, Margaret latched on to Zachary. "So you're the tour guide Tiffany told me about. I'll have to sign up for one of your tours."

"Sure," Zachary muttered as he glanced at Tiffany, who now made small talk with Jason.

In her best southern accent, Margaret asked Zachary to suggest a few exciting things she could do during her stay in Costa Rica.

"Sure," Zachary said, recalling how Tiffany stood to the side that morning in the hotel lobby for a couple of minutes before joining the group, her sweet, tentative smile revealing an orthodontist's dream.

When Margaret finally heaved a deep sigh and turned away, Zachary had a twinge of guilt over his rude behavior. Tiffany had distracted him with her beauty and charm. Meeting her again had thrown his mind into a tailspin. He wanted to know her—know her hidden thoughts and dreams—the secrets of her heart.

The mysterious web surrounding Tiffany made him an easy prey for her charms. Was this love at first sight? Surely not, he thought, for wouldn't that be ridiculous!

# CHAPTER 12

Meeting Zachary again so soon after the hike was an unexpected bonus for Tiffany. A profound gladness overtook her as she recalled the kindness he showed her that morning on the bridge. She wanted to know where he lived before moving to Costa Rica and why he had come. For that matter, she wondered how long he planned to stay. She liked that they apparently had similar interests, and yet, her premature interest in Zachary frightened her, for she knew nothing of his trustworthiness—knew nothing about him at all. She hoped her practical side would serve as a lifejacket in the current of emotions flooding her tonight. After all, she had once proven to be a poor judge of character.

Turning from Jason to speak to Nellie, Tiffany glanced through the large picture windows at the lush backyard. Even bathed in shadows, the flowers were bold and beautiful. "Everything is a blaze of color—inside and out," she said. Then she pointed to a credenza that held a tall blue urn filled with exotic flowers. "Did the flowers in that stunning arrangement come from your backyard?"

"Indeed, they did," Nellie said. "Are you familiar with tropical flowers?"

"Aren't the tall red flowers torch ginger?"

"That's right. And the yellow flowers are oncidium orchids and the orange ones are heliconias. And I added a few green anthuriums as background to make the color stand out."

"Your living room reminds me of a jungle," Tiffany said, "and I mean that in a good way."

"That's what it's supposed to do. We wanted our home to be in keeping with the rainforest, so we gradually brought in colorful decorations and appropriate pictures to bring life and drama to the room."

Tiffany eyes fell on three photographs hanging on the wall behind the sofa that appeared to be a small representation of the flora and fauna of the Costa Rican rainforests. The first picture was of a fat black monkey looking down with a quizzical expression from a tall tree wrapped in thick green vines. In the next one, a lazy sloth clung to a tree that was home to a number of exquisite white and purple orchids. "All of your pictures are striking, but my favorite is this last one," Tiffany said as she stared at a beautiful bright blue butterfly edged in black that was nestled into a massive fern. The butterfly's fragile-winged glory was spread over lacy green fronds laden with sparkling raindrops.

"That incredible butterfly is a blue morpho," Nellie said.

"So is all of this your handiwork?" Tiffany asked.

"Photography is my new favorite hobby. I sell a few around town and give some as gifts."

On the wall adjacent to the sofa, Tiffany noticed a photograph of the legendary quetzal, known for its smooth, melodious sound and magnificent appearance. "I hope to see a quetzal someday, but Zachary made it clear they're hard to spot. He said that even though most tourists want to see a quetzal more than any other bird, only a few people actually do."

"Yes, as a rule that's true, but with a good guide—or at the right moment—it can happen," Nellie said.

"So you've seen one?"

"Oh yes, more than one. But I'll never forget my first time to see one. I was with George when we spotted this incredible quetzal perched high in a tree at the edge of the rainforest. It looked so regal; a divine aura seemed to surround it."

Tiffany lifted her eyebrows as she forced her gaze away from the special bird. "Maybe spotting one is reserved for certain people."

"Maybe so," Nellie said, "or for special times." Then Nellie led her guests outside to visit on the patio for a while before dinner.

Right away, Tiffany noticed how the dim light of dusk had softened the colored flowers and brightened the white ones. "Someone has evidently worked hard to achieve these wonderful results."

"Growing flowers is another one of my hobbies, but Mother Nature controls the outcome of plant life here in the tropics. I just help when needed."

It appeared to Tiffany that someone had tossed a variety of seeds into the air and allowed them to land at will. The random color spoke to her of a free and gentle spirit dwelling in the garden. "Your patio is lovely. It's like an outdoor living room."

Nellie smiled. "That's because we live out here, as weather permits."

When Tiffany sniffed the air, Nellie pointed to the right side of the patio. "That sweet fragrance comes from the yellow blossoms of the small tree over there."

A garden path, bordered by flickering votives, snaked toward a little white wooden arbor in the corner of the yard. The slight tinkling of the musical chimes swinging from the tree blended with the melodic sound of chirping katydids that were hidden in the nearby raspberry-colored bougainvilleas. The lovely backyard emanated with peace.


Soon after Nellie set out the assortment of cheese and crackers, George waved a hand over the entire tray. "All of this, the Provolone, Swiss, and Gouda was produced at the Monteverde Cheese Factory just up the road."

"Zachary mentioned the factory," Jason said. "Now when did it open?"

"We established the factory in 1953, not long after we arrived," George said. "We purchased fifty Guernsey heifers from some of Costa Rica's prime herds down in the Central Valley. And later, we combined the milk from our dairy cows with the milk produced on neighboring farms to begin making cheese. At that time, cheese was the only product we could safely store and transport along the muddy oxcart roads."

"What kind of cheese did you first produce?" asked Jason.

"Aged cheddar. It held up better than other cheeses. We had lots of challenges founding the factory, but almost from the beginning we produced and sold about twenty-two pounds of cheese every day. Eventually, the factory prospered and provided an important source of cash flow for the rural area around here."

"I've heard a few of your stories of how you got the factory going during those early years," Zachary said, "but your courage to persist through so many problems and setbacks still amazes me. So how would you say you managed to stay with it? Lots of people would have given up."

Looking thoughtful, George leaned forward in his chair. "It's true the project presented many challenges. In the beginning, we ran the factory by trial and error, making improvements as we learned from our mistakes."

Margaret placed the palm of her hand alongside her cheek. "Oh my, it must have been a huge undertaking, and certainly a burden to start a factory under such crude conditions. I can't imagine being involved in such a big project."

"My parents and grandparents have talked about tough times on the farm," Jason said. "I've even heard all about the Great Depression in the United States back in the thirties. But the way you started from scratch to build a new way of life in a foreign land really impresses me."

George looked Jason in the eye. "Young man, if you grew up on a farm in Iowa, I'm sure your family had crops drown from too much rain or burn up from not enough."

"Yeah and sometimes freezes or hailstorms took their toll."

"And insects damaged crops and animals died, right?"

"Oh yeah, we experienced tough times growing up on the farm, all right, but what you faced sounds much worse—completely out of your element, and all."

George relaxed into his chair and crossed his legs. "Well without comparing one situation to another, your family must have found it very hard to make a living on the farm. It's tough work."

Tiffany twisted a stray strand of hair at the nape of her neck. The Baldwins and their faith stories attracted her like a moth drawn to a flame. "How did you continue to believe the factory would prosper and grow in the face of so many challenges through the years?" she asked, humbled by their endurance. "Where did you find the courage to stay with it?"

Glancing at Nellie, George took his time answering. "Yes, it's true we didn't always know where our next meal would come from, but we worked hard and took life each day as it came. We trusted good things would happen as we pushed on through our discouraging situations. But it wasn't always easy to continue trusting when the low odds of succeeding made it hard to believe things would work out."

"So how did you learn to trust?" Tiffany asked.

"God's faithfulness to comfort and encourage us through our failures—crude conditions and tough circumstances—inspired our faithfulness to trust Him. His loyalty to give us the courage we desperately needed to keep working to make the factory a success helped nudge us to continue trusting Him. His faithfulness helped us plug along the best we could. And we tried to remember to thank the Lord for His help and all of our successes, even the small ones."

Nellie stood. "I don't mean to interrupt this serious conversation, but I need to go indoors to tend to dinner, and I would like it if you girls would keep me company and lend a hand with cooking the *tostones*."

"Cook what?" asked Margaret.

"*Tostones*—that's Spanish for fried plantain chips."

As soon as they went to the kitchen, Nellie asked the girls to peel the plantains while she gathered the supplies needed to fry them.

Margaret picked up a plantain and squeezed it. "Are these ripe? I mean are they ready to peel? They're so hard. Bananas are never this firm, are they?"

"The plantain isn't the typical banana. It's a fruit that looks like a banana, but isn't as sweet. It's under-ripe on purpose—makes it easier to slice for frying. Try a bite after you peel one. It tastes like a raw potato."

Nellie fried the plantains and ran them through a small press. Then she returned them to the pan to fry again. "This added step makes them extra crispy," she said, lifting the last batch from the pan to drain. "I doubt either of you will ever bother to fry plantains, but I thought you would enjoy helping me prepare something that's common to this culture."

"You've got me pegged. I'm too lazy for all this work, but I've enjoyed watching you." Margaret popped a fried chip into her mouth. "Hmmmm, not bad at all. They're much better cooked."

Tiffany reached for a chip. "It's easy to see you've done this before. I'm glad you invited us to help."

"Yes, I've fried plantains many times, but I doubt I've ever had more fun preparing them than I have tonight with you girls." Then Nellie handed Tiffany the plate of *tostones* to carry to the dinner table.

When Tiffany entered the dining room, Zachary caught her eye and winked. At the sight of his lazy, sensual smile, she almost dropped the dish full of plantains on the floor.

# CHAPTER 13

After the guests were seated at the dinner table, George remarked that not all Quakers bless every meal out of concern praying could become a habit rather than a sincere expression of gratitude. "But Nellie and I usually bless our meals, so if there are no objections, let's bow our heads in prayer."

Following a brief period of silence, George delivered a short, though meaningful prayer. He gave thanks for the blessing of every good gift in life, and in particular, the bounty of food from God's providence.

After George prayed and Nellie started the platter of pork around the table, he caught her eye and nodded. And from the warm smile on her face, he suspected the presence of the young folks had stirred her motherly instincts in a good way, as he had hoped it would.

By the time Zachary and Tiffany received the entrée they chatted like old acquaintances. And although George seldom jumped to conclusions, he did not doubt for a moment they would make a great pair.

On the other side of the table Jason had captured

Margaret's attention with a description of the eye-catching blue morpho butterfly. "The morpho is a bright iridescent blue color that's edged in black. And it's the largest butterfly in the world with a wing span of five to eight inches. Can you imagine that?"

Margaret spooned a serving of beans and rice onto her plate. "I can't wait to see one in person."

"Don't worry; I'll take you through the gardens myself," Jason said, "and make certain you see a morpho. They're spectacular, but you should also see the leafcutter ants while you're there. They aren't beautiful like the morphoes, of course, but far more interesting."

"How so?" Margaret asked.

Jason danced his fingers in a trail across the tablecloth as he explained how the leafcutters march in a long line with a grandiose sense of purpose to their movements. "Leafcutters slice off a tiny piece of a leaf with their teeny jaws to create a compost of fungus to eat. And this tiny bit of leaf is up to thirty times their weight, if you can believe it." By now, Jason's voice squeaked. "And I've read they can vibrate their jaws up to one thousand times per second, which is hard to imagine."

By this time, Jason's descriptions commanded everyone's attention, including George's, and he had seen and heard it all. He appreciated Jason's enthusiasm and wondered if Margaret did as well.

Margaret fluttered her hands in the air. "Now wait a minute. How do the little buggers know where they're going?"

"When they go in search of leaves to cut, they leave a strong scent trail so they can find their way back to the nest. Now I ask you, is that not crazy amazing?"

Margaret giggled. "They sound like a marvel."

"They are. Can't you just picture them?"

"Yes, I actually can. In my mind's eye I see itty bitty armed soldiers lined up for combat."

"That's perfect," Jason said, "because if you ask me the behavior of the leafcutter ant *is* somewhat human-like."

"Human-like? What do you mean?" asked Margaret.

But before Jason could answer Tiffany chimed in. "What you've just described about ants moving with a sense of purpose and working hard to co-operate with one another to create a positive living environment demonstrates how we as humans should—"

"And what's that supposed to mean?" Margaret asked as she rolled her eyes.

Tiffany held her hands up, palms facing away. "If you'll give me a chance, I'll explain. I mean their ability to live and work in harmony for the good of all provides a profound lesson for how we as humans should behave, don't you think?"

Wrinkling her forehead, Margaret flipped a hand through space. "You know, Tiffany, we're trying to have a simple dinner conversation. We're not involved in a class lecture on biology or philosophy."

Tiffany flashed Margaret a sharp look. "Well I beg your pardon, but I see a worthwhile correlation between leafcutters and humans."

"Excuse me, girls" Nellie said, "but Margaret, have I mentioned that I'm also from Alabama? I grew up there and I love to reminisce about home. Would you share a few stories from your youth with us?"

George almost cheered when Nellie spoke. The girls' not-so-subtle sarcasm made him fidgety. Besides, in his opinion their behavior was unbecoming for girls of their age.

Margaret sat straighter in her seat. "Well let's see,

have you ever gone crabbing?"

"I have, but do tell for the benefit of those who haven't," Nellie urged.

"Crabbing?" Tiffany asked. "You've never mentioned this before. What does that mean?"

"Yeah, what did you do?" Jason asked.

Smiling smugly, Margaret explained that her family spent many summers vacationing at various creamy white sandy beaches around Gulf Shores, Alabama. "We played at the beach off and on all day long, swimming, sunbathing, or riding the waves. And most days, we also enjoyed a game of volleyball or badminton at the beach. But crabbing was our most fun night activity. We competed to see who could catch the most crabs as they came in on the tide. And boy, did we have to act fast as they skittered over the sand at lightning-speed!"

Jason's eyes bugged. "That must have been crazy fun."

"It was. Can you picture dozens and dozens of crabs racing willy-nilly at high speed all over the beach? They looked like those toy cars people maneuver by remote control."

"So how *did* you catch them?" Jason asked.

"Sometimes we used nets and sometimes we popped a bucket over them to scoop up several at once."

Jason snorted. "Man! Did you take them home to cook? And eat?"

"Some people do, of course, but we always turned them loose. Actually, we dumped crabs by the bucketful on one another's feet."

Tiffany's mouth fell open. "You didn't."

"We did! That was the best part—squealing and running to dodge the crabs."

Margaret's story reminded George of his carefree days

of living near the Gulf of Mexico and all the times he had gone crabbing around Mobile. Without doubt his early years in the United States held a special place in his heart, but he kept his thoughts to himself.

George thought about Margaret as he helped Nellie serve the dessert. She said little about the rainforest and contributed nothing to Tiffany's remarks about the similarity between ants and people, but her eyes sparkled when she described crabbing and playing on the beach. Sometimes Margaret seemed a bit flaky, but he had a hunch she had substance. For certain, she had a fun, spunky spirit.

When George set a piece of apple pie before Jason, he nearly laughed aloud. Jason appeared about to drool as he stared at the tiny rivulets of rich vanilla ice cream oozing over warm cinnamon apples that spilled from the crust.

"Oh man," Jason whispered to Margaret, "this looks delicious! And the crust looks like my mom's—all golden and flaky."

Margaret giggled and sniffed her pie. "And it smells good, too. The aroma takes me back to my grandma's kitchen."

It pleased George to see Margaret and Jason interacting, but something told him they would never make it as a couple. They talked easily enough, but parts of their conversation made him doubt Jason ever gave much thought to girls. He seemed more interested in his leafcutter tales, blue morphoes, and apple pie than asking Margaret questions about herself.

Not long after coffee and dessert, as the guests prepared to leave, Nellie said, "Now since all of you are a long way from home, George and I would like for you to consider us your surrogate family. We would love to help you in any way we can. Right, George?"

"Absolutely!" George exclaimed. "Our door will always be open. You can drop by anytime."

Moments later, George noticed Zachary and Tiffany exchanging cell phone numbers. And the expression of bliss on Zachary's face made him think of someone swallowing something smooth and creamy—even intoxicating. It inspired him to give thanks for an evening gone well.

As the door closed behind the young folks, George chuckled out loud that he had fallen heir to the opportunity to introduce Zachary to his mystery girl. Not much to the game of matchmaking, he decided, although the look of envy on Margaret's face as she watched Zachary and Tiffany talking low together made him wonder if he might have helped create a budding rivalry.

## CHAPTER 14

"Margaret? Margaret, are you awake? We need to be out of this hotel room by noon." Eager to move to the furnished apartment Mr. Baldwin helped them locate, Tiffany tossed her duffle bag onto her bed and began folding clothes to the sound of snoring.

Margaret had kept her up late last night talking about the dinner party, but especially Zachary, making it clear she planned to pursue him. Tiffany was also interested in him, but she did not want to risk ruining their friendship over a new acquaintance.

She envied Margaret's strength and courage and considered her a good influence in many ways. Several times on the long flight to San Jose, she stiffened at a strange noise or a change in the flying pattern. But when she focused on Margaret's relaxed demeanor, after a bit, she could let go of her exaggerated assumptions and relax.

When she was with Margaret in an uptight situation, if she observed her nonchalant attitude, it helped her be less anxious. Margaret's confidence and innate ability to

present things in a good light helped ground Tiffany—
helped her trust more and doubt less, at least for a time.
In that regard, she needed to be more like Margaret, but
she didn't so much admire her shrewdness when it came
to getting her way. Margaret knew how to keep the upper
hand in most situations. She would not have a chance
with Zachary after Margaret wrangled a date with him.

Tiffany glanced at her watch. "Margaret? Do you plan
to sleep all day? Seriously? The morning's more than half
over. We have to move out of here in a couple of hours."

There was still no answer. But she had a hunch that
by now her lazy friend only pretended to be asleep. She
removed her jeans from hangers, kept the creases lined
up, and folded them into a neat stack. She had never
competed with Margaret over a guy, and since they were
in a foreign country with only one another to rely on, they
should not start now. They shouldn't let anything come
between them. Tiffany pulled her underwear from a
drawer and tossed them onto the bed. "I'm serious,
Margaret. Are you going to wake up, or not? You haven't
even started packing."

Margaret groaned and rolled over. "You shouldn't
have kept me up so late last night."

"I kept *you* up? You're the one who rehashed the
dinner party at length, discussing Zachary, Nellie, George,
and Jason—and in that order, I might add."

"Yeah, and by the time we turned off the light tension
filled the air so thick it took my breath away. I had
trouble going to sleep."

"Please don't start," Tiffany begged.

"Zachary's still fair game, you know."

Tiffany bristled at Margaret's insolence. "And the way
you flirted with him off and on the entire evening, batting
your eyelashes at though you had something in your eye,

surely clued him in that you're interested."

Margaret threw back the covers and stomped toward the bathroom, stopping only long enough to grab something to wear. "Who are you kidding? You practically drooled all over him."

Tiffany growled. "How would you even know? Your eyes were glued on Zachary."

Though the impossible situation disturbed Tiffany, after Margaret disappeared into the bathroom, she had an *"aha"* moment—she could not control the situation. And neither could Margaret. The next move belonged to Zachary.

Tiffany started folding her bubble gum pink sundress, and as she wondered how she'd ever chosen such a bold color, a loud popping noise from the window startled her. Dropping the dress onto the bed, invisible bugs crawled over her at will as she darted her eyes around the room. Although she saw nothing more than the curtains billowing in and out in the breeze, a shadow of concern drifted over her.

For some unexplainable reason, fear often lurked nearby her, sometimes funneling in without warning to attack her peace of mind or suck the joy from her soul.

She had never suffered a trauma. A masked gunman had never accosted her; nor had a snake ever crawled into her bed. However, she had been a victim of the unmerciful wrath of Mother Nature when a tornado destroyed her family's home one long ago hot summer night.

She could still hear her mother's urgent voice echoing through their wood frame farmhouse as it had that night. *"Tiffany! Tiffany Faith! Get down here right now! A tornado's coming and we've got to take cover. Bring your book and come on before we're all blown away.*

*Do you hear me? Hurry!"*

With her heart pounding like a hammer on a nail, she fled the bedroom and bolted down the stairs as she clutched the favorite of her Carolyn Keene mystery series, *The Hidden Staircase*. She loved to assume the role of Nancy Drew, the irrepressible heroine, and found it difficult to stop reading in the middle of a mysterious plot that would lead to thrills and an unexpected outcome.

*"Run, girls, run! You need to—,"* her mother had shouted that night. But the wind whistling around them sucked away the last of their mother's instructions as she ran ahead to light the way.

Tiffany tucked her head down and raced alongside her sister Karla through pellets of pea-sized hail and cold sheets of horizontal rain. A circulation of debris swirled around them as rumbling thunder shook the earth and lightning lit the sky.

Their father waited at the door to the musty cellar to light the way down the steep, narrow steps. She hated the creepy, cavernous hole in the ground, filled with cobwebs, and who knew what else.

And when she saw her mother searching in the corners and under the hard, narrow benches with a hefty flashlight, her heart nearly stopped.

*What was she looking for? Tarantulas? Scorpions? Centipedes?*

Tiffany shuddered at the images of the horrible insects that surely lurked all over the cramped cellar that stunk from mildew. Built at the turn of the century, the aging cement walls of the cellar suffered from cracks and leaks. But worst of all, the light was too dim to read.

Though it happened many years before, the dread and insecurity of that night had become a part of Tiffany. Maybe it was the reason she became jittery about the least thing that seemed different or unexplainable.

The hair on her arms stood on end as she looked around the room again.

Actually, on more than one occasion since arriving in Costa Rica, she had had a premonition of impending doom—far stronger than ordinary fear. But she was unable to explain her ill-fated feeling.

Perplexed, she shivered as she folded the last garment, a blue knit pullover top, and slapped it into the duffle bag. She zipped the bag shut, and cocked an ear. But she heard only Margaret splashing in the bathtub.

Did a gust of wind pop the curtains? Or was someone waiting right outside the window to catch her off guard? Was the room haunted? But she didn't believe in ghosts. Did she? Maybe a messenger from another realm had come to warn her of potential danger. Suffering from a powerful premonition that something horrific would happen, Tiffany trembled from head to toe.

Finally, she let go of the zipper and pushed the duffle bag aside. Dropping to the edge of the bed, she bowed her head and closed her eyes, but words to pray would not come. Only a pitiful moan escaped her lips as she rocked back and forth in a posture of pain.

# CHAPTER 15

Morning had come far too soon for Margaret, so she pretended to be asleep when Tiffany opened her bags and rustled her clothing. With her back to Tiffany, she stared at the three-toed sloth in the tree right outside the window. It still galled her that Zachary wanted Tiffany's cell phone number instead of hers last night after dinner.

She had nursed a growing frustration, plus a nagging headache, all the way to the hotel, which set the stage for her approach to rehashing the dinner party.

When they finally turned out the lights, Margaret, smitten by Zachary's charm and sexy good looks, easily imagined herself the victor in a battle over him. The thought comforted her like satin sheets at the end of a long, hard day.

But now in the bright light of morning, Zachary's obvious preference made her question her chances of attracting him. Most people viewed her as a confident person, but like anyone else, she had times of self-doubt. Was something wrong with her? Had her flirting techniques suffered from lack of practice? How did

Tiffany *always* attract the guys, while she was left wanting?

When Tiffany hollered for the third time, Margaret groaned and rolled out of bed. A snippy exchange occurred between them as Margaret gathered her clothing and headed to the bathroom.

With the perk of daily maid service at the hotel, Margaret was not particularly motivated to leave. She could eat every meal out without compunction, but Tiffany had budget issues that prompted the need to move to an apartment.

Margaret *did* need more storage space, however, for half her clothing covered the chairs, and her shoes cluttered the floor or straggled out from under the edge of the bed. Her hair care products filled the skimpy space by the bathroom sink, while her makeup covered the desk in the bed area. And it would only worsen after her first shopping trip to San Jose.

She needed to pack, but she gave in to laziness and slid deeper into the frothy soap bubbles to soak and plot how she might attract Zachary.

"Are you planning to spend the day in there?" Tiffany's sarcasm pierced the airwaves.

"Cool it!" Margaret shouted back, shaking her head at how Tiffany's uptight, worry-wart ways did not match up with Zachary's lighthearted and confident air.

Moments later, at the shrill tone of Tiffany's cell phone, Margaret jerked up through the bubbles. Holding her breath, she listened, unable to imagine who had the nerve to call so early in the morning.

When Tiffany hollered through the bathroom door to report Zachary and Jason would be there in a half an hour to help them move, Margaret stood, slung her slight frame from the tub, and grabbed a towel in one rapid movement. She would have to rush, for she refused to let Zachary catch her with wet hair or without makeup.

# CHAPTER 16

Upon entering the tiny apartment they had rented sight unseen, Margaret's wealthy upbringing flashed before her eyes. When she saw the small bedroom that would be hers, she stared at the pasty white walls, longing for the bright, spacious bedroom of her youth. The last couple of years she lived at home, the raspberry and cream color scheme in her bedroom, along with a splash of lime green had bored her silly, but now she thought fondly of her old room. "Is this place small and humble enough for you?" she asked Tiffany.

"It's great—so cozy and cute." Tiffany acted as though they had rented a mansion.

Disgusted, Margaret slumped into a chair, while Zachary and Jason carried in the girls' personal belongings. Unable to bear the thought of spending the afternoon in the cramped apartment, she blurted out, "Let's go see the butterflies where Jason works. The gardens sound like a place Tiffany and I shouldn't miss while we're here."

"That's a great idea," Jason said. "I lead my first tour

group in the morning and I need to practice what I'm supposed to say. Plus, I can show you a blue morpho and the leafcutter ants I told you about last night." After a brief chuckle, he added, "And there's another thing I'd like to show you that's rather special."

So after a quick run for groceries and a light lunch, the four headed for Monteverde to check out the butterflies. Speeding along the rut-filled road, bone-jarringly rough in places, caused a trail of dust to kick up behind them. "Geeeezzz!" Margaret cried from the backseat. "I'll need another shower tonight." She waved her hands in front of her face, hoping her bright idea to drive all the way up the mountain to look at a bunch of insects would be worth the miserable trip.

"But you suggested the outing," Tiffany said, looking unruffled from the front seat beside Zachary.

Margaret glared at Tiffany, wondering how her friend managed to find center stage, while she groveled for the back row.

When they arrived, Jason ushered them into the insect area, and after a few lead-in remarks prepared for tourists, he turned his back to them and lifted the lid of a large glass case. Jason rested something in the palm of his hand and turned to the girls with a mischievous grin, asking who wanted to hold it first.

Tiffany gasped audibly and recoiled to a safe distance.

Jason chuckled as the insect wiggled its long, hairy legs. "I promise this type of tarantula isn't poisonous."

Glancing sideways at Tiffany, whose eyes bulged as she shook her head slowly back and forth, Margaret saw her chance. She held out her hand. "I'll hold it. I'm not afraid."

"Oh wow, are you serious?" Jason asked. "Most girls I know freak out big time over spiders. But tarantulas are the worst—they're so scary looking. I must tell you, I shook like a frightened rabbit the first time I held it."

Margaret received it into her tiny hand. "Ahhhh, it's just a big ol' hairy spider." But in spite of her brave veneer, when the tarantula lifted its legs to creep up her arm, she wasted no time passing it to Zachary, batting her eyelashes at him during the transfer.

"All right, I'll hold it," Tiffany said, her voice quavering.

"Are you sure? You look like you're about to pass out," Margaret said, noting the alarm in Tiffany's eyes and her pale appearance. She guessed Tiffany wanted to take back her offer as soon as the words left her mouth.

Zachary reached for Tiffany's hand. "Here, I'll hold the spider and you cup your hand underneath mine. That way you won't have to touch it."

Margaret tapped her rigid fingers over the glass case. "I've seen enough here. Let's move on and find the butterflies."

After Jason bedded the tarantula back in the case, he took them outside to the winding, forested pathway that led to a small covered pen with mesh on the top and all four sides.

Margaret could not stop smiling as she observed the beautiful butterflies, either fluttering through the air or resting among the flowering shrubs and twisted vines. "Oh my! What a magical place! There are so many different kinds—colors and sizes."

"Yes, we have more than fifty species of butterflies here in the garden from all over Costa Rica," Jason said, explaining they were divided into four separate confined areas according to their habitats.

About six feet into the fenced area, Jason glanced up to his left and pressed a finger to his lips. "Shhhhh, it's a glass wing butterfly." Then he pointed to the tallest shrub near the path, and spoke under his breath. "Glass wings are hard to spot, but it's on the top branch—way up high. Do you see it?"

"Oh yes," Tiffany whispered. "It's so different."

Margaret whispered, "I've never seen anything like it before. It's so delicate, so transparent. You can see right through it—like glass."

"Hmmm. Like glass?" Tiffany asked.

Margaret snickered. "I know. I know. That's how it got its name—glass wing."

Tiffany cupped her hand toward Margaret's ear. "All too often I'm as transparent as the poor little butterfly."

"Yes, that's how you sometimes behave. And I can usually see right through you," Margaret said, keeping her voice low. "And so can everyone else."

"Thanks a lot," Tiffany said as they followed Jason and Zachary to another area to watch the leafcutters at work.

Margaret shifted her weight from one foot to another as Tiffany asked endless questions about the ants. Soon, Margaret felt as antsy as the ants. And when she noticed Zachary staring at Tiffany the way a small child looks at a Walt Disney movie, she lost her cool. "Okay! I've seen all I need to see here. Jason told us all about the leafcutters last night. And yes, they're interesting little critters, but let's move on."

Such heavy silence filled the air following Margaret's outburst that you could almost hear the teensy leafcutters marching along. Jason hastened to move them to another protected area for butterflies.

Upon entering, Margaret stopped dead in her tracks. Hundreds of butterflies of all sizes, shapes, and colors swirled and dipped gracefully through the air. She took in the beautiful, surreal scene like a nature lover admiring a rainbow after a storm. And when a black butterfly with yellow stripes and long black antennae landed on her arm, she held her breath for several seconds.

"It's a zebra-wing butterfly," Jason mouthed.

The fragile butterfly moved its long, narrow wings in and out in slow motion. The intricate details of the tiny creature filled Margaret with an unfamiliar reverence. She watched it for several seconds, but her sweet encounter with the lovely insect ended the instant she caught a glimpse of Zachary whispering in Tiffany's ear. The starry-eyed expression Zachary gave Tiffany made him as transparent as the glass wings butterfly they had just seen.

Margaret looked back at her arm, but the butterfly had flown away. For a moment, she felt as though one of the little insects had worked its way inside her tummy. Filled with frustration and ready to leave, she turned toward the gate. The breathy whispers and long gazes between Zachary and Tiffany were a bit more than she could stand.

But her mood shifted when she caught sight of an iridescent blue butterfly edged in black. Perched on a tropical hibiscus shrub a few feet away, the beautiful butterfly stretched elegantly over a large satiny rose pink hibiscus blossom. She gasped. "Oh Jason, it's a blue morpho, isn't it? It's wonderful! Simply wonderful!"

A few seconds later, it moved on, but somehow, as the morpho soared and dipped throughout the garden, Margaret's doubt diminished a little, and she suddenly had a ray of hope to savor.

Unexpected things still happen from time to time—if she could only learn to exercise more patience. Maybe she needed to adopt Tiffany's subtle approach. But no, that didn't sound nearly as fun.

## CHAPTER 17

Humming softly, Margaret sat on the edge of the couch polishing her toenails a bright chili pepper red, a shade deeper than the red polo shirt Zachary wore for his dinner date with Tiffany. She waved a perfunctory goodbye at the sappy couple as they left for the evening. "Have fun. Without doubt, I will. I'm knee-deep in a great novel."

But when the door closed behind them, Margaret heaved a big sigh and screwed the cap back on the nail polish, tightening it by tiny increments. Tsunami waves of disappointment washed over her as she left the living room. Desperate for something to soothe her soul, she propped against the back of the bed and groped in a box of assorted chocolates.

"Oh no, they're almost gone," she cried out to the empty room. She closed her eyes and popped a chocolate, chocked full of almonds and sweet, soft caramel into her mouth.

But as she savored the silky rich dark *chocolate*, a

slight concern tiptoed in—an entire summer in the sweltering tropics could be a long and lonely one if Tiffany and Zachary became a hot item. She gulped as she swallowed a bitter tear along with the sweet gooey candy.

For a brief moment she wondered if Jason had plans for the evening. He did not have Zachary's finely chiseled good looks, but he was far from homely. His thick, black hair often settled awry on his forehead in a sexy sort of way. And his heavy, dark eyebrows—a little thick for her taste—arched over chocolate eyes, alive with curiosity. *Chocolate!* She managed a smile.

She had nothing against Jason, who was of average height and a bit stocky, but not a single spark had passed between them. Even though she had glimpsed his caring nature—his sensitivity—she knew he wasn't her type.

She was drawn to Zachary like steel to a magnet. But could her southern charm compete with Tiffany's understated charisma and obvious vulnerability? She loved Tiffany, but smarted with envy that she hadn't been the one to attract Zachary.

Margaret thrust her hand into the box of candy for another chocolate. And as she munched on the sugary delight, she played around with a number of engaging scenarios, starring her with Zachary as her leading man.

But in reality she knew only one person well in this foreign land, and it would not be wise or proper to allow anyone or anything to damage her relationship with Tiffany. Would it? She should relax her hold on her fantasies and march on like a leafcutter ant.

*But am I that noble? Or responsible? Really? Can I just ignore my feelings and give up that easily?*

Her ridiculous thoughts made her smile. She retrieved her airy romantic novel from the nightstand. Delving into the story to identify with the book's heroine sounded like a delicious endeavor, especially since she had a lot of time on her hands and wanted to forget something unpleasant. She would read about romance instead of living it—at least for tonight.

She reached for another chocolate—just one more. Gulping, she sat straight up in bed and hurled the empty box across the room. "This is the capper," she shouted. But no one was there to hear her or to see the desperate tears that teased her eyelashes.

A mass of contradiction, Margaret pulled a sigh from deep in her gut and flipped open her juicy romance novel—an intriguing story of star-crossed lovers set in the south of France. She would drift into a fantasy world set in the Loire Valley to try to shake her disappointment.

She had lost the first round of a battle that had only taken place in her mind, but there was always hope of winning the next one. After all, who knew what tomorrow might bring.

## CHAPTER 18

"You're looking great this evening!" Zachary said as he climbed into the jeep beside Tiffany.

"You're too kind," Tiffany said, peering at him through long thick eyelashes. "I'm just wearing plain denim shorts and a simple white cotton T-shirt, but thanks anyway."

"I wasn't trying to be kind. I'm serious—you look super." Then he started the jeep, backed out of the driveway, and headed for the small diner where he had recently met Jason.

A clear balmy night hung over the rustic town as tourists and locals strolled down the sidewalk past a number of businesses and restaurants. Tiffany had never been more pumped on a first date. Even the noise from revving car engines, squealing tires, and barking dogs clattering into the open vehicle excited her. She just hoped the evening lived up to her expectations.

"I'm Wendy," the waitress said after seating them in a corner booth and handing them each a menu. "So are you new in town?" she asked Tiffany.

"Yes, I'm here to attend classes this fall."

"Oh? I see. So you've come to stay awhile." Then Wendy sighed and asked for their drink orders.

"Iced tea," Tiffany said. "With lemon, please."

Zachary held up two fingers. "Make that two."

Wendy wrinkled her forehead. "You want lemon, Zachary? Since when do you drink tea with lemon in it?"

"Since right now."

Wendy scribbled on her order pad as she turned and flounced off.

"Are you dating her?" Tiffany asked.

He tossed his head back and frowned. "Her? Land's no. I haven't dated anyone for months."

"Oh? For months? Seriously?"

"Well, I did go out with Wendy a couple of times not long after I moved here and then again a few weeks ago, but she's not my type."

Tiffany lifted an eyebrow and smiled at Zachary. "You have a type? And what might that be?"

Zachary grinned as their eyes locked. "Who knows, maybe I'm looking at it." Then they began to visit like old friends sharing a secret, speaking low and eye to eye.

"How did you learn about the institute?" he asked.

"The university I attend in California has a sister program with them, so I inquired about coming to study tropical biology."

"And do you plan to teach?"

"I'd like to, but it's doubtful I'm cut out for teaching."

"What do you mean? Why not?"

Tiffany hesitated. She had not known Zachary long, but she wanted to be upfront with him from the start. She was determined to be open and authentic this time, since her last relationship had ended on a disastrous note, partly because she hadn't been honest about her feelings. "I hate to admit it, but I have a phobia about public speaking."

"A phobia? Is it that bad?"

"It's that bad. So as much as I want to teach high school biology, I may need to work in some other area of the science field."

"Like what?"

"Maybe research?"

*Now why did I say all that? I'm telling too much too soon. He already knows I'm afraid of heights. He's so confident he cannot possibly understand my ridiculous concerns over things I cannot touch or see.*

"But my mom who teaches high school Spanish thinks teaching is a worthwhile career choice. She believes that as a teacher you not only have the opportunity to teach, but you have a chance to influence your students in positive ways and encourage them to pursue their dreams."

"The premise of inspiring students to make brave and determined choices for their lives sounds noble, but the thought of opening my mouth in front of others makes me freeze. Let's talk about you for a while. Where did you go to college? Tell me something about your past."

Zachary fingered his glass for several seconds before he answered "I graduated from the University of Florida in the School of Natural Resources and Environment."

"And what brought you here?"

"My college buddy and classmate, Adrian Gomez, aroused my interest in Costa Rica. His colorful stories about his homeland and information about the rainforests inspired me to come find work."

"And where is he now?"

"He went home to San Jose to be near his family. I

haven't seen him in ages."

If Zachary had not moved to Costa Rica to be near his friend Adrian, she wondered if he had another reason for locating so far away from his family and home. Maybe he was hiding something. Or even running away from something. "So you're happy with your job and enjoy living here?"

"Yep! I have everything I could ever need or want right here."

"And do you plan to stay here?" she asked, secretly questioning whether anyone could possibly have everything he or she needs or wants right out of college, or for that matter at any point in life.

"Why not? I'm crazy about this place."

"It's easy to see why." Then she shared how much she enjoyed watching movies and documentaries filmed in mysterious, faraway jungles around the world. "I love watching the big cats—the lions, cougars, and jaguars as they run wild through the jungle. And seeing the monkeys swing through the trees—they're very entertaining. But now that I'm here in person, I've discovered the tropical birds thrill me more than anything. They are *so* bold and colorful."

"Jungles aren't always as active and exciting as the documentaries make them out to be, but spending time in the rainforest can be exciting."

"I must confess that I've thought about staying here after completing my studies. Maybe I could work a year or so for the Monteverde Reserve before I return to San Diego to finish my degree."

Zachary wiggled his eyebrows. "I'd see to it you had a good time."

Tiffany shook her head. "No, I could never lead groups. Never. It's silly to even think such a thing."

*There I go again—I'm whining and isn't pretty, but he makes it so easy to spill my guts.*

"Tell me about Kansas," Zachary said. "I've never traveled that far west of the Adirondacks. What was it like living on a farm in the Midwest?"

"I loved growing up on a farm—all the fresh air and open sky. I spent a lot of time outside. When weather permitted, I rode my bike on the dirt road past my dad's wheat field or explored around the farm on foot. I often stopped to study the clouds to try to make them into something—a flower or a dog, or whatever I could dream up. And I loved going out after dinner to catch the sunset. The bright purple, red, and orange colors that swirled across the sky were so gorgeous it made me happy."

Zachary looked surprised. "Well, I won't admit to that much joy, but I do agree sunsets are quite showy. And sunrises too."

"Sunrises? I've only seen a few of those—they come kind of early, you know." Then she told him about one summer morning during church camp when she was awake early enough to catch an incredible sunrise spreading soft shades of pink, coral, and lavender all over the sky like some fabulous Monet painting. "It was stunning."

"I also spent a lot of time in nature," Zachary said. "I grew up in a small town near the Adirondacks and often went backpacking in the mountains and canoeing on the lakes and rivers. We had great family picnics, school outings, and even church functions in the mountains, but what I loved most of all was camping out overnight."

"Why is that?"

"That's when I really had the chance to think about all the mysteries of the universe. I spent a lot of time studying the stars to find the big dipper and, of course, I always looked for the man in the moon."

"Weren't you afraid to sleep outside in the forest at night?"

"Naahhh. We slept in a tent and assumed the critters that came into camp were harmless, or at least we believed they couldn't get to us. We just trusted we would wake up the next morning in one piece."

"Trusted?" She had such a difficult time trusting in challenging or scary situations. "Seriously? You weren't afraid of the dark?"

Zachary shrugged. "What can I say? Call it innocence or ignorance—take your pick."

Tiffany wished she could confront life with innocence or ignorance. Then maybe dread would not be her frequent companion. She loved all the celestial wonders of the universe, especially the bright stars that glittered against the inky black night sky, but she would not sleep outside for anything.

"So anyway, after I shut my eyes," Zachary said, "I let my mind slip into overdrive to consider all kinds of extra-terrestrial possibilities on Mars, or wherever."

"Camping overnight sounds so brave. I don't know how you did it." Tiffany wanted to slide under the booth at how wimpy she sounded. But she felt the tension drain out of her when Zachary asked about her parents.

"As I've said, my dad is a wheat farmer and Mom stays home, but she does a lot of volunteer work at our church. What about your family?"

"I'm an only child. I keep in touch with my mom by email and cell phone. She knows how to text, but she sometimes writes the old-fashioned way with pen and paper. It's a mystery to me, though why she wants to take time to write a long letter by hand and go to the post office to buy a stamp when there's a faster way to communicate these days."

"And your dad?"

"Haven't seen him in ages."

Zachary's curt response aroused her curiosity, but she did not push. Instead, she mentioned her sister Karla. "She's six years younger, blonde, and much shorter than me, but we think a lot alike."

"Is she also interested in biology?"

"Not so much, but she would have loved the black and white faced monkey that entertained me and Margaret every morning at the hotel."

"Sounds like a capuchin."

"The little monkey jumped from a tree onto the window ledge right by our table and sat for several seconds to watch us eat before moving on. He returned over and over like hired entertainment for the breakfast hour."

Zachary laughed. "Yeah, tourists love them—they're such fun to watch. Almost every morning, right outside my bedroom window, three of them scamper across the tree limbs like trapeze artists at a circus looking for fruit or insects for breakfast. And I might add that the inquisitive capuchins are the smartest of the Central American monkeys and favored by organ-grinders all over the world."

"Karla would have enjoyed watching them in their natural habitat."

"It's clear to me you miss your sister. How old did you say she is?"

"She turned sixteen this summer—driving a car now."

"If she's sixteen and six years younger than you, then you must be about twenty-two?"

Tiffany grinned. "Great math! I turned twenty-two in May of this year. So how old are you?"

"Twenty-four in May."

"You're kidding." Their growing list of commonalities perked her interest all the more. "So what do you do for fun? What are some of your favorite pastimes?"

"Hmmm..." Zachary drummed his fingers on the tabletop. "You go first—you brought up the subject."

"I'd rather watch a sunset than a movie," Tiffany mused. "Or stroll in a flower garden instead of the streets of New York City. Not that I've ever vacationed in the Big Apple. And you?" she asked, noticing how his gorgeous long wavy locks caressed his shirt collar. "What do you enjoy doing?"

"Besides hiking and camping, I like fly fishing in rivers and streams. And I enjoy flowers. Like you said— nature calls out my name the way it does yours."

As Tiffany watched Zachary fondle his glass of iced tea, she easily imagined his long, slender fingers touching her. "Of course, not everyone feels as we do about nature, but somehow I'm not fully alive unless I'm in touch with Mother Nature."

Zachary's eyes lit up. "That's me! I'm more engaged in life when I am outdoors. For me, spending time in nature and enjoying it in countless ways is time well-spent."

While they waited for dessert, Tiffany leaned her head back against the booth. As she stared at Zachary's dimples, she wondered how a smile could be so sexy.

"Would you have time to tutor me this summer on the plants and flowers common to the tropics?" she asked. "And brief me on some of the animals that live in the rainforest? Maybe it would give me a jump on my classes this fall."

As they shared a single scoop of vanilla ice cream it occurred to Tiffany she was more at ease with Zachary after two or three times together than she had been after dating her college boyfriend Eric most of last year.

She marveled at her good fortune to meet someone as nice as Zachary on her first full day in the tropics. A special chemistry seemed to bubble between them. But was she crazy to entertain the notion he could be her soul mate so early in their relationship? Probably! But she couldn't dismiss the warm glow she felt that had persisted throughout the evening. Tiffany reached for her backpack. "I hate for the evening to end, but it's been a long day."

After they had chatted so easily over dinner, Zachary was unusually quiet on the drive home. The awkward silence frustrated her.

Drawn to Zachary's smooth ways and handsome looks, she wondered what she should do when he tried to kiss her goodnight. Should she let him or move more slowly this time?

At the door to her apartment, Zachary took her hand in his, looked into her eyes, and promised to call again. Then he turned and sauntered off.

Tiffany went inside and leaned back against the door, feeling both relief and disappointment that he hadn't tried to kiss her.

*Now, how can that be? I'm glad to he didn't try to kiss me, and yet I wish he had?* But worst of all ... *Why hadn't he tried?*

## CHAPTER 19

Tiffany woke to a morning so perfect she could scarcely believe Monteverde ever had a rainy season. She'd never seen the sky a deeper blue or the sun a brighter yellow. Even the leaves rippling in the tropical breezes just outside her window seemed a bolder green than usual.

Savoring the sweet interlude between waking and rising, she listened from her bed to the birds fluttering from branch to branch. She loved it when they stopped long enough to sing a bar or two.

Right outside the apartment window, the familiar sloth slept like the dead as it clung to a tree. Then a spider monkey came bounding into view to entertain her with a few gymnastics. And when she smelled the sweet fragrance of the Ylang Ylang tree drifting through the open window, her senses went on overload.

With high expectations for the day, she grabbed her cell phone to see if Nellie's schedule would permit a morning visit. She wanted to know her better. Plus, she sensed an incredible faith about Nellie that she hoped to plug in to.

Nellie answered on the first ring. "Wonderful! Your timing is perfect. George just left to run errands. How soon can you get here? I'll perk fresh coffee."

Tiffany threw on her clothes and rushed out the door. As she putted up the mountain, she clutched the wheel with both hands, keeping a close eye on the narrow road leading to the Baldwins' home near the Monteverde Reserve.

Nellie met her at the door. "It's so lovely outside this time of day that I thought we'd visit on the patio."

"That's what I hoped for. Your backyard caught my eye the other night, and I'm quite sure your flowers called out my name to come visit them this morning."

Nellie giggled as she led Tiffany outdoors. "And I'm so glad you heard them. You know they're the loudest before all the dewdrops evaporate in the early sunrays. Now how about a cup of coffee? And would you care for a cinnamon roll?"

Tiffany held her hand over her heart. "Oh my goodness! I'm crazy about cinnamon rolls."

"Why don't you take a quick stroll to check out the flowers while I fetch breakfast," Nellie said.

"Don't ask me twice." Tiffany started down the path for a quick swing through the yard. She returned just in time to open the patio door for Nellie, who carried a large wooden tray loaded with steaming hot coffee, golden pineapple slices, and warm cinnamon rolls.

Tiffany helped Nellie empty the tray onto the green and white checkered table cloth. Then she leaned over to sniff the purplish-pink petals of an exquisite orchid nestled in a simple clay pot in the center of the table. "I saw several tree orchids in the rainforest the other day, but I don't recall seeing this one."

Nellie touched the side of the clay pot. "There are

about thirteen hundred species of orchids in Costa Rica, and this one is called Guaria Morada. It's our national flower. Some people believe the Guaria brings good luck. Plus, this particular species is supposed to evoke peace, love, and hope, which is why I keep one around."

Tiffany cut into her roll. "Do you bake cinnamon rolls every morning?"

"Oh my, no," Nellie said. "Most mornings George and I eat a thick slice of my homemade bread, toasted and spread with jam or jelly. But of course we always have a selection of fresh fruit. Papaya. Mango. Pineapple."

"And do you eat together out here on the patio?"

"We drink a cup of coffee together, but we go our separate ways for a while to do our devotionals in private before we eat breakfast."

"Devotionals?"

"Yes. Through the years I've discovered reading the Bible and spending time in prayer in the morning grounds me for the day ahead."

"I don't often pray," Tiffany confessed, "unless I need help. Actually, I don't really understand prayer."

"Prayer *is* somewhat mysterious; considering we pray to someone we can't see. But for me, prayer is about sharing my heart with the Lord and listening quietly for what I call His whispers of love."

"Whispers of love?"

"Yes, the Lord's love whispers of encouragement or reassurance. Or guidance and conviction."

"You pray and then sit in silence? I can't imagine sitting quietly for very long. A hundred things would run through my mind to distract me."

"Well, of course, I don't always find it easy to remain quiet and listen for the Holy Spirit, especially if I have a lot of things on my mind I need to do or I'm wrestling with a problem. But with a lot of patience and dedication, I've developed the habit of meditating at a specific place and time each day, which makes it easier to focus and listen, as well as speak."

"I'd like to learn how to pray, but ..."

"There aren't any rules. You may pray about anything. And you may pray anytime, anywhere, for God is always near. There's a scripture, I believe it's Psalm 46:10 that says, *"Be still and know that I am God."* It reminds us to listen in silence and remember who God is. Besides sharing our hearts with the Lord, we can praise Him to show our respect, and of course, we can thank Him for all of our many blessings."

"I'm a believer, but I must say that God is abstract in my life right now—always at a distance."

"Are you saying you know of God, but you don't know Him on a personal level?"

"How did you know?" asked Tiffany.

Nellie smiled. "I haven't always known God as a personal friend. Even after I believed in God, it was a while before I formed a relationship with Him."

"But now that you have, do you always feel a connection to the Lord?"

"No, not always. Sometimes, I become complacent and lose sight of God. Sometimes, I focus more on my problem than I do on His power to help me. But for the most part, I make a conscious effort to stay focused on the Lord and to remember that hope found in Him is what sustains me and helps me persevere."

"I just wonder if I'll ever know the Creator first hand the way you seem to."

"I believe you will. Your questions indicate a hunger to know Him. You may not find Him how or when you expect to, but I believe He'll find you. He knows your heart, and some day, perhaps when you least expect it, you'll hear His love whispers inspiring you to respond."

"I don't fully understand, but I do appreciate you sharing with me this morning. I had a strong hunch I could talk to you about spiritual matters, but I still have so much to learn about a faith journey."

"I did, too, at your age, and I still have plenty to learn. No one has all the answers. And for that matter, no one ever will."

"It's all a bit daunting right now," Tiffany said. "But you've given me plenty to mull."

"Well our talk has reminded me how easy it is to become complacent. As I said, I also have times when I need to refocus." Nellie reached out and patted Tiffany's arm. "Now, before you leave, shall we stroll through the yard so I can cut a bouquet of mixed flowers for you and Margaret?"

Tiffany longed to draw on Nellie's wisdom and learn how to trust more. But most of all, she wanted to learn how to face down feelings that threatened to block her from realizing her dreams.

## CHAPTER 20

"How about sharing a small pizza with everything on it?" asked Zachary after he and Tiffany were seated at a table at a cozy Italian restaurant located near the edge of Santa Elena de Monteverde.

After the waitress left to turn in their order, Tiffany said she had exciting news to share. "I've signed up to do volunteer work at the Monteverde Cloud Forest School."

"Doing what?" he asked.

"Garden maintenance chores like pruning, planting, and weeding, and I'll also help with some of the land stewardship projects on campus."

"What's your schedule?"

"Monday through Thursday, so that gives me three days off in a row."

"That's good; you'll still have time to explore the rainforest."

"That's the plan," Tiffany said, "although getting Margaret to go with me may be tough. She's not into nature like we are."

"I'll take you anywhere you want to go," Zachary said,

his heart skipping a beat. The late evening sun that spread glorious shades of purple, red, and orange over the sky formed a perfect womb for nurturing their budding relationship.

"Tell me more about your work as a naturalist," Tiffany said.

Zachary stared at her as she spoke through full, luscious lips the color of red raspberries. Her demure charm and gorgeous face now dominated his days, and every night before he slept titillating thoughts of her danced in his head. In a short period of time she had made substantial inroads into his heart. He could hardly wait to kiss her and feel her long, slender arms wrapped around him.

Tiffany slipped a stray strand of hair behind her ear. "Zachary? Did you hear me? I asked about your work as a naturalist."

"What do you want to know?" he asked, picturing her long, golden brown legs stretching beneath the table.

"What are some of the advantages of the job besides getting paid to work outdoors around plants and animals?"

"Well, I'm seldom bored. I rarely tire of the sights and sounds of the jungle. And it's quite an experience to meet people from all over the world. Some are nice and interesting, but others, not so much. For certain, I've never met anyone as nice and interesting as you." Zachary reached for her hand.

Tiffany smiled and pulled her hand back. "But you handle uncooperative and demanding tourists with such ease."

"Oh?"

"Miss Lucy? The day we met?"

"Oh, right. She took the prize. Yes, it's important to

be friendly and courteous—behave professionally, regardless of how difficult some people are."

"I'm sure you need to stay in top physical condition, since there's a lot of hiking. And be prepared to handle emergencies as they arise, which would require a lot of confidence. It all sounds exciting, but I don't know why I'm pushing for details." Tiffany tugged at her ear. "It's beyond what I could ever do."

When Tiffany went to the ladies' room, it occurred to Zachary that he had never met anybody like her before. He wondered if she was actually interested in his work or if making polite conversation was her forte. She was a mass of contradiction, hyped one minute and doubtful the next. But he loved how she pulled at her ear when a wave of nerves hit her or how her long graceful fingers danced in the air for emphasis when she spoke.

He was not only enamored by her sharp mind and innocent eyes, but he also liked how she filled out her blouse. She did not make it easy to concentrate on their conversation.

When Tiffany returned, Zachary slid a piping hot slice of pizza onto her plate. "Say, how about sharing a favorite story from your youth while we eat? I'd like to know you better."

"I'm not sure it's a favorite story, but as you probably know tornados are quite common in Kansas where I grew up, and when I was nine my family lived through one."

Zachary leaned forward in his chair. "What happened?"

"One Saturday night in May—I was in the fourth grade—a tornado swept across the Kansas plains, leaving a path of destruction that included our family farm, as well as several neighboring farms." Tiffany described how they huddled underground, drenched to the bone from

running through cold rain, while the air roared above
them like a hungry lion. "It felt like we were down there
for hours, but actually the storm passed over in a matter
of minutes. And when we left the cellar, our home was
gone. We were devastated. There was nothing left. Sheet
metal, lumber, and piles of crumbled brick and mortar
littered the yard. And many of our trees were uprooted.
Even tall, strong ones were helpless against the powerful
winds."

Zachary's jaw dropped. "What about your livestock?"

"Many of them, cattle and horses, lay dead or dying in
the pasture. Our farm looked like a battleground. We lost
our home and all of our possessions. Everything was
gone, except for a handful of pictures and mementos that
turned up a few weeks later."

"That sounds like a miracle. How'd you ever find
them?"

"Several people returned things that dropped from
the funnel onto their property. And yes, it was a miracle,
but the real miracle was that we survived. Poor old Mr.
Campbell on the neighboring farm died before he
reached the storm cellar—struck down by a huge tree
limb. Grandmother Connor spoke often of the faith that
got Edna Campbell and her boys through that awful
summer. Night and day, she reminded us to lean on the
Lord for comfort and strength, but I don't recall feeling
comforted or strengthened because of Grandmother's
convictions or prayers."

Even after the many years that had passed since that
awful event in Tiffany's life, Zachary heard the angst in
her voice as she spoke of the storm that destroyed their
home. Though touched by her story, he wasn't sure what
to say. "It must have been awful for you—for all of your
family."

"My mother was inconsolable for days and not herself for months. And we lost our dog Ring, an old black mongrel with soulful eyes and a white ring around his neck. It haunts me that we weren't able to take him to the shelter with us. He hid out somewhere and never turned up."

Zachary reached for her hand. "I'm sure your life changed a lot after the tornado. Do you suppose your tendency to worry about everything relates back to that awful experience?"

Tiffany pulled her hand away. "Or maybe there isn't a connection at all. Maybe I'm just a big worrywart."

"But who wouldn't have a healthy respect for a tornado? Or any of Mother Nature's disasters—hurricanes, earthquakes, or whatever that threatens lives?"

"But I hate it when I'm afraid and don't even know why." Tiffany tugged at her ear. "I was more anxious about everything after the tornado. A friend talked me into enrolling in a speech class a few years later, and I'll never forget the first time I tried to stand before the class to give a speech."

"But you got through it?"

"No. I had sweaty palms and stuttered for several minutes before I gave up and ran out of the room."

"Was it a bad speech?"

"Quite the contrary. In my opinion, the premise of the speech held promise, but I was too nervous to pull it off. So I dropped the class and have since avoided all circumstances that would require me to speak before others.

Zachary drummed his fingers on the table. He considered himself a good conversationalist, but responding to deep inner feelings did not come easily for him. "You are convinced that you can't do something you want very much to do—teach school. But I've a hunch you'll find a way to overcome your phobia of speaking before others. And when you do, you'll figure a way to make your dream come true in spite of yourself."

"That's easy for you to say."

Zachary chose his next words carefully. "It isn't easy to change, but I believe that change is possible with the right help and a lot of hard work."

"Now how would someone as confident and courageous as you recognize how hard it is to change?"

"That's me," he said, "confident and courageous." Although feeling like a coward, he decided not to answer her, for he would rather not unearth what had long been buried. Some of his childhood secrets were too painful or dreadful to recall. So he asked her about the morning they met in the rainforest. "Why were you so uncomfortable? Nothing I said seemed to help. Did something frighten you even before the tour began?"

Tiffany grimaced. "I didn't like how high the bridges were above the ground. Plus, all the swinging and swaying frightened me. It's that simple."

"It didn't look simple. Do you mind talking about it?"

"It's just that you can usually count on me to anticipate the worst in any situation."

"So you tend to let your imagination run away with you?"

"You got it. Several times that morning I pictured things unlikely to occur, letting my imagination spoil what could have been some nice moments. What else can I say?" Tiffany fidgeted with a tendril of hair. "That's enough about me. I'm blabbing too much. Tell me more about yourself."

"What do you want to know?"

"You've told me a few college stories and mentioned

how your friend Adrian influenced you to move here, but you've been mum about your high school days."

"There's not much to tell," Zachary said, hoping that would satisfy her. He was content with their narrowed world, and he wanted to keep it that way. He loved being with Tiffany more than any girl he had ever known. Her insightfulness and ambition, as well as her beauty had him in a dither to get her alone. But something told him he better move slowly with her. He wasn't a patient person, but he vowed to keep his distance tonight, just as he had on their first date.

However, by the time they finished dinner and drove to her apartment, his vow turned out to be wishful thinking. His conviction to move slowly had waned, while his desire to hold her close and kiss her had increased.

Tingling with desire, he killed the motor and reached for her. But she pulled away and insisted they call it a night. She turned to rush from the jeep.

When Zachary caught up with her at the apartment door, he reached to pull her close, but she stretched out her arm to ward him off.

"What's wrong? What did I do?" he asked.

Tiffany pulled her keys from her bag. "Nothing. Thanks for a nice evening."

Uncertain how to interpret her cool vibes, he simply took her hand in his and gave it a gentle squeeze. She didn't pull her hand away this time, but when he leaned in to brush his lips over her cheek, she ducked her head and hurried inside. "Goodnight," he said as the door closed behind her.

Damn it all! On the drive home, Zachary felt like stopping at a bar. Had he irritated her at some point? Or did he ask too many questions at dinner? Or not enough? Maybe he was too casual about her concerns. She appeared relaxed and genuinely interested in their conversation, but clearly, she had discouraged all physical contact.

Although he pictured a star in his crown for good behavior, he swerved around the last curve before home in frustration. He wondered where such nobility to exercise restraint would continue to come from. And for that matter, how much longer could he refrain from having a few beers to help him forget the negative crap in his life?

He wasn't used to being rejected. When he roared to a stop at his apartment, he began to plot his next move. It might take him a while, but one way or another, he would remove the barrier she so carefully erected.

# CHAPTER 21

"I know that yummy smell. Cinnamon rolls!" Tiffany exclaimed as Nellie opened the door.

"And I wanted to surprise you."

Tiffany had not wasted time making her way up the mountain for another early morning visit with Nellie. And as soon as they had settled on the patio she mentioned her most important recent news—her job as a volunteer. "I have all summer before classes start, and I want to make good use of my free time. There are several places I want to explore, but I'll still have plenty of time if Margaret will stop sleeping the day away and go with me."

"Was she asleep when you left this morning?"

"Actually, no. She woke early today because she plans to paint. She's working from a photograph of a coati that she took on the grounds of the hotel."

"Oh, that's the funny little guy with a long snout that looks like a raccoon."

"Yes, and it has a tail longer than its body."

"You tell Margaret I want to see her painting when she finishes," Nellie said. "I used to paint some, but not since I was a girl in Alabama."

Curious about Nellie's ability to move so far from her homeland, Tiffany said, "I'm fascinated you were able to leave everything familiar behind to move to a foreign country at such a young age. Were you ever afraid?"

"Oh my yes, many times. In the beginning, I wanted to bolt every time a new challenge came along. To believe good things would or could happen in the face of such uncertainty wasn't second nature to me."

"But you were so brave to leave the United States to move here. It must have taken a tremendous leap of faith."

"Faith? Faith had hardly entered my mind before I left the United States. I was clueless about hardships back then. I led a sheltered life as a girl. I left home with innocent dreams and plundered blindly into a reality that wasn't easy—even harsh sometimes."

"So why did you come?"

"I loved George and thought coming here with him was my destiny."

"But how did you find the courage to stay?"

"It wasn't easy, but as I matured in my faith, I learned to rely on the Lord. In Him, I found the courage and strength to do the things I thought I couldn't do or was afraid to do. The Lord was patient with me. He remained faithful—always near and ready to help—even when I whined. And believe me, I whined aplenty."

"Did you return to the states to visit through the years?"

"Oh my, yes. And some of my family traveled here. My parents passed on years ago, but I think of them often. Sometimes when I close my eyes to relax out her on the patio I hear Mama's sweet voice playing in my head. I can still hear her calling, "Nellie, where are you?

Can you hear me? It's time for dinner. Are you and your little friends hiding behind the lilacs again?" Nellie smiled wistfully. "My childhood was such a sweet and carefree time. My daddy was a physician, so he was able to provide a comfortable life for us."

"So do lilacs remind you of your mother?"

"Oh yes, I always think of Mama when the sweet smell of lilacs slips up my nose. She often stopped to sniff a cluster of blossoms from the hedgerows of lavender lilacs in our backyard. And when Mama worked in her flower garden, she always wore a wide-brimmed, floppy straw hat to shield her face and garden gloves to protect her hands."

"And your daddy?"

"The smell of vanilla makes me think of Papa. He used this stuff called pomade on his hair that smelled like vanilla. It gave it a silky shine and made him look rather dapper."

"It's neat how our memories of people or events are often triggered through our senses. The other day in the rainforest I caught a whiff of a mild, pleasant aroma—tree orchids, I think—that reminded me of Grandmother Birdwell. I loved snuggling up to her in church every Sunday morning as a girl. She always smelled so nice."

Nellie's eyes widened. "Come to think of it, the scent of mint reminds me of Grandma Haeger. I loved her so. When she smiled, her papery thin face was lined like a road map. Many hot summer afternoons, we played *Old Maid* on Grandma's sun porch and ate chocolate chip cookies, fresh hot from the oven. She served me cold milk, but she always sipped iced tea, never failing to put a sprig of mint in it."

Tiffany smiled. "I have another memory to share that's still ongoing. The smell of cinnamon reminds me of

Glenda Potts

my mother. Every Christmas Eve, my sister Karla and I help Mother prepare cinnamon rolls. They are similar to yours, Nellie—very yummy. Mother pops the rolls into the oven on Christmas morning before we gather around the tree to investigate Santa's generosity. Afterwards, we eat a hearty farm breakfast of scrambled eggs, crispy bacon, buttered toast, and fresh grapefruit, and top it off with Mother's wonderful cinnamon rolls."

"What a lovely tradition! And may the smell of cinnamon always remind you of your mother," Nellie declared, smiling warmly. "And as far as keeping our loved ones alive in our hearts through our senses, the same applies to keeping the Lord alive within us every day, don't you think?"

Tiffany twisted her ponytail around and around on her fingers. "Are you saying we can be reminded of God through our senses as we experience Him in creation?"

"It's something to ponder," said Nellie. "So I think we've analyzed enough for one day."

Tiffany held up one finger. "I'd like to tell you one more thing? Grandmother Connor, who died several years ago, loved to quote an old Chinese proverb that went something like this: *We mustn't forget our ancestors, for to do so will make us like a stream of water without a source, or a tree without roots.* And after all these years, it's beginning to make sense."

"Yes, and the Lord is our ultimate ancestor, for we are all rooted in His love," Nellie said. "And as such, He will empower us to withstand the storms of life and strive to be all He created us to be."

Tiffany's heart had warmed from the large helping of soul food Nellie had dished her. "May I ask you one last question about when you came to make Costa Rica your home?"

At Nellie's nod, Tiffany said, "It's easy to see you consider this your home now, but have you ever regretted moving so far away from your family?"

"Oh, I suppose we all regret some of our choices along the way, but there's no use in it, since regret doesn't change anything. But actually, no, I don't regret moving here. It's a wonderful place to live. It's my home. Like I've said, there were major adjustments, but once I learned to lean on the Lord, I discovered an ongoing and invaluable source of hope. When I truly believed in God's power to help me, I was better off."

"Believe. That's a powerful word."

"Believing is the essence of a faith journey."

"Once again, you've given me a lot to think about," Tiffany said, letting a smile validate her appreciation.

Nellie tilted her head as she looked at Tiffany. "I am honored to be your spiritual mentor, but why all these questions?"

Tiffany tugged at her earlobe. "And believe it or not, there are more."

"I'm not surprised, but what prompts you to be so inquisitive this morning?"

"There's just *so* much I don't know about spiritual or religious matters, or for that matter, life in general."

Nellie took off her glasses and rubbed the bridge of her nose. "Few do at your age. But what in particular are you dealing with right now? Something challenging? Frightening?"

"I hate to do anything new. It doesn't take much to set me on edge. It frightens me to leave my comfort zone—the life style and situations I'm used to."

"You're here. You've come a long way from home to study. That's good, isn't it?"

"Yes, but it took a *lot* of courage and Margaret

goading me. Then, lo and behold, in spite of my countless reservations about coming, and my anxiety on the bridge that first day, I fell in love with this place."

"There's a special allure about Costa Rica for many of us. So, what's the problem?"

"I wonder where my feelings will lead me. The rainforest is so compelling with its endless green trees and beautiful flowers. And I love the sounds of the animals and birds—even the mist. To me, the thrill of being in the jungle is larger than life. And I find myself actually entertaining thoughts of living here, if you can believe it." Tiffany felt her face redden over her premature comment.

"What's your incentive to move here besides your new infatuation with Costa Rica? Is something else beckoning you?"

"Uhhhhh… Well I met Zachary on my second day here, and we've been together several times since your dinner party. I like him a lot."

Nellie sipped her coffee and then looked Tiffany square in the eye. "Yes? Go on."

"Well you've known Zachary for a while now. Surely you can see why I'm attracted to him."

"Of course I can. He's a nice young man."

"And besides the obvious, I value his opinion. He's smart, as well as good-looking," Tiffany said. "In fact, he may be too perfect to be real."

"I've wondered that about George from time to time, especially back when we … What am I saying? I still do. His craggy good looks and stalwart ways are still attractive to me. But your relationship with Zachary is brand new. Just take your time and be prayerful about your choices."

"You've given me a lot to process. So how did you get to be so wise, Nellie?"

"If I'm wise, it comes from years of living as I've

gained insight from my experiences and as I've observed others. I believe most people gain a deeper understanding about life as the years pass. You'll grow wiser with the passing of time. You're already an insightful and lovely young woman, Tiffany. You'll figure things out."

Tiffany stood to leave. "It's hard for me to see beyond today and my tendency to fret about everything, but I hope you're right about me growing wiser."

In truth, she couldn't imagine gaining the kind of insight about God that Nellie seemed to have. It was hard to believe she could ever connect with a higher power as Nellie described.

# CHAPTER 22

"Are we absolutely certain riding horses is what we should be doing with our time?" asked Margaret as she and Tiffany rode with Zachary and Jason to a farm to go horseback riding. She supposed one could call it a double date, but she knew better. She enjoyed Jason, but trying to pair the two of them would be a waste of time. She had no interest in him, although it disheartened her that he apparently felt the same about her.

"You'll love it, and I dare say it'll be a fun, action-packed experience that you'll never forget," Zachary said. "The experienced guides will lead us over private trails for a couple of hours. And by the way, I'm not a cowboy, but I rode with these people the first summer I lived here and I had a great time."

Tiffany patted her hands together and glanced into the backseat. "It'll be such fun. The scenery should be great and the company even better. I'm crazy about horses. I once had a horse named Patience that was so sweet and gentle that it made riding a horse a breeze."

"Well, I'm glad you're hyped about all of this. I'm not

so sure," Margaret said. "I haven't ridden a horse since I was five; if you could even call it that—my dad held the reins and led the horse around in circles at a dude ranch in Colorado on a family vacation one summer."

Not long after they arrived, one of the guides said, "All of our horses are gentle and well-trained. And we try to match the size and temperament of our horses to the rider."

But Margaret did not buy it. "Hey, my horse has its head hanging down low and it's breathing evenly in and out. What does that mean?"

The guide chuckled. "It means your horse is relaxed. It'll be fine."

Trembling inside, Margaret shifted back and forth in the saddle. She dreaded the ride worse than she had ever dreaded anything, including college finals. Swallowing hard, she sat stiffly on her small, blond horse while one of the guides gave basic riding instructions.

Finally, they were underway. As they rode along, it became clear to Margaret that the others considered the pasturelands a paradise for horseback riding, but she could have lived without the breathtaking views. She did not enjoy the lapis blue sky overhead or the mountain peaks that pierced puffy white clouds. She failed to appreciate the verdant meadow, dotted with massive boulders, or the tall trees that lined the path. Annoyed that she had come, the clear, gentle air did not impress her either.

But after plodding alongside Tiffany for a half an hour without a mishap, Margaret began to relax enough to move more in rhythm with the horse's stride. She even caught Tiffany's eye and giggled when her horse whinnied and swished its tail.

Tiffany hollered. "Did you hear a bird cawing a few

minutes ago? Or see the creature scurrying through the pasture off to the left?"

"No. By then I was studying the clouds. Have you noticed how they sometimes dip so low into the valley only a crescent remains visible?"

Tiffany looked over at Margaret. "You noticed the scenery?"

Margaret grinned. "Now don't get your hopes up."

"Smell that?" Tiffany asked, sniffing the air.

"You mean the stench of the sweaty horses?"

"No, I mean the aroma of coffee plants mixing with the sweet smell of sugar cane."

Margaret noticed Tiffany sat upright with her back straight, and that her feet were a third of the way into the stirrups, with her heel pointing downward. So she relocated her feet and moved in to a more upright position. For a few minutes she rode like a regal queen on a throne. But her mood changed in a flash when big gray clouds rolled in and began to drop a heavy mist. And when she spotted a big, ugly black bird circling overhead, a tremor shot through her. She hated vultures. She considered the lurking bird an omen of something awful to come.

She couldn't imagine what motivated the group to continue riding under such dire circumstances. It was about to storm, for goodness' sake. Where had their good sense gone? Or did they even have any? If only she had worn a helmet—or better yet, refused the invitation to ride a horse in the first place.

Margaret shifted her weight in the saddle and snuggled her feet deeper into the stirrups. She reached into her bag for a rain poncho, but accidentally dropped one of the reins. When Margaret's startled horse shot forward and stumbled on uneven terrain, she let out a heart-stopping scream.

"Oh no! Oh no! Hang on Margaret!" Tiffany hollered as Margaret's terrified horse reared up on muscled haunches and pawed the air, pitching her to the ground.

Margaret landed face down on the unyielding earth, her head striking mere inches from a large boulder.

"Margaret! Are you all right, Margaret?" Tiffany cried as she jumped from her horse. Zachary and the guides were already in attendance as she knelt beside Margaret whose arms and legs were spread awry.

"Margaret! Can you hear me?" she shouted. "Wake up! Oh please, speak to me … Please?"

With only an eerie silence following Tiffany's outburst, she whimpered and ran her fingers through Margaret's long blonde hair that fanned around her stony face.

# CHAPTER 23

Trembling, Tiffany slumped toward Zachary. "Dear Lord in heaven, she's not dead, is she? We've got to do something."

Zachary caught her in his rock-solid arms and held her head against his chest. Even in her worried stupor, she felt Zachary's fingers catching in her tousled, kinky strands as he murmured reassurances in her ear.

A gash on Margaret's scalp had already begun to ooze blood onto the grass by the time the guides could provide a first aid kit. They eased Margaret to her back and applied pressure to her wound with sterile gauze. Then they checked for a pulse and examined her pupils.

The horses whinnied and trampled the earth, while a howler monkey barked faintly from afar. Even above the squawking covey of birds circling overhead, Margaret's moan, softer than a baby kitten could be heard.

"She's coming around! Can you see me, Margaret?" Hope filled Tiffany when Margaret tried to open her eyes.

Jason knelt and spoke low in Margaret's ear. "Hang in there; we're all here with you. You're going to make it.

You're too tough to let a horse have the upper hand. So don't do it. You hear me Margaret? Don't do it."

One of the guides nudged Jason aside. "We need to check for broken bones and clean and bandage her wound."

Margaret blinked. "I'm bleeding?"

"You'll be fine—just try to relax," said the guide. "We'll fix you up enough to get you back to the farm. Then we'll take you to the emergency center to be checked. Tell us what you can see."

"Everything's blurry. And my head hurts," she said, fingering a goose egg that had popped up on her forehead.

When she tried to sit, one of the guides gently restrained her. Margaret groaned. "Where's my horse? Shouldn't I get back on?"

Tiffany had swung between worry and hope for several minutes, but now with Margaret's questions she was stuck on sweet, glorious hope.

Margaret tried to pull herself upright. "Ohhhhhh … I feel sick. And dizzy." Then she passed out again.

But this time Tiffany did not have enough time to entertain a litany of morbid thoughts before Margaret regained consciousness and asked how far they were from the barn.

Tiffany forced a laugh. "I can't believe you, Margaret. You have scared us enough. Let's get you back to have you checked out ASAP."

When they determined Margaret could be safely moved, Zachary volunteered to take her on his horse. Tiffany flinched and looked away when Margaret's head lolled backward against Zachary's chest and nestled into his neck.

During the return trek, Tiffany had plenty of time to

think. It was ridiculous to be so jealous of Margaret. Why couldn't she believe in her own self-worth? She needed to gain more confidence—be more self-assured. And she certainly needed to be more trusting. Insecurity held her back from doing the things she wanted to do.

Tiffany plodded down the trail behind the others, longing for a miracle to change her attitude and approach to life.

# CHAPTER 24

"They tell me you'll be fine," Tiffany told Margaret when she noticed her sagging on the edge of the examining table.

"But my wrist ... Is it broken?" Margaret asked holding her sore wrist against her body.

"It's sprained," answered a nurse. "And you've suffered a mild concussion. Also, a wound in your hairline just above your left eye required several stitches."

"But I'm all right?"

"Yes, the wound is only about an inch long. You're a lucky young lady. We've seen much worse in here. You'll have several ugly bruises and will be quite sore for a few days, but you'll mend. We're sending you home with a prescription for a mild analgesic. And you need to rest, but don't go to sleep for a while. Call us if you start vomiting or have any questions or problems."

Margaret didn't speak a word all the way home, which unnerved Tiffany. For one who had the nickname "miss chatter chin" as a young girl, Margaret was surprisingly quiet.

At the apartment, Margaret announced a slight headache and went straight to her room to rest.

"But remember, don't go to sleep," Tiffany said. "I'll bring you a cup of hot tea in a few minutes. Sound good?"

A half hour or so later, when Tiffany took in the tea, she found Margaret in bed, but awake and staring out the window. "What's on your mind? Do you want to talk?"

"Maybe …"

"About the accident?"

"The curtains are so pretty—such a bright floral fabric. I can sometimes see patches of sky as they move back and forth in the breeze. It's all so lovely." Margaret blew on her tea and looked around. "Life's a miracle, isn't it?"

Tiffany pulled the curtain aside and looked out the window just as the last sliver of sun slipped behind the trees. "It's such a nice time of day—that special time when the sun still lights the world even though it has dropped from sight."

"Do you see the lazy sloth?"

"He's alive and well—moving just enough to keep you company."

Margaret's eyes watered. "And is that a little songbird I see in the tree?"

"Oh yes, it's high on that crooked branch angling upward to the left—right above the sloth. It flew from perch to perch, but finally stopped to roost right in your line of vision. That should lift your spirits. And by the way, you've just proven there's nothing wrong with your eyesight."

Margaret gulped. "I've never spent much time analyzing the events of my life, but this has given me a lot to think about."

Something important had happened to her friend. Margaret appeared unusually vulnerable and extra thoughtful. "We're grateful your injuries weren't serious. You'll be fine."

"As it turns out, my pride suffered more than anything."

"What do you remember about the ride back to the farm?" Tiffany asked, hating herself for doing so, but the image of Zachary holding Margaret close in his arms was still etched in her mind.

"Not much, except I rode with Zachary on his horse. And isn't it interesting that if he'd held me in his arms a few weeks ago, it would have thrilled me beyond words, but today I saw it as nothing more than an act of human kindness." Margaret sniffed and reached for a tissue. "I'm so grateful for no broken bones."

"You could have broken your neck or split your head open on that rock."

Margaret blew her nose. "Or the horse could have kicked me."

"Right. But none of that happened."

Margaret massaged her neck. "If I'm fine, why am I crying?"

"Even though the accident didn't result in serious injury, it has you thinking about serious things."

"I feel so grateful. I ... I suppose my experience could be labeled a wake-up call. You know I'm not easily frightened, but from the first mention of riding a horse, I wanted to beg off and stay behind. I was terrified when the horse bolted."

"It scared me, too. It all happened so fast. And when your horse pitched you off toward that boulder, I imagined the worst. Your head hit with such a thud that I pictured it breaking open like a watermelon dropping to the hard ground."

Margaret gave Tiffany a half-smile. "I've been doing a lot of thinking. I've always been so impatient with you and your phobias. And for that, I am sorry. I'm beginning to see I've taken life for granted for far too long."

"We all take life for granted sometimes and become complacent." Tiffany said. "In fact, Nellie made the same remark to me the other day."

Margaret pointed toward her dresser. "Will you hand me my cell phone? I want to call home."

"Of course, I'll leave you alone to rest. We'll pick up on this conversation another time, if you'd like. Let me know if you need anything."

Tiffany had never heard Margaret talk this way before, as though she did not want to lose sight of a miracle she had just witnessed.

# CHAPTER 25

George laid the newspaper on the breakfast table to add an 's' to form the word *brans* for the clue 'fiber-rich cereals.' He enjoyed working the daily crossword puzzle. Besides, he had read somewhere that doing so might help his brain cells stay healthier longer.

A long time ago, he discovered spending time in prayer and reading scripture every morning kept his soul fueled. As for his body, he tried to remain active and eat a healthy, balanced diet, although Nellie's handiwork in the kitchen sometimes played havoc with his good intentions.

George set the newspaper aside and stabbed at his gooey cinnamon roll. "You've made these a lot lately, Nellie. You know how I love them. I bet you could sell them, if you had a mind to."

"Psshaw! You flatter me, George." Nellie refilled his coffee cup. "But now that I have your attention … Did you finish the crossword puzzle?"

"Yep, I zipped right through it this time. So what's on your mind?"

"I'd like to talk about my recent visits with Tiffany. This is a huge time in her life. She seems to be at a crossroads and searching for something."

George furrowed his brow. "Like what?"

"It's my opinion she seeks, not only guidance for her future, but also spiritual understanding. She's a Christian with many questions about a faith journey."

"She strikes me as being a bright and sincere young lady," George said, and then he told Nellie how intently Tiffany listened the night he spoke at the hotel about relocating to Costa Rica.

"The other morning she quizzed me at length about moving here. She asked how I managed to persevere through so many hardships to make a new life so far from home."

"Ohhhh, now that's verrry interesting. Did she mention Zach?"

"Indeed she did. Their relationship has progressed quickly, like ours did all those years ago." She smiled. "Not that I minded your prince charming ways that rushed matters."

George grinned and winked at Nellie.

Nellie tossed some bread crumbs onto the patio for the birds. "But I urged Tiffany to go slowly in their relationship. Some things shouldn't be rushed, you know."

"I wonder how Margaret is this morning. She must have taken quite a tumble."

"I'll call and check on her before I leave for the ladies' gathering at the Meeting House. And just so you'll know, right after the meeting, I plan to stop at the Butterfly Gardens to see Jason and capture a few butterflies with my camera."

"Say, why don't you take Jason a cinnamon roll? Or

maybe two—he'd love it."

"That's a good idea. Now another thing ... Do you suppose Zachary feels responsible for Margaret's accident? Or that he might need to talk about what happened?"

George downed the last of his coffee. "Hmmmm. Well there's certainly no reason he should feel guilty, but I'll give him a call—see if he can meet me over his lunch break. That'll give him a chance to open up, if he needs to."

"Zachary respects your opinion, so I doubt your words would fall on deaf ears. I'm sure you could say something helpful."

"You think so?"

"I know so. Oh, he may dismiss your remarks at first, but something wise you say could pop into his head later on."

"He's such a fine young man. I'll see if I can catch him between tours. I don't run in to him like I used to, since Tiffany's been in town. I really miss being around him."

George met Zach at a café specializing in Spanish cuisine located not far from where he lived, and only minutes from where Zach worked at the reserve.

After ordering lunch, George asked Zach about his tours. "Do you have any new experiences to tell about? Met any interesting people lately?"

"Oh, I've had new experiences, all right. Every tour is interesting and every day is different—different wildlife sightings, different people." Then he talked about the growth of tourism in Costa Rica and the growing number of visitors that come specifically to visit the Monteverde area. "I guess the word has spread about our beautiful rainforests and great climate."

"But I understand it isn't only tourists who come here. Some folks are moving here to work or to retire here."

"And building tree houses in certain areas has also become a popular thing to do," Zachary said.

"I'm pleased people want to come. Tourists are a boon to our economy, but I hope the environment doesn't suffer from all the new development."

Zachary scowled. "Right. I hate it that clearing the land often disturbs some of the creatures."

George clenched his mouth and shook his head. "It's wrong to bother the wildlife that's lived in the rainforests for eons. I mean, it's great to grow and change, but not all change is good."

"And I'm sure as one of the founders of this area you have a special interest in what happens around here. I've noticed how you stay involved in community affairs. So what are you up to these days?"

"It's nice of you to ask," George said, touched by Zach's rare inquiry about how he spent his days. "It's a rewarding time in my life. Most nights I sleep like a baby and wake up rested and ready to pursue the hobbies I enjoy. But I spend the main chunk of my time volunteering at the Monteverde Friends School. It's gratifying to help my fellowman in whatever way I can."

"Is that the school the Quakers founded back in the early fifties?"

"Yes, and it now serves Costa Ricans and North Americans, as well as Quakers. The school places a strong emphasis on hard work, community development, and personal growth."

"Do you speak to the students about the history of

this area?"

"Yes, and I also touch on spiritual awareness, when it's appropriate."

"Well, they're lucky to have you. Say, I just spoke to Tiffany about Margaret before I met up with you.

George noticed Zach always steered clear of any talk of religion or spirituality. "So is she going to be all right?" he asked.

"Tiffany says Margaret has improved, but is quieter than usual—rather reflective, in fact. Which I understand is out of character for her."

"I would guess the accident has her wrestling with priorities," George said. "A close call can do that to you. It can grab your attention and remind you to wake up and appreciate life."

Zachary ran his fingers through his hair. "I feel so guilty about what happened to Margaret."

"Guilty?" George asked, as he looked Zach in the eye. "And why is that, Zach?"

"Because I suggested we go."

"It was an accident. There's no reason for guilt. Sorry it happened? Yes. But you needn't view it as anything but an accident."

"I appreciate your comments, but guilt is a hard thing to kick. I feel bad about the entire situation.

"Go easy on yourself, Zach. The accident wasn't your fault just because you suggested the outing. Just let go, you hear? Hanging on to unnecessary guilt won't solve a thing." George said. "Now tell me about Tiffany. How is she doing since the accident? I'm sure it upset her."

"She freaked out at first, but she's an amazing person."

George narrowed his eyes. "And what's that supposed to mean?"

"I'm crazy about Tiffany. I think about her day and night. So tell me ... What do you think about her?"

"Tiffany? Why I've grown quite fond of her," George teased.

Zachary tapped his spoon handle against the table. "I'm serious. I've never been in love before, but she's everything a guy could want."

"So you think she's more than a pretty face, huh?"

"No doubt about it, she is very special. Besides being beautiful and sharp, she's deep and insightful."

"Sounds like you're in a bad way, my boy."

"Yeah, but one thing bothers me. She's so uptight about everything—about us."

"You mean she's cautious about becoming too physical too soon?"

"Yeah, if you want to be blunt about it. How did you know?"

George smiled at his memories. "Maybe she's cautious with good reason. Maybe she doesn't want to jump into a serious relationship. And who could blame her with the divorce rate climbing all the time? Folks ought not to get in such a hurry. They ought to take it slow and easy and get acquainted before they rush in to making serious decisions that involve a lifetime."

"And that would require patience and understanding that I'm not sure I have."

"Just give it time. It's not an easy situation you're in, but you're a fine young man and you'll do the right thing."

Zachary glanced at his watch. "I've got a tour starting in less than half an hour, so I better run."

"And I need to make a run to town to do a few errands for Nellie. She made a list for me in case I had extra time on my hands after lunch." George chuckled at the notion he would ever have extra time. He never had enough time for all the things he wanted to do. But long ago, he decided it wasn't about how much time he had to spend, but rather, how he spent the time he had. He wanted each day to count for something and he had a good feeling about the time he had just spent with Zach.

"I enjoyed our time together, son," George said as they left the café. "And Zach, another word before we part—not to repeat myself, but remember that it wasn't your fault Margaret was thrown from a horse. We must take responsibility for our own actions, but we don't have to go through life carrying unnecessary guilt. Now you take care and keep in touch, you hear?" Then before George sauntered off to his jeep, he gave Zach a big, warm bear hug that lasted several seconds.

## CHAPTER 26

"Hey, Jason, if you don't have anything better to do today, what do you say we buzz up to the cheese factory for a tour?" A heavy rain had forced Zachary to cancel all his morning tours. Besides, he needed to shake a restless mood.

"Sounds great," Jason said into his cell phone. "I'll watch for you in front of the gardens."

After the rain slowed, Zachary zipped up the hill, eager to see Jason's reaction to the factory, and in particular, his enthusiasm over the ice cream samples available at the end of every tour.

Zachary usually thought of George when he thought about the cheese factory. George's display of affection yesterday made him feel like a little boy loved and a man revered, all at the same time. He couldn't recall the last time a man had hugged him. The embrace had given him a warm fuzzy feeling that he wouldn't mind hanging on to.

He was grateful for George's willingness to listen to him like a dedicated father, but like any good parent,

George expected him to do the right thing with Tiffany. And he wasn't sure he could trust himself to refrain much longer from putting moves on her.

When he and Jason arrived at the factory, they discovered the last tour of the day had just ended.

Crestfallen, Jason asked, "So when can we reschedule?"

"Next time it rains?" Zachary said.

George entered the factory, shaking raindrops from his umbrella. "Hey, guys, what's going on?"

"I brought Jason to check out the factory," Zachary said, "but the tours have ended for the day."

"You're in luck," George said. "I happen to know a little something about this place. I'll take you around."

"Wow!" Jason exclaimed. "Zachary tells me you know more about the factory than anybody else does, anyway, so it would be a real treat if you had time to do this."

"Well, then, what do you say we get started?" George said. "But first, let me give you a brief overview of the founding of the cheese factory."

George explained that they signed legal papers to build in the spring of 1953, but construction on the excavated site didn't begin until later that autumn. The narrow, unpaved roads leading to the remote site added to the overall burden of bringing the extensive plans for the factory to fruition. It required the work of many people to complete the massive undertaking, but they were fortunate to have a man who had majored in the dairy industry at college to come on board early as plant manager.

"Of course, we had to learn how to make cheese," George said, "but several families in the group were dairy farmers back in Alabama, so even before we left the United States we considered the possibility of producing cheese. One family, before they came, even visited a processing plant in Wisconsin to study how to make superior cheeses."

"And how many different types of cheese does the factory currently produce?" asked Jason as George led them to the area where the tours began.

"I believe it's around seventeen, including Baby Swiss and Parmesano. Incidentally, Gouda was the first pasteurized cheese produced in Costa Rica." Then George elaborated on a few of the many changes that took place over time, including replacing Quaker Oat tins for the cheese molds when more modern technology and equipment became available.

"You must have been determined to make it a success. It sounds like you worked hard as a team."

George smiled and nodded. "That, we did. We meant business. And it was an advantage that Quakers are devoted to helping one another in any way possible. We produced good products and built a favorable reputation that eventually led to shipping products to all parts of Costa Rica, as well as exporting them to other Central American countries. The factory now employs at least one hundred Costa Ricans. That's a fact we're quite proud of."

Jason chuckled. "It sounds like you worked together the way my leafcutter ants do—diligently and in harmony with one another for the good of all."

George shook with laughter. "I like that comparison. We were determined to work as a unit to provide for our needs as a whole. We pushed on with a cooperative spirit in spite of setbacks and challenges."

With a serious look on his face, George added, "And if you don't mind my saying so, I believe the success of the cheese factory is a prime example of what happens when we trust a higher power to provide for us. We believed in ourselves and the project from the beginning, but more importantly, we believed the Lord would carry us through."

With a pensive look on his face, Jason said, "Ahhhhh, the power of steadfast faith, my grandpa would say."

Zachary noticed George always gave credit to a higher power for all his successes, but he could not wrap his mind around that kind of faith—believing in a helping power that is only in your head. "Say, George, how about showing us how they process the cheese and make the ice cream."

"I'd be glad to. And if you'll hang in with me to the end, we'll have a chance to sample some of the cheese and several ice cream flavors."

Jason grinned like a student hearing the bell mark the end of a long school day. "Are some of the ice cream flavors produced from crops that are grown locally?"

"Sure enough," George said. "We have coffee. Coconut. Pineapple. Orange. Mango. And several others. You can sample them all, if you're up to it."

Jason's eyebrows shot up. "Now you're talking. Let's go."

# CHAPTER 27

Holding a glass of orange juice with the chill long gone from it, Tiffany stared into space recalling an article she had read several times that compared a soil garden to a soul garden. Of course, she couldn't remember the details, but she recalled the basic premise was that the crusty earth of a soil garden must be loosened, and rocks, sticks, and weeds removed before vegetable or flower seeds can adhere to the soil and take root. And that in a soil garden, rain, sunshine, and proper pruning help produce vegetables and flowers worthy of harvesting for man's purposes.

Similarly, the hardened human heart of a soul garden must be softened, and indifference removed before seeds of faith in God and His love can adhere and germinate. And that in a soul garden, spending time reading God's Holy Word, worshipping Him, and communicating with Him through prayer help produce Christian virtues—the fruit of the Spirit—worthy of harvesting for God's purposes.

She could not think of all the virtues, but

remembered love, joy, and peace topped the list of the fruit of the Spirit. This abstract comparison helped Tiffany understand that the heart must be open and willing to receive God's love and goodness. And that it must be tended in order to thrive. Although the two gardens varied greatly, she liked the correlation that linked the human heart to an earth garden.

After nibbling on stale toast, she walked to the sink and dumped the warm orange juice. She poured a cup of coffee and carried it to the kitchen window to stand for a minute in the warm morning sun. As she sipped the coffee, while listening to the distant sounds of waking wildlife, she noticed the lazy sloth still sleeping soundly in the tree. It reminded her Margaret was also still asleep on this quiet Sunday morning.

*Sunday!* Tiffany suddenly had an urge to attend a worship service. But where? The Catholic Church down the street? She did not think so, for the one time she visited a Catholic service with a college friend, although it was a lovely service, it proved too formal for her taste. Then she remembered the Friend's Church Nellie and George attended. Interested in how Quaker services were conducted, she decided to call and ask about visiting with them.

"We'll meet you at the front door of the Meeting House in about an hour," George said. "It's near our house on the road to the rainforest. You can't miss it."

Before they entered, Nellie briefed Tiffany on what to expect, explaining that instead of a sermon, Quakers sit in silence for the duration of the worship service in an effort to seek God's presence. "Think of the worship service as a special time set aside for silent meditation and prayer," she told Tiffany.

An hour or so later, Tiffany returned to the apartment to find Margaret sitting cross-legged on the floor. "You're awake? And actually out of bed?"

"Of course I am. Did you think I'd sleep all day? I read your note. Tell me all about the Quaker service you just attended. And don't spare me the details."

Margaret's rare show of interest in anything religious surprised her, but she managed to keep a straight face. "Well, unlike mainstream protestant churches, the Quakers have a meeting rather than a service. And by that I mean, they do not have a minister with a prepared sermon, but rather, they gather at the Meeting House to worship as individuals."

"What do they do at the meeting? Conduct business?"

Tiffany smiled. "I guess you could say that. They conduct spiritual business by listening for a silent message from the Holy Spirit that they believe lives within them."

"What?" Margaret asked as she cut into a slice of mango. "And no one ever breaks the silence?"

"Oh, yes, if a person receives a divine message from the Holy Spirit that they want to share, they may break the silence."

Margaret commented on how different it seemed from the church her family attended. "Do you see their methods as inappropriate or wrong?"

"I have no idea what's right or wrong when it comes to worshiping God," said Tiffany. "Or even if there is a right or wrong way to worship. I mean, who's to say that one approach is better than another? But overall, I'm more comfortable with the method of worship I grew up with—listening to sermons and Bible readings, and, of course, singing the old traditional hymns."

"Yeah, I loved to sing hymns. I still do sometimes."

Margaret's voice had grown soft, as had her face. "So did you enjoy the service? Did it change you in any way?"

"I hate to admit this, but at first the silence distracted me. I kept wondering when someone would speak. But toward the last, although I can't say that I ever felt a special connection to God, the utter stillness did have a unique and calming effect on me. The silent devotion to the Lord that I witnessed was impressive."

"Let me know if you plan to visit the Friend's Church again, I want to join you."

Again, Tiffany suppressed her surprise. "So tell me about your morning. Been up long?"

Margaret stood to set her empty plate on a nearby table. Then she took a chair near Tiffany and grinned. "I have a wonderful idea to share. What would you think about going on a night hike in the rainforest with the guys as soon as we can arrange it?"

This time Tiffany let her mouth fall open. "*What? A night hike?*"

"You heard me. So, what do you think? I'm sure Zachary would love to lead us."

Completely caught off guard, Tiffany could not imagine what had gotten into Margaret. She had never expressed an interest in touring the rainforest in the daytime, let alone at night. She had already thrown her a curve ball by asking about a Quaker church service. Now she had proposed a *night* hike in the *rainforest?*

"Don't you know lots of creatures would be lurking out there in the dark?" For a moment, Tiffany thought she would upchuck.

"But it's surely safe or they wouldn't have organized tours for night hiking," Margaret said.

Tiffany wanted to please Margaret, and certainly, being with Zachary offered the best incentive of all to cooperate with Margaret's harebrained notion. But ...

Margaret snapped her fingers near Tiffany's face. "Hey, will you at least consider it?"

Yes, thought Tiffany, it could actually be a positive experience, but she wasn't ready to go night hiking, not yet, anyway. "I ... I'm not sure it's such a good idea."

"Come on now. You'll love it."

"I ... I don't think so."

"Please?"

"Oh, Margaret, for heaven's sake, I ... All right, I'll give it some serious thought."

Margaret stood. "Good. Let me know what Zachary says. I'll be in my room for a while."

"But Margaret, are you sure you're up to it? You're just getting over your accident."

"I'm fine. Just call him. It'll be fun."

"I don't know about this. I ..."

"Now Tiffany, you can do this. And while you're on the phone, I'm off to spend time thinking about my future."

"That's always good, but different for you." Tiffany wanted to retreat to her room and forget Margaret ever suggested a night hike.

"I'm serious," Margaret said. "I've been reflecting on the meaning of life in a new way. I want to figure out what to do next. Like where I should go from here, and whether I actually want to teach school. I'm confused about what I want out of life."

"But you've always been so decisive. You never worry about anything."

"Not as a rule, but since my accident I have more empathy for those who do."

"Like me?" Tiffany hated the inferior feeling that often accompanied her anxieties or the mention of them.

"I didn't say that. But yes, like you. Anyway, I shook inside at the thought of riding a horse that day. I felt like a wet noodle the whole time, but I wanted to follow your lead, so I forged ahead."

"What do you mean?"

"I mean, it impressed me that you stretched yourself to come so far from home to study. I've never seen you so anxious about anything, but you came in spite of your many reservations."

"You can't imagine how scared I was."

"But it was your example of courage to step out of your comfort zone and come to Costa Rica that inspired me to go horseback riding against my better judgment."

"So now it's my fault you fell off a horse?" Tiffany laughed. She wasn't sure if she should feel sorry she had influenced Margaret to go horseback riding or happy that her rare show of courage had had a positive influence on someone.

"I'm not trying to be funny. From the start I had a negative attitude about riding a horse—expected the worst—but I wanted to appear brave. Sound familiar?"

Tiffany snorted. "Familiar to me? Hmmmm …" Margaret almost sounded like a different person. Evidently her accident had brought on some sort of awakening.

Margaret turned to leave the room. "So about the night hike—it'll do us both good. I'm leaving you to it—call Zachary."

The mention of her coming so far away from home to study made Tiffany homesick. She glanced at the clock. Her family would be home from church and finished with the Sunday dinner that always followed the church services. In the past, she had taken their family traditions for granted, even found them boring at times, but this morning she longed to be a part of them.

When Tiffany's mom came on the line, Tiffany launched into a lengthy description of her recent explorations in the rainforest and her work as a volunteer. She even mentioned Margaret's nasty fall. But mostly she babbled on and on about Zachary as though his existence controlled the quality of her life.

After her mother shared the news from home, her dad got on the line. "You missed the wheat harvest a couple of weeks ago. You should have been here; I hired some good looking guys to drive the trucks again this year."

"Oh, Dad, you're ever the kidder, aren't you?" Tiffany giggled, and then a lump filled her throat when her dad said he loved her and that they missed her.

When Karla got on the line, she told big tales about her part-time job at Wal-Mart, and her recent dating and driving experiences. "I don't know what part of my life excites me more, work or play. And you never told me driving was such a hoot. I love it."

After the conversation ended, she looked at the phone, still in her hand. It is now or never, she thought. Karla's fun-loving, adventuresome spirit, along with her parents' love and encouragement that came across the many miles, cheered her so much she decided to rethink the night hike. Maybe following through with Margaret's absurd suggestion would do her good.

She punched in Zachary's number in slow motion, giving thought to stopping after each number. She nearly dropped the phone when he answered on the first ring. But somehow she managed to relay Margaret's crazy suggestion.

"That's a great idea," Zachary said. "I really dig hiking at night."

"Have you led groups at night before?"

"Absolutely! I've had special training to lead tours in the rainforest, day or night. We'll have a great time."

*Phooey, I'm committed.*

Shaking her head in disgust, Tiffany resented her tendency to fret every time an opportunity came along to try something new or different.

## CHAPTER 28

When Tiffany's cell phone rang a couple of evenings later, even though Zachary was identified as the caller, she gripped it as if a stalker was on the other end. "Hello?"

"Can you and Margaret be ready around five tomorrow evening?" he asked. "I've already checked with Jason."

"Why so late? It'll be almost dark by the time we start."

"Yes, isn't that the idea? It's a night hike. Remember? We need to leave for the rainforest before the sun sets."

Rolling her eyes into the back of her head, she wondered what she had gotten herself into. Plans for the night hike had progressed too fast. "Will you have a flashlight?"

"Of course. One apiece, in fact. You can't manage in the jungle without one after the sun goes down. Oh by the way, we can only explore a couple of hours. Will that be enough time for you?"

She heaved a big sigh and flopped back against the sofa. "What should we wear?"

"Wear long pants, long sleeves, and boots. And don't forget to bring a rain jacket. I promise you'll love it."

"But is it safe? I mean, really safe?"

Although Zachary assured her safety would be his primary focus, she still regretted agreeing to the plan. But as the budding biologist, she had no choice but to carry on. Besides, Margaret's bravery had forced her hand.

The next evening, Tiffany secretly fretted all the way to the reserve. She wanted to trust everything would go well, but she was convinced the hike would be disastrous.

She hoped the cozy glow from the sinking sun would soothe her into a more positive attitude, but upon entering the jungle her heart sunk to her stomach like a stone in water. It was even blacker than she imagined it would be. The dense overgrowth blocked all but small patches of the late evening sky. She wanted to turn and bolt, but she mustered the will to keep shuffling alongside Zachary in the awful, eerie darkness. *I can't cave in. I've got to do this. I have to.*

Margaret and Jason's constant chatter got on her nerves. Their voices could easily drown out the sound of a nearby animal. Besides, she needed to think. About what, she did not know, but she wished that they would hush.

Zachary spoke as though he had read her mind. "We'll need to keep our voices low so we won't scare off the wildlife."

Jason snickered. "Or stir them up."

"That wasn't funny," Tiffany said, waving her flashlight back and forth and up and down to reveal a predator or perhaps ward it off.

Zachary stopped. He turned toward Tiffany and

placed a hand on her shoulder. "Look, people and lights frighten the animals. For the most part, they're just as afraid of you as you are of them. And yes, they're nocturnal, and they forage for food at night, but they aren't going to attack you unless you threaten them."

Tiffany sucked air. "Threaten? Oh my, I—"

"I've found something!" Jason's squeaky voice pierced the darkness. "Come take a look and see what you think."

Margaret squealed. "What? What is it?"

When Zachary swung his sturdy lantern low to the ground, Tiffany cringed. He knelt on the ground and pointed to several small animal tracks in the dirt where hikers had worn away the vegetation. "These tracks are from a harmless prehensile-tailed porcupine. It's a small nocturnal vegetarian rodent."

"Vegetarian?" Tiffany asked.

Zachary looked up at her and grinned, his face glowing in the lantern's light. "Yes, that means it doesn't often eat humans."

"Not funny," she croaked, swatting his shoulder.

Only a short distance further, Zachary stopped again. He knelt to study several claw marks that covered a large area. In only seconds, he announced they were from a three-toed sloth. "The sloth has weak hind legs, so it has to drag its body along the ground and pull itself forward with its front claws." Zachary described the sloth as the slowest mammal in the world, and that even though it claws and bites in defense, it's powerless against a large predator.

"Doesn't a sloth sleep more than half the time?" asked Margaret.

"Yes, up to fifteen to twenty hours a day. In fact, it spends most of its time in a tree, sometimes even giving birth in a tree."

"I like to watch the sloth that's usually outside my bedroom window," Margaret said. "It's nice to learn more about them."

Several yards further along, Zachary stopped and swung out an arm to slow them. He lowered the lantern and scanned the area around the base of a massive and strange looking tree. "I thought we might find one."

Margaret yelped and jumped back. "Oh my heavens, I've never seen one loose in the wild before."

Tiffany stopped dead in her tracks. Her encounter with a tarantula in the Butterfly Gardens was not her first, for she had seen several growing up on the Kansas prairie, but had never gotten used to them. Trembling at the sight of the hairy spider, she prayed it would not jump. "It's so big—so creepy looking."

Margaret gave Tiffany a quick squeeze. "We've got to remember we're much bigger and we're wearing boots that are laced high and tight around our ankles. I don't see how anything could possibly bite us."

Shuddering, Tiffany let out a high-pitched giggle. "But you won't make me hold it, will you?"

After the tarantula crawled out of sight, Zachary lifted his lantern to point out the tree they stood under. "Now if the spider didn't spook you enough, this strangler fig tree with its snake-like tendrils and sinister name ought to give you a thrill."

Wearing slim-cut blue jeans and a form-fitting gold T-shirt with *University of San Diego* plastered across the front, Tiffany edged closer to Zachary. "Oh my, what can you tell us about this gruesome tree? Why is it called a strangler tree?"

"Uhhhhh ... Why is it called a strangler fig tree?"

"Yes, isn't that what you just said?"

"Uhhhh … Well it, uhhhh … Well it has a wonderful and fascinating form."

"Is that all?"

"Oh, well…" Then Zachary described the strangler fig tree as atypical, for it grew downward toward the forest floor, rather than upward. "Monkeys, bats, or birds eliminate a minuscule seed from the ripe fruit of the strangler fig tree into a compost garden at the top of a different type of tree," he said. "So are you with me, so far?"

"Barely, but go on," Margaret answered.

"So the seed germinates and a new strangler fig tree grows down around the unwilling host tree. Then after a long time—many, many years, in fact—it strangles the tree that's inside."

Jason shook his head. "No, I think the host tree dies from lack of light rather than strangulation."

"You're absolutely right." Zachary laughed. Then he looked at Tiffany. "So what do you think of the strange tree?"

When Tiffany did not answer, he repeated his question. "Tiffany, what do you think of the tree?"

She only shrugged. During Zachary's lengthy description of the tree, she had been fanaticizing about his kiss and what his muscles pressing against her in a long embrace might feel like.

Zachary lifted the lantern to spotlight her. "Did you hear what I just said?"

The tarantula caught her attention, as did the strange tree, but Zachary interested her more than anything else had thus far. As far as she was concerned, he was the most fascinating creature of the entire night. She smiled and nudged the lantern away.

Zachary sighed. "Let's backtrack to the entrance and

call it a night. Maybe we'll find something even bigger and better next time."

After a few minutes, Tiffany edged close to Zachary, hoping he could not hear the wild beating of her heart that had nothing to do with apprehension.

Tiffany would long cherish the memory of the night hike with her buddies, for in the end, Jason's infectious enthusiasm and Margaret's bold excitement provided antidotes for her anxiety. And Zachary's charisma had distracted her beyond words.

Tonight in this untamed jungle, she had tamed her anxiety a little with the help of her friends. The small victory spurred her on, and she discovered that the occasional night sounds accompanying their footsteps as they returned to the entrance of the rainforest actually thrilled her in a comfortable way.

## CHAPTER 29

"You're going to be impressed with this place," Zachary said as the Tree House Restaurant and Café came into view. "They built the restaurant around a huge tree that towers over the roofline."

Tiffany craned her neck to see. "You aren't joking. It's gigantic."

"And wait until you see inside the restaurant. The limbs sprawl in every direction," Zachary said, angling the jeep into a parking space.

Tiffany stopped right inside the entrance to the restaurant to stare at the long, twisted branches that appeared to be clawing their way to heaven. "I don't know if the food is good or not, but it's worth coming just to see this crazy tree."

As they studied the menu, Tiffany danced her fingers on the table in rhythm with the Latin music playing in the background. "Let's bring Margaret here. She'll freak out over this place—especially the wild tree."

Zachary's eyes grazed over Tiffany's face and down the length of her body to the point it disappeared under the table. "You look gorgeous tonight."

Tiffany only smiled as she adjusted one of the slender spaghetti straps of her hot pink sundress.

Zachary's head filled with romantic visions of holding Tiffany close and peppering her mouth with hot kisses. "You were the best part of waking up today, and you know how much I love the tropics." Smiling generously, his mind whirled with high hopes for the evening— particularly the end of the evening.

Tiffany blushed. "Thanks. But I'm shocked I won out over the rainforest."

"You did. You won, hands down." Then Zachary mentioned their recent night hike. "Did you have a good time?"

"Of course, although in the beginning anyone standing within three feet could see me shuffling around like something would pounce on me at any second. But in the end, I loved it. And so did Margaret."

"She seems to have recovered from her accident."

"Yes, but I think it has changed her, at least a little. When I recently visited a Quaker service with the Baldwins, even though Margaret hasn't gone to church for years, she wanted to hear all about it. She even expressed an interest in going with me some Sunday."

"Yeah, well some of us aren't in the habit, I guess."

"Not in the habit of what?"

"Going to church. I never go."

"I've noticed you're antsy when the subject of religion comes up. Mind telling me why it makes you squirm so much?"

Zachary's antenna shot up. "Squirm? I'm just not in to talking about church or a higher power. You don't mind, do you?" Trying to believe in something imaginary did not appeal to Zachary, but he chose not to risk upsetting her by saying so.

"Never mind—we'll talk about something else." Then Tiffany mentioned calling home to visit with her family. "Listening to Karla share some of her driving experiences took me back a few years."

"You make it sound like you're old, but look at you— you're young and lively." Zachary wanted to take Tiffany behind a big limb of the sprawling tree for a lingering kiss. But he reached for her hand instead. When she pulled back, it irritated him. What was with her? She sent too many conflicting messages, with coy looks one minute and the cold shoulder the next.

"Let's have a cup of coffee with dinner," he suggested, making an effort to be cool. "The restaurant is known for its gourmet Italian-style brew. They grind fresh prime beans that are grown locally."

After lingering a while over dinner, Zachary began to wonder if he should tell her about his first year of high school—his "lost year." He wanted her to know everything about him, just as he wanted to know everything about her. Maybe he would suggest a moonlight stroll along the fringes of the rainforest after dinner. It would be easier to talk about his tainted past in the dark. But who was he kidding? What he really wanted was to be alone with her—to hold her close and kiss her until she was breathless.

Although Zachary was seldom anxious, he was stymied about how to proceed, for she had rejected his every effort to touch her. By the time the dinner bill arrived, his hands shook so much he dropped his billfold on the floor. And as he leaned over to pick it up, he bumped his head on the corner of the table.

Tiffany's eyes were wide with concern. "Are you all right?" she asked.

He rubbed his head. "I'm fine. It didn't hurt a bit."

"Are you sure? You look a little pale."

He drew back his hand and glanced for blood. "It's nothing. What about a stroll in the rainforest before I take you home?" As soon as the suggestion was out, his body sagged.

"I should probably refuse, but all right, if we make it a short one. I just hope we're not alone, and that you have your big lantern with you," Tiffany said as she took the tanned hand he held out to help her from the booth.

As Zachary drove along the narrow road leading up the mountain, Tiffany jiggled like a statue had been strapped to the seat. But in spite of her cautious demeanor, Zachary's fantasy of holding her in his arms in the dark and deserted jungle took flight.

Delighted to see the nearly empty parking lot at the mouth of the rainforest, he jumped out and ran around to help her from the jeep. "We will turn back anytime you want to, especially since we are not dressed for night hiking."

"Oh, no, I don't have on boots. My ankles are bare," Tiffany cried. "I can't do this."

"We'll only go for a short walk," Zachary insisted. "Just long enough to stretch our legs."

"I don't need to stretch my legs."

"We sat for hours over dinner. Come on, it'll do us good," he said, plotting how he would help her loosen up.

Fortunately, the lantern's strong beam and the soft celestial light trickling through the overgrowth adequately lit the trail.

Over the next several minutes, only a chorus of insects broke the awkward silence as they moseyed along the forested path without speaking. When he dared, he slipped his free arm around her waist and pulled her close. Too his surprise, she not only let him, but she actually leaned her head toward him. Intoxicated by her presence, and the smell of gardenias in her hair, his desire to kiss her escalated with each step they took.

A few moments later, when a howler monkey cried out in the distance, Tiffany jerked away from him so fast she lost her footing. He caught her just before she fell, and without a word he set the lantern on the path and cradled her in his arms.

At first, Zachary's lips barely grazed Tiffany's. But when her shape melded with his, a powerful longing for more coursed through him, and in seconds his feathery kiss became firm and sensual. And her soft, compliant mouth transported him to a place he never wanted to leave.

A tidal wave of emotion swept over him that went beyond physical desire. He wanted to take care of her— protect her. He wanted to be her hero. He wanted to relieve her anxieties and allay her fears. Caught off guard by such powerful feelings, he murmured in her ear. "I've never felt this way before, Tiffany. I don't want to stop kissing you."

"Me either, Zachary, but ..."

As he held her close, the intensity of his emotions surprised him. "That first day on the bridge—I felt the electricity between us. Did you?"

"Yes, Zachary, I did. I was breathless whenever you came near. You made me feel like I'd caught a falling star."

"And I recall you, not the swinging bridge took my breath away. It happens every time we're together. Sometimes just thinking about you—"

Tiffany suddenly pulled away, trembling as though hit by a blast of cold air. "I'm flattered, Zachary, but let's stop right now. Let's turn back."

"I'm sorry. Am I rushing you?"

She feathered long strands of hair from her eyes. "Oh please don't misunderstand. You surely know that's not what I want to say. I'd love to stay here with you, but it wouldn't be wise."

Zachary sensed a weak moment in her and moved in to take advantage of it. And to his surprise, as he leaned in to kiss her, she moved into his arms and offered her lips.

But seconds later, she again pulled back as though some puritanical restraint had surfaced to squelch her desire. "It's clear what's on your mind and I'm simply not ready. Let's get out of here," she said.

Zachary was stunned, but without a word he took her trembling hand and led her back over the moonlit path to the parking lot. He had never dated a girl like Tiffany before. She seemed so confused about what she wanted. Her ambivalence sparked a desire in him to stop and pound his fist against a tree.

She had set the pace for their relationship, and he didn't like it. But even though he didn't agree, not even one iota, he didn't doubt she would be worth the wait.

# CHAPTER 30

Tiffany flopped around in bed reliving the previous night with Zachary. Especially the last kiss, the sexiest kiss she had ever known. Although Zachary clearly wanted to fan the embers sparking between them, she had chosen to douse them.

She was torn between desire for him and the conviction to move slowly this time, for the previous year Tiffany had ended a college romance that soured after a sweet beginning. Eric was witty and fun, even thoughtful at times. But after dating a few months, Eric's underlying self-centered arrogance overshadowed his few redeeming qualities when he pressured her beyond casual intimacy one night.

She harbored guilt and regret over yielding to him, for she had intended to remain chaste for the man she would marry. Disappointed in herself, as well as in him, she ended their relationship.

After several worrisome weeks, she received the sign that indicated she was not pregnant and could move on with her life. But for months afterward she did not date.

And when she did begin to go out again, no one of interest had come along—until now.

Last night in the rainforest, her desire for Zachary had verged on igniting, but an inner voice encouraged her to slow down. She resisted Zachary's charms. But would she next time? Or would a virile body and dreamy blue eyes in a handsome face derail her from her logical track? And would his bright mind and their common interests add to the challenge of trying to move at a more reasonable pace this time?

Without doubt, strolling alone with Zachary in the seductive moonlit darkness of the rainforest had added to the struggle to stay grounded in her convictions. She swayed on the edge of a steep precipice of powerful emotions, but this time was different, for she sensed that should she slip over the edge with Zachary the experience would be filled with beautiful, scented rose petals and sweet enticing honey.

She wanted to talk to someone, but Margaret had slept in. Besides, she questioned whether Margaret would care to hear her romantic tales about Zachary. Her mother would listen, of course, but she needed to speak face to face with someone.

She called Nellie, who urged her to come. And as always, Nellie greeted her with a warm welcome that comforted her soul like her mother's chicken and rice soup had always soothed her tummy.

"I love it here," Tiffany said as they stepped out back in the morning air. "Your flowers are so beautiful. I suppose caring for them is a labor of love for you."

"Yes, I think that's fair to say," Nellie said as she offered Tiffany the plate of fruit.

Tiffany selected a couple of slices of juicy papaya and several chunks of golden pineapple. "Your love of flowers reminds me of my Grandmother Birdwell. She has a lot that come back year after year. I especially love her four o'clock flowers that don't open until late in the afternoon. They make me think of how Margaret operates most days, or would if she could."

"Was Margaret able to go on the night hike?" asked Nellie.

"Actually, Margaret suggested the outing. And I'm glad she did. I was scared at first because it's *so* dark in the jungle at night, but I loosened up as we went along."

Nellie wiggled her eyebrows. "You never know what might end up prowling in your path on a night hike in the rainforest, huh?"

Tiffany grinned. "Yeah, and Zachary took me for another walk last night after dinner—just the two of us."

"Oh, that sounds romantic," Nellie said.

"Maybe too romantic, since I'm drawn to him in all the normal ways." Tiffany felt a blush creep over her at what she had implied.

Nellie smiled. "Don't let the fact you're normal bother you. The challenge is what to do about your natural feelings."

"Things started to get out of hand between us, so I ended our walk early," Tiffany said as she shifted in her chair. I'm attracted to him but ... Oh never mind."

Nellie reassured Tiffany she was not easily shocked. "It's good you want to move slowly—your relationship is young. Try to follow your instincts and continue using your best judgment. And don't hesitate to pray about this. You may talk to the Lord about anything."

When Nellie went inside for napkins, Tiffany watched a hummingbird hover over a feeder, while it beat its wings so fast they blurred.

When Nellie returned she described the tiny bird's

behavior. "It reminded me of you," Tiffany said.

Nellie spread mango jam on her toast. "Oh? How's that?"

"The little bird was quite persistent in pursuing its goal. And it is clear to me from listening to your stories that you persisted in trusting a divine guidance for your life when you moved here to make your home in a foreign land. You had to learn to keep beating your wings regardless of what happened or how discouraged you became at times, didn't you?"

Nellie answered without hesitation. "Yes, and as I've practiced the awareness of God's powerful presence in my life, I've become more tuned into His whispers of reassurance and encouragement."

"What do you mean by practice the awareness of God's presence?"

"I try to remember God is the creator of all things good and lovely and practice seeking Him in ordinary places day to day, such as when I bake a cake, tend to my garden, photograph flowers or butterflies, and so on."

"But that sounds like a choice that requires practice and dedication," Tiffany said.

"Yes, it is a choice that requires practice and dedication, but regardless of what happens in my life, whether good, bad, or boring, I've discovered it's in my best interest to remain conscious of the presence of God throughout the course of a day. Remaining aware of the Lord's presence off and on throughout the day helps me to keep 'beating my wings,' as you said earlier. It's what feeds my soul."

"And I suppose there are countless ways to connect to God."

"Yes, I believe we can connect to Him through all His living creations—people, animals, and plant life. I happen to feel a special connection to the Lord in nature, such as when I smell a sweet sea breeze or look at a rainbow after a storm. But I also think of Him when I hold a baby, watch our dog Bailey at play, or listen to a friend in need. And there's more—so much more," Nellie said. "I believe seeds of awareness of a higher power are planted in our souls in many ways through creation."

Tiffany rested her elbow on the table and supported her chin with her fist. "You've given me a lot to think about. This morning when I noticed the sun bathing your colorful flowers, I felt so peaceful. They danced in the breeze like they were alive, but I didn't give credit to God for their loveliness. I can't say that I've ever felt His presence as you have. At least, I've never been aware of hearing His love whispers of encouragement and guidance." Then Tiffany asked Nellie to pray for her to experience God in a more meaningful way.

Nellie stressed that above all else, a personal relationship with God, founded on love and trust is the essence of a faith journey. And although accepting God's love into our heart may only take a moment, it takes a lifetime to nurture a relationship with Him.

As Nellie's insights began to penetrate Tiffany's soul, hope for her relationship with Zachary, but especially hope for achieving her goals began to trickle into her heart and an inkling of freedom bobbed in the gentle flow.

## CHAPTER 31

The sun was barely up, but Zachary was due any moment to take Tiffany to look for a quetzal. They hoped to beat the throngs of tourists that usually arrived at the rainforest by mid-morning.

Most weekdays Tiffany kept busy as a volunteer, but on her days off she set her sights on exploring in the rainforest. She enjoyed spending time with Margaret and visiting Nellie, but time spent with Zachary ended up in a special category.

Her heart quickened when she heard the roar of the jeep motor. She grabbed her backpack and rushed to the door, high on the possibility of a big find. And the mild temperature and blue sky matched her sunny mood as they made their way up the mountain.

After they arrived and gathered their gear, Zachary said, "Now just a reminder—quetzals are easily spooked. So if we spot one, we need to stay still and keep our voices low."

She held up her right hand. "Scout's honor, I promise you silence. And I can make like a statue, if I need to."

Zachary laughed. "I hope that won't be necessary."

Then without another word, they moved with a serious purpose toward the bowels of the rainforest, the sound of their footsteps blending with the cawing birds and chirping insects. A small critter scurrying through the dense undergrowth or a troop of howlers barking close by from a tree, sometimes added to the noise. Once, they caught a glimpse of an endangered Baird's tapir as it ran swiftly through the undergrowth. "That was an adult," Zachary said. "You can tell because the adults have black leathery skin and only a sparse amount of short black hair, while the young ones are brown with white spots and stripes."

When Zachary stopped now and then to scour the trees with binoculars, Tiffany listened with baited breath, often photographing smaller, less significant birds as she waited.

Tiffany wanted to stay hopeful, but time crawled as they maneuvered the path that had been cut through the forest floor by thousands of hikers. As the quetzal remained elusive, the sound of their feet crunching on leaves and twigs began to ring loudly in her ears.

After more than an hour had passed, and they had forged deeper and deeper into the jungle, still without spotting the famous bird, Tiffany began to wonder if Zachary had something more than finding the regal bird on his mind. Why had he brought her so far into the forest that the dense growth overhead created a dark and forbidding atmosphere?

"Zachary? I once read quetzals are easier to spot in the fringes of a rainforest where the light shines on them as they sit high in the branches."

"So?"

"So why have we walked so far in?"

"They can be anywhere."

"Maybe they're still asleep. Or we came too early," Tiffany said. "The forest is so deserted."

Zachary swiped his hand in a forward motion. "Come on, let's push on."

"But we haven't seen anybody else the entire time."

He turned to stare at her. "That's how I like it."

Perceiving a furtive look about him, she had a sense of foreboding that twisted around her heart with the same tenacity as the green vines wrapping the trees.

*What did Zachary have on his mind? Why had they walked so far into the jungle? Did he have a plan for her that had nothing to do with a quetzal?*

"I want to go back. I …"

Zachary glared at her. "What's the matter? You act like you're scared. You're not afraid of me, are you?"

"Should I be?" she asked. For some unknown reason she had the sensation of stepping into a spider web, whose wily weaver planned to trap her. Something about Zachary's tone frightened her. Maybe he expected more from her than when they were last alone in the dark and secluded rainforest. Or maybe her present apprehension had nothing to do with being alone with Zachary, for several times since arriving in Costa Rica, a sense of foreboding had overwhelmed her when he was nowhere near.

But on the other hand, she had not known him long. On more than one occasion he avoided talking about his past. Or changed the subject at odd times. What was he hiding? What was his real motive for bringing her to this deserted place today? Could he be trusted?

Confused, she suddenly blurted, "Can we turn back? Now?"

"No! I'm not ready to give up. Let's keep hiking," he

said, trudging on.

She whined. "We're not going to find a quetzal this morning. I want to—"

"What makes you so sure?" Zachary hollered as he walked ahead of her. "What's the matter, don't you trust me?"

*"Will you stop? Right now? I want to go home,"* she shouted, uneasiness mounting.

Zachary whirled around and took a step toward her.

Frightened by the strange look she saw in his eyes, Tiffany turned and darted down the path away from him.

Shouting her name, he chased after her, his footsteps echoing loudly in her ears.

Pumping her legs with all of her strength, she soon ran at her top speed. Her breathing grew ragged, while her heart raced with fear.

Even toting a tripod, Zachary, with his long strides and unusual strength, easily narrowed the distance between them. In the grip of heightened anxiety, she pushed on, but within seconds, he was so close that the sound of his heavy breathing caused the hair on her body to stand on end.

"Stop right now," he growled, throwing his equipment to the ground. Then he grabbed her.

Gasping, she stumbled on exposed tree roots and fell to the ground. Her heart pounded from dark assumptions as she screamed, "No, no, no … Please don't … She flung her arms wildly about, fighting him with every ounce of strength she could muster.

After they had scuffled for several seconds on the forest floor, and she had delivered a few punches to his chest, she stopped fighting. She gave, in, for she was no match for his strength.

As he held her tightly against his chest, anxiety froze

her every nerve. Anticipating the worst was yet to come, she held her breath for several seconds, while her imagination went places that curdled her blood. Her whole body ached with dread. But moments passed and nothing happened.

Zachary finally relaxed his hold on her and pulled back to look into her face. He lifted her chin. "Look at me. What's wrong with you? Answer me, Tiffany. Why are you so afraid? Why were you running from me?"

She thought briefly of things she hadn't done—things she would never do. Fear for her life was more than she could bear.

"Surely you're not afraid of me," Zachary shouted.

Whimpering, she squeezed her eyes shut and stiffened her body against the blows she thought would come. "Please don't hurt me," she begged.

"Hurt you? For heavens' sake, what are you talking about?"

Tiffany swallowed the bile that rose from the depths of her belly. "Don't hurt me. Please? I—"

"Dear Lord in heaven, how could you think I want to hurt you? Listen to me, you crazy fool! I love you, Tiffany. I can't believe this. You've misunderstood everything."

Gasping for air, she glanced up at Zachary. What she saw confused her. Hurt or disappointment, she couldn't be sure which, filled his eyes. His pained expression was clearly not the look of someone who wanted to do her harm. "But I thought ..."

He let go of her and stood on the trail beside his backpack and equipment. "I'm beginning to see what you thought. Go, if that's what you want. I won't stop you."

"But I ... I don't understand," Tiffany said as it slowly dawned on her she had made a horrible mistake.

Zachary tossed his hair out of his eyes. "That makes two of us. I certainly do not understand any of this or what brought it on."

"I'm sorry. I don't know what got into me."

"Neither do I, but I'll give you this—I'm the one who's sorry right now. More than anything, I wanted to find a quetzal for you today. I couldn't bear to give up. I pushed on, refusing to turn back because I wanted to make you happy."

His voice had changed. It was softer. Lower. She stood and slowly slid her backpack from her shoulders and let it drop with a thud alongside his. "It's not your fault we didn't find one."

"But what did I do wrong?" he asked. "Why were you so terrified? You acted crazy."

Feeling foolish now, she said "Now that I've calmed down, I can see you didn't do anything wrong. It's not your fault that I lost my mind. I don't know what to say. Except that my imagination got out of hand. Again." He was right. She did behave crazily—like one possessed.

Zachary reached out for her. "But what happened? What got in to you? We need to talk."

"I … Oh Zachary, I …" Tiffany fell in to his arms. He pulled her close, cradling her head against his chest. They stood that way for several seconds, his chin resting in her black curls. Then she shifted in his arms and looked up at him. He leaned toward her and kissed her just below a damp eye. She hiccupped. Then their lips met in a warm and tender kiss.

At first it felt like a consolation prize, for she could almost taste his regret that he had not found one of the special birds for her. But then his kiss turned passionate, and without hesitation, she moved her lips in rhythm with his. Her rising desire melted away any remaining tension, leaving her oblivious to the possibility of hidden wildlife or inappropriate choices. Mindlessly, she focused on need—the need to express something that had grown larger than life.

At last Zachary ended the kiss, and looked at her with great longing. "I'm so in love with you, Tiffany. Don't you know that? Can't you tell by my touch? By my behavior? I've tried to be so patient, but you confuse me. You're frustrating."

The hunger she felt for him was in his eyes. In the space of a heartbeat, her feelings for Zachary became crystal clear. "Heaven help me, Zachary, I love you, too. I love you and I'm so sorry about how I acted. I—"

Zachary put a finger to her lips. "Shhhhhhh," he whispered. Then he leaned toward her and like magnets, their lips pulled together in a deep and meaningful way. Rapid breathing and swift movements narrowed her world as they stood in the heart of the jungle locked in a fierce embrace as though some powerful force would soon part them.

But even as her passion reached a high threshold and her reasoning powers a decided low, she remembered another time and place when she wished that she had waited. A powerful inner sense warned her that their physical relationship had advanced far faster than it should have.

Zachary no longer frightened her. She trusted him, but she did not trust herself. Smoldering with desire for him as every inch of his body pressed against her, she was tempted to throw caution aside and let him lead her into a nest of tangled vines far from the beaten path.

He murmured in her ear. "Come on, Tiffany. Come on …"

She wanted to stay in his arms forever, but a soft

whisper urged her to hold back. Later, she would wonder where the strength came from, for in that moment deep in the heart of the jungle, though consumed by raw emotion and strong desire, Tiffany stood her ground. "No … No, Zachary. Let me go," she said, trying to wiggle free of his embrace.

Moaning in her ear, Zachary held her tight as his hand strayed down her back. "I love you, Tiffany. I want—"

Unable to block out that night with Eric, she raised her voice. "I mean it, Zachary, let me go."

"But Tiffany, I thought—"

"Don't you understand? I can't do this. You're moving too fast," she hissed, wedging her palms against his chest to push him away. "This is not what I want. Not here. Not now. Do you understand? L-e-t me go!"

Zachary dropped his arms and stepped back, fanning his hands in the air, palms facing her. "I'm sorry. You're right. Let's go."

She reached down and grabbed her backpack, slinging it hard against her shoulders. "Let's get out of here, right now."

Zachary gathered his belongings. "I'm sorry I've upset you. Somehow I've done everything wrong this morning. But can we end on a better note? Would you consider stopping at the hummingbird reserve with me? It's right at the edge of the rainforest."

Tiffany couldn't find her voice.

"I know you'll love it," he said. "It's just a few yards up an embankment and through a grove a trees from where we parked. I promise I'll behave."

During the long, silent walk to the jeep, Tiffany gradually relaxed enough that her head began to clear. Admitting to herself that she had sent him too many mixed signals, she determined that she would soften her attitude toward him and be more consistent in her behavior. But she would stand firm in resisting his physical advances.

They dropped off their gear at the jeep and walked up a slight incline to the hummingbird reserve. Tiffany lifted her eyebrows at the sight of dozens and dozens of hummingbirds bombarding feeders dangling from tree limbs or metal poles. The tiny birds, attacking the feeders filled with nectar, looked like eager children diving for a plate of warm cookies. "This is absolutely amazing!" Tiffany exclaimed. "And there are so many of them. And look at their wings—they're an absolute blur."

"I must say your excitement is contagious—I'm enjoying the birds as if I'd never seen them before," Zachary said.

Recalling the hummingbird in Nellie's backyard, Tiffany said, "I've seen plenty of hummingbirds before, but never anything like this. I'd read there are about fifty species in Costa Rica, but I didn't expect to see them all at once. They're amazing."

Zachary stuffed his hands deep into the pockets of his shorts and stood tall. "They're incredible, all right. I never tire of watching them. It thrills me every time."

She pointed to a tiny bird splashed with red, yellow, purple, and blue, its shimmering green body as rich and stunning as hand painted silk. "They're so colorful and their heads are so teensy."

"And did you know hummingbirds can rotate their wings to hover in place while feeding on nectar? And that they can fly backwards?"

She shook her head. "The only thing I knew for certain was that they can beat their wings up to eighty times a second. They're simply amazing."

Zachary leaned toward Tiffany. "Do you think you could use a word other than amazing to describe the hummingbirds?"

She laughed and slapped at his upper arm. "I'm sorry, sir, but there is no better word. I tell you, they are amazing!"

"Actually, I agree with you. They' are amazing." Then he gestured toward a pole on their left. "There's a Rufous-tailed hummingbird. They're the most common of all."

After taking several snapshots of the little bird, she turned to find Zachary standing inches away. Her breath caught as their eyes met and held for several seconds.

Zachary looked away first and pointed at a nearby feeder on a tree limb. "And there's a Black-crested Coquette hummingbird—one of the tiniest birds in the world. What a treat! You rarely see one of those."

With lingering frustration over the way their hike ended, Tiffany resisted the urge to ruffle Zachary's tousled hair as he spoke tenderly about the tiny bird.

"You're adorable, Tiffany," Zachary said as he reached out to brush away a strand of hair that had fallen low over her forehead. "I love you. You know that, don't you?"

Her heart soared and the last of her frustration evaporated. In that magical moment, any remaining doubt about his honorable intentions faded away. And even though she resisted kissing his charming face, she believed the wonders in creation knew no end, and that one specific creation excelled in beauty and worth above all others.

## CHAPTER 32

Near dawn, Tiffany woke to the mournful sound of a relentless rainfall beating against the roof. And as the wailing wind whistled eerily around the windowpane, an old enemy began to seep into the bedroom and slither into her being. Rigid with apprehension, she looked cautiously around the room.

Vivid images of floating angels from the dream she had had toward morning began to take shape in her mind. She considered fetching paper and pen from the chest opposite her bed to journal the details of the dream, but anxiety too deep to wade through had flooded the room.

The dream began with her weeping hysterically in Grandmother Connor's living room, but the sound of the door to the adjacent bedroom popping loose, startled her into silence. The door creaked as it slowly opened, finally revealing several women who laughed gaily as they floated above the floor with their arms moving reverently through space. White grosgrain ribbons swung back and forth from their long satin dresses that hung softly around them. She held her breath as the angelic-looking women came near her, swirling with unbridled joy and dipping with marvelous grace.

Like a feather drifting from the sky, Grandmother Connor floated downward to land beside Tiffany with the same confident smile and love on her face she had had when alive. And even though dead for many years, she recognized Aunt Ethyl's warm and caring face as her feet grazed the floor. Then Tiffany's heart nearly stopped when Cousin Kara plopped down beside her and giggled. Regardless of her circumstances, Kara had always brought a ray of sunshine to Tiffany's life, and the many others who knew and loved her.

These dearly departed family members whispered to Tiffany of a divine life in the hereafter, reassuring her that she need not be afraid of heaven. "The forever life with the Lord is a blissful existence," Grandmother Connor had said, as the others smiled and nodded.

She only vaguely recalled her grandmother telling her to be brave enough to trust the Lord to light the way. But she distinctly remembered her saying, "Rejoice in God's presence and lean on Him for comfort no matter how deep your sorrow or dark your days. Invite Him to bring you hope that is as vital to the soul as rain to a thirsty earth."

When the women ascended into the ceiling and disappeared, an unusual peace filtered like air into every crevice of the room. Tiffany could not see it or touch it, but she felt this important peace radiating through her and nudging joy to the surface.

As Tiffany relived the details, if seemed as though the strange dream had centered on hope. She had been sobbing hopelessly at the beginning of the dream, and by the end of the dream, hope had prevailed.

She questioned why she had been in such a sad state.

Why did she need comfort and encouragement? Or hope? She loved Costa Rica. She was happy this summer.

Exhausted by the baffling experience, Tiffany welcomed the distraction of her ringing cell phone. She answered it without a trace of trepidation, even though it was still quite early in the morning.

## CHAPTER 33

A loud scream woke Margaret from a sound sleep. In a fuzzy, startled state, she crawled out of bed and stumbled into Tiffany's bedroom. Her heart lurched at the sight of her friend bent double on the floor.

"No … No … No …," Tiffany wailed pitifully as she clutched her stomach.

"What's wrong? What's wrong?" Margaret yelled as she grabbed the cell phone from the floor. "Hello? Hello? It's Margaret. Who is this?"

"Oh, Margaret, this is Mrs. Birdwell, Tiffany's mom. My poor Tiffany … What have I done?"

Margaret suddenly felt clammy. "What's happened? What's wrong with Tiffany?"

"There's been a horrible accident and I shouldn't have …" Mrs. Birdwell began to sob.

"I'm listening. Talk when you can." Margaret closed her eyes as she waited for Mrs. Birdwell to speak.

Several seconds passed before Mrs. Birdwell spoke. "Oh, dear merciful heaven, I …"

Unexplainably calm, Margaret said, "Just take your

time, Mrs. Birdwell."

"This is unbearable. I ..." Mrs. Birdwell sobbed, her cries piercing Margaret's heart. Margaret stiffened and waited.

Eventually, Mrs. Birdwell explained their daughter Karla had been in a horrible accident. A young man driving a pickup truck had slammed into Karla's car, killing her and a friend instantly. "Our Karla ... Tiffany's sister is gone."

"I'm so terribly sorry. Can you tell me what happened?" Margaret asked as 'stay calm, stay calm' rang in her head over and over.

"He was drunk. A drunk driver killed our baby," Mrs. Birdwell said, between pain-filled sobs.

Margaret later reflected that it seemed an invisible hand replaced her shocked cry with appropriate words. "I won't leave Tiffany's side. I'll help her pack and make the necessary arrangements to catch a plane out of San Jose the first thing tomorrow morning. And I will come with her."

"Oh thank you. I ..."

Tiffany's father came on the line. "We'll be forever in your debt if you'll help Tiffany come home. She'll need you. Or should a family member come for her?"

Margaret reassured Mr. Birdwell he need not worry, for she would accompany Tiffany to Kansas. Then she expressed condolences with words she did not know she had, and said goodbye with an unfamiliar composure, promising to stay in touch as travel plans progressed.

At the end of the phone call, Margaret reached for Tiffany, who still sobbed on the floor. Speechless, she held her friend close as they rocked back and forth.

In time, Tiffany's sobbing turned to babbling, and then her babbling changed to moaning. Tiffany's agony sobered Margaret more than anything ever had in her young and sheltered life.

Karla's life had been snuffed out like an extinguished candle flame. *Pooofff!* A lovely young girl was gone forever. She grieved for Tiffany and her parents, but because she had never experienced a terrible loss, she could not begin to imagine the pain they would bear.

When Tiffany's breathing started coming in rapid, shallow spurts, Margaret wondered if she had suffered a severe psychological shock. She did not know much about such things, but knew enough to ask a few questions.

Relief flooded her when Tiffany gave a negative response to her inquiries regarding nausea, chest pain, and dizziness. At least nothing was seriously wrong physically.

Tiffany's well-being was in her hands now, and would be until they arrived in Kansas. She shuddered over falling heir to such a serious responsibility—an unbelievable situation that would require her to do things she had never done before.

Drawing from a hidden reserve of strength and self-control uncommon to her, Margaret efficiently purchased bus tickets to San Jose for late that afternoon, booked a hotel room near the airport for that night, and bought airline tickets to Kansas City for the next morning. Then after making a number of necessary phone calls, she packed Tiffany's bag, as well as her own.

"Here, you're going to need this—it's a long flight," Margaret said, handing Tiffany a blanket and pillow as they boarded the plane early the next morning. Margaret stowed their carry-on luggage in the overhead compartment. Then she sat next to Tiffany, who had already slumped like a ragdoll against the window. "Don't forget to buckle your seatbelt," she said as she snapped her buckle in place. Sighing audibly, Margaret settled into her seat. There would be no changing her mind—she was committed to seeing Tiffany through a difficult time.

The plane taxied onto the runway, picked up speed and nosed upward for takeoff. San Jose quickly faded from sight as the airborne jet glided higher and higher and faster and faster.

When the plane had leveled off and the captain had turned off the seatbelt sign, two flight attendants rolled beverage carts into the aisle to begin their in-flight service. "And what would you like?" one of the attendants asked Margaret. "Coffee? Tea? Orange juice? Apple juice? Or tomato juice? Maybe a Bloody Mary? Or a soft drink? We have—"

"A diet coke, please."

"And what would you like with that? Pretzels or a cookie?"

Margaret bristled at the prattle. Ready for the cart to move along, she accepted a tiny bag of pretzels. And when Tiffany only stared into space, Margaret also requested a bag of pretzels for her, along with a bottle of water, just in case.

Attempting to take her mind off the tragedy, Margaret settled into her seat to relive her recent fall from a horse. The accident had birthed within her a surprising gratitude for life, inspiring her to rethink priorities and goals for her future. As a person inclined toward laziness and selfishness, Margaret wondered if she had changed enough to come through for Tiffany. The time and emotional energy that would be needed to help Tiffany called for unselfish behavior. It called for patience and kindness. She would have to put Tiffany's needs before her own. Could she come through for Tiffany?

Earlier, when she spoke to Zachary about notifying the Baldwins and Jason of Tiffany's family crisis, Zachary's insightful remarks indicated he had learned a lot about Tiffany in a short period of time. And since she had known Tiffany longer, she should be better equipped to help her through this crisis. But in truth, she did not consider herself capable of dealing with a situation of this magnitude. What should she say or do to try to help? She did not know how to take care of others—others always took care of her.

Although ordinarily blasé about life, mounting concerns about the rough days ahead made her body rigid with apprehension. The prospect of trying to console Tiffany without saying something stupid filled her with dread. If only the entire tragic scenario would disappear, she thought.

Then over the next few minutes, she daydreamed of flying to Disneyland or Tahiti or home to Mobile, Alabama. She would settle for anywhere, just not to a funeral.

Unable to fathom the depth of Tiffany's pain, Margaret longed for advice about how to respond to her. In past similar situations, she had heard people offer to pray for the bereaved, but she seriously doubted that would help.

She considered herself a Christian, but for quite some time she had ignored her church upbringing. Although she could actually quote a few scriptures from Sunday school, she seldom picked up a Bible. Not a spiritual person, she never spent time in prayer, and in fact, she had to admit she did not know how to pray. What do you say to someone you can't even see?

But when she leaned back on the headrest and closed her eyes, pleading words formed in her mind: *Help me? Help me be sensitive to Tiffany and know how to help her during this terrible time. Help me do and say the right things. Please...*

Somewhat calmed by these thoughts, she shifted to a more comfortable position, hoping to block everything from her mind to nap. She took a deep breath and closed her eyes.

*Sometimes it's better to say nothing at all, than to say the wrong thing. You can't fix this. The only thing you can do for Tiffany is to be there for her. Listen and be yourself.*

This important message whispering into the solemn silence of her frazzled mind helped her relax enough to doze between the muffled sounds of heartache coming from the seat next to her.

*CHAPTER 34*

At Margaret's urging, Tiffany buckled her seatbelt. Then she leaned toward the window and pulled the blanket up to her chin. She pressed her face into the pillow and let her tears trickle quietly at will, while her mother's voice from yesterday morning rang in her ears. "Tiffany? Tiffany? It's Mother. I ... I ...."

An unbearable sense of doom, even stronger than she had had several times since arriving in Costa Rica, came over her as she clutched the phone. "Mother? Mother, what is it? What's wrong?"

If she lived to celebrate her hundredth birthday, she would not forget how the tragic news of Karla's death shocked her sensibilities, leaving her feeling disconnected from her own body and from the world she had known.

She remembered Margaret speaking to her mother. And when they finished talking, Margaret dropped to the floor and held her close. They sat that way for a long time, sharing their disbelief and sorrow.

With a broken heart, as she huddled by the window in the plane that carried her closer and closer to Kansas for her sister's funeral, she tried to recall a conversation with her beloved Grandmother Birdwell about the pain of losing a son when he was young.

A bright and insightful woman, Grandmother Birdwell's wisdom had mounted over the years as she not only relied on Jesus during sad or disappointing times, but also through good times. She longed to draw on her grandmother's strength and courage, or remember Nellie's wise reflections. But ugly speculations about the horrible accident churned inside her head like grains of sand tossed about in an ocean wave, making it impossible to think.

The plane rapidly gained altitude on its northerly course to take her home. After it settled into a smooth flying pattern, Tiffany listened to Margaret breathing beside her, longing for the oblivion of sleep to come to her, too. But numb with grief over her sister's death, reality kept intruding during the long flight to Atlanta.

Unable to rest on the layover in Atlanta or during the second leg of the flight to Kansas City, Tiffany's body cried out for rest as they began the car trip to the farm. Weak from hunger and sore from the inside out, she longed to stretch out and sleep for days.

In the past, when Tiffany returned home from college for a visit, the lights glowing through the windows of home offered a breath of fresh air. But tonight, as they approached the brightly lit farmhouse beckoning from the prairie, she felt nothing but dread.

Tiffany stepped from the car, her mind stagnant from sorrow. But when Goldie, the family's golden Labrador retriever bounded over to greet her, she felt an involuntary smile part her lips. She knelt to pet Goldie, and when Goldie whined with delight and nuzzled Tiffany's legs and licked her arms, she experienced a strong connection to Karla that made her cry. In that bittersweet moment, as tears trickled down Tiffany's face, she kissed the top of her beloved dog's head, and said, "Good girl, Goldie. You're such a sweet, good girl."

Drying her eyes with the back of her hand, she introduced Margaret to Goldie. Then she lumbered alongside Margaret to the front door where family and friends welcomed them with loving hearts and open arms.

Although she wanted to help her parents, she could barely muddle through her own discomfort during the remainder of the evening. The tragic news of her sister's death had violated her soul, robbing her of peace and joy. Time stood still. And time disappeared as family, friends, and neighbors trickled in and out.

Wonderful, caring people brought enough food to feed multitudes, but she only picked at the plate someone set before her.

In the midst of forced small talk and sobering silences, many unanswerable questions loomed in her fragile mind. *How did this happen? Did Karla suffer? Where is she now?* She longed to wake up and say with certainty an unbearable nightmare had come to an end.

As soon as possible, Tiffany went upstairs to escape the pain permeating the living room. Her mother had already retired for the evening, and someone had shown Margaret to what would be her bedroom for the next several days.

"I'll unpack your bag," said Aunt Karolyn, while Cousin Diana helped her dress for bed. Then Aunt Marie rushed in, "I thought a glass of warm milk might help you sleep."

She couldn't even respond as they hovered around her like mother hens, offering everything they could think of, including prayer, to help her relax enough to sleep.

She loved her family and always enjoyed their company, but tonight, grief penetrated every organ of her body. Her thoughts were locked inside. Her chest ached. Her stomach roiled. Even the pores of her skin cried out in despair.

When they finally turned out the light, leaving her alone to toss and turn, she whispered to the empty room. *"Why? Why? Why did this have to happen?"*

She slept fitfully as nightmare intermingled with reality. And each time she woke, the truth stabbed her in the heart as intensely as it had upon first learning of the fatal accident.

*Karla's dead? Dead? She's gone? Gone forever?* "Nooooo … nooo … nooo …," she moaned, her mind in a fog.

Tiffany survived the night, but when morning spread its light over the earth, darkness remained inside her.

A Kansas summer thunderstorm rumbled low in the distance. The small grandfather clock that had hung in the hall outside her bedroom for years released a slow, muffled tick-tock, tick-tock. Cows mooed low in the barnyard. And chickens clucked for food. But the familiar noises did nothing to distract her from a heart broken by circumstances she ached to change.

Shifting in bed, she looked at the digital clock. *Seven-twenty?* She had hoped for noon. Better still, she wished that it was noon the day after the funeral. Or noon of another life.

Someone had apparently slipped in and out of Tiffany's room without her hearing them, for a light breakfast of buttered toast, orange juice, and milk stared at her from the night stand. Her stomach churned as she pushed the tray aside.

Through her bedroom window, she noticed a house sparrow braving the wind as it clung to a small limb of a massive old tree, one of the few trees that survived the tornado. The delicate bird would flee to hide from the brewing bad weather, but her sweet and innocent sister had been caught in the eye of a storm from which she could not escape.

As the story went, on a clear, star-studded night Karla, only sixteen and a brand new driver, drove to a girlfriend's house to hang out for a couple of hours. Halfway into the visit, she and her friend decided to drive to an ice cream shop in the nearby town. Witnesses reported Karla stopped at a four-way stop near their destination, but when she entered the intersection, a twenty-year-old boy, drunk and speeding in a heavy pickup truck, ran a stop sign and broadsided her little red car. The boy survived, but Karla and her friend died as the car crumpled upon impact.

*The drunk driver survived! And two innocent girls did not. Now where, dear Lord, is the justice in that? Why did you let this happen? Where were you, God? Why did he live and the girls die?*

As she longed for answers, the thunderstorm passed but a storm still raged inside her. She would never forgive the drunk driver who took her sister's life. Her head ached from weeping. Her eyes felt like she had walked through a sandstorm.

Finally pulling herself from bed, she tried to yank on her jeans. But with limbs like jelly, she stumbled and fell. Pounding the floor in desperation, her anger and resentment toward the driver now included God. *Where were you when Karla needed you? And where are you now?* His betrayal nearly squeezed the life from her.

Later that morning, after recovering enough to make an appearance in the kitchen, several of her mother's longtime friends arrived with hot casseroles, steamed vegetables, and chocolate goodies. In addition, they brought soul food, for they kindly, with loving concern urged her to vent her sorrow. And for a sweet blessed while, their quiet presence and listening hearts shed a ray of light on her dark mood.

The next day the Women's Ministry at their family church brought meals and condolences. The minister came to pray on behalf of the family: *"...help them endure and find hope and peace in your love."* Tiffany wondered what that meant. God had abandoned them.

The days grew long, every hour lasting longer than the one before as they prepared for Karla's funeral. One day a few high school buddies paid Tiffany a visit. They cried together over Karla's senseless death, but they also laughed at shared girlhood memories, providing Tiffany with a much-needed respite from pain.

By the time the funeral service took place five days after Karla's death, mingled sorrow and resentment weighed heavily on Tiffany's heart. Her tears spilled out when someone sang *It is Well with My Soul*, for she knew nothing about her sister's view of heaven. She knew only that nothing seemed right with her own soul.

The final straw came when one of the funeral directors at the graveside service handed Tiffany a single rose from the flower spray on her sister's casket. No one could console her as she sobbed hysterically.

Karla was on the verge of blooming into a wonderful young woman. For Tiffany, the blood red rose was a symbol of her sister's death, an unfathomable loss.

## CHAPTER 35

"How could this have happened?" Tiffany shouted as she grabbed a bed pillow and slung it across the room. It was the morning after the funeral and a deadly combination of sorrow, anger, and resentment had placed a strangle-hold on her mind. "How could this unspeakable thing have happened to Karla—to all of them?" Even the silent room angered and frustrated her.

She needed to talk to someone. Her parents would listen, but she hesitated to add to their burden of grief. Margaret was a good listener, but she had never suffered a loss of this magnitude. She needed to talk to Grandmother Birdwell, who had had a lot of experience with loss and grief.

Tiffany looked around the room, searching for something that would bring comfort—some sort of relief from the unbearable ache that started in her stomach and rose to her throat. She had always loved her second floor bedroom at the end of the hall, especially when she decorated it with some of her favorite colors in nature—grass green, sky blue, and sunshine yellow.

During high school, she thrived in this special haven with its wonderful view of the wheat fields and prairie grass. But looking out the window this morning at the picturesque farm scene offered no comfort and her brightly colored room did nothing to soothe her. Not even her stuffed animal collection perched on shelves over her old desk held her interest. The silly critters looked frivolous—too incidental for words.

When Tiffany went downstairs to breakfast, she only pushed her scrambled eggs around and around on the plate.

"Tiffany, maybe you should take your coffee and go sit on the patio," her mother suggested. "You can listen to the birds. And I'll join you later."

Though Tiffany longed to crawl back into bed and ignore the rest of the day, she went outside to please her mother. She plunked her weary frame onto the chaise lounge that commanded a view of the entire backyard.

She had always enjoyed sitting on the patio to catch a few sunrays or to listen to the birds singing, but this morning the warm sun annoyed her and the warbling birds hurt her ears. "Shut up! Just shut up," she shouted at the red cardinal perched high above her. To her dismay the little bird stopped singing and flew away, which only served to fuel her sorrow.

Her mom's colorful flowers that usually brought such pleasure looked like nothing but hard work. As she nursed this grey mood, Grandmother Birdwell slipped onto the patio and pulled a chair close to Tiffany. "Good morning, Tiffany, may I sit with you for a while?" She reached out to stroke her granddaughter's curls. "Your hair is so beautiful, my dear."

"It's too curly—kinky. It's unruly."

Her grandmother smiled. "Karla's death is too

horrible for words, isn't it? I wondered if we could share a little of our sorrow this morning, if you're up to it."

Tiffany closed her eyes. She had wanted to talk to her grandmother, but did not know where or how to begin.

Grandmother Birdwell patted her arm. "It's difficult to believe Karla is gone and even harder to bear. Everything seems dark and frightening, even pointless right now, doesn't it?"

Turning tear-filled eyes toward her grandmother, Tiffany said, "It's unreal and I can't accept that she's gone. I don't know what …" Tiffany stopped, for she was riddled with an emotional mix she could not label.

"It's hard to sort out your feelings when you're struggling to stay afloat in a sea of painful emotions and everything familiar is gone, isn't it?" asked Grandmother Birdwell.

"I don't know what to think anymore. I mean, when all hope is gone and you're drained of joy, what's left?"

"You need something to hold on to."

"Like what?"

"Hope. Hope that you'll survive your terrible loss. Hope that life will go on, regardless of pain."

Tiffany spoke through thin lips. "I could wring the driver's neck—or worse. I don't understand why God let this happen. Why didn't He prevent it? Karla was just a baby."

"We all ask 'why' when bad things happen to us. It's natural to ask questions when we don't understand. You're entitled to your feelings. But there isn't a good answer for why it happened." Grandmother Birdwell was quiet for a moment. A grim look crossed her face as she said, "Do you remember me telling you about losing my son, your Uncle Earl?"

"Some of it, but I can't remember the details."

"Earl's death at the age of ten from Rocky Mountain spotted fever left me floundering in a world without meaning. I took to my bed for days, nursing my sorrow and asking countless questions. Sometimes I was so frustrated that I beat my pillow and screamed. And there were times I walked the floor, feverishly lamenting my loss every step of the way. I was desperate to have Earl back. Over the weeks and months, my resentment built. I needed to blame something or someone for his death. So I blamed God for not saving Earl—for taking him from me."

Tiffany had listened carefully all along, but when she heard this, she sat up straighter and looked her grandmother in the eye. "You felt that way, too?"

"Oh yes. Angry. Resentful. Frustrated. Hopeless. Did I say angry?"

Tiffany gave her grandmother a pensive look. "Yes, you did. So you were also mad at God?"

"Yes, for quite awhile. Losing Earl tore my heart out. My hope died with my son, and certainly, peace and joy became a distant memory. I didn't want to go anywhere or see anyone."

Somehow it helped Tiffany to know someone else had felt as she did. "So how did things finally improve for you?"

"For a long time I felt alone even when I was with other people. Your grandfather—God rest his soul—grieved by withdrawing into a world of his own. He wouldn't talk about Earl, as if things would change if he didn't mention his name."

Tiffany so longed to hear the hope in the awful tragedy of Karla's passing. "So what ended up making a difference for you?"

"Neither the time, nor the effort I put forth to face

things on my own was helpful. I longed to accept Earl's death—accept what couldn't be changed and come alive again, but I needed help. So one night many months after Earl died, I cried out in desperation to the Lord. I spent a long time on my knees in the dark, sharing my pain from unbearable heartache. And that night, I finally heard the Lord's reassurance. I recommitted to trusting Him and believing in His goodness to show me a better way to handle my feelings—a better way to live."

"But did praying really change anything for you?" asked Tiffany.

"I would say, yes, prayer changed things for me in the sense that it changed me. Certainly my circumstances went unchanged—Earl was gone—but through prayer, I finally opened up to God's whispers of encouragement. I had stopped participating in life after Earl died. I was still alive but living as though dead. But after well over a year of agony, I drew close to God and bared my soul. And I eventually began to experience periods of peace and to feel hopeful that I could learn to live in the present. I even began to have moments when I wanted to take a peek at the future and consider how to put routine and purpose back in my life. Most of all, I wanted to learn how to let go of impossible dreams."

Tiffany could not identify with her grandmother's testimony of how she was helped. "I certainly don't doubt you, but it's hard to understand."

"Of course it is. In a nutshell, I would say God's love and merciful grace transformed me from a gray, lifeless person into one who could smile again—one who still had much to live for. It's hard to articulate what happened. It might be a stretch, but I would compare my experience with what happens when delicate snowflakes drift from the sky and change the gray, barren earth of winter into something bright and lovely."

Tiffany longed to glean something helpful from her grandmother's words. "I understand your metaphor, but it didn't happen that fast. Did it?"

"Oh no, of course not. It was a gradual process, and I took many steps backward before I finally noticed I had more good days than bad. But that night of meeting the Lord in the bottom of my pit of sorrow marked the beginning of real change that eventually made a positive difference in my life."

Tiffany clung to her grandmother's every word like a drowning victim clings to a life preserver but couldn't fully process what she had heard.

"I don't want to sugarcoat how difficult it was to accept the irreversible," said Grandmother Birdwell. "It took time. It took energy. It took patience. It took prayer to understand that God didn't take Earl away from me. He didn't cause my sorrow. But He was there to help me find the strength and courage to make peace with my heartache and move on."

"It's hard for me to imagine experiencing what you've described, Grandmother. Or believe the way you do."

"I understand, Tiffany. And I don't mean to oversimplify things. Even though I received help, a part of me knew I would always miss my son and grieve on some level. But God, who is all-powerful, applied His salve of love to my hurting heart, and one glad day it finally happened—I wanted to dance again."

"You make it sound like a miracle."

"Yes, that's how I see it."

"So you're saying you believe in miracles?"

"I do. God restored my life when I thought it had ended. To me, that was a miracle."

"And so you believe it is possible to survive a terrible

loss? I mean, in the sense of being happy again some day?"

"Yes, I've had many good times through the years since Earl died. I still miss him dreadfully. Life isn't the same without him. My heart carries a scar and my soul has a vacant place, but I've learned how to appreciate life again in spite of my loss."

Tiffany had heard some of her grandmother's story, but now that she suffered it had become personal—it took on a different meaning. "I know you speak from your heart, Grandmother, but it all sounds impossible. One thing is for sure, I can't forgive that drunk driver. And it's hard to imagine being happy again without Karla."

"I understand. My heart is also broken. Just give yourself time and stay open to help. Everyone deals with grief differently. There's not a formula or a timetable for surviving a loss."

"Right now, peace seems impossible."

"Don't expect the tears to stop miraculously. Your pain has to find a way out. Just remember, I will listen anytime you want to talk. And one more thing, dear Tiffany—listen for God's love whispers, for He wants to help you accept what you cannot change."

Tiffany shifted uncomfortably in her chair. "My friend Nellie said much the same thing, but I don't know how to listen for help from a source I can't even see."

Grandmother Birdwell had her work cut out for her, and for that matter, so did the Lord, for helping her would be a challenge.

## CHAPTER 36

A few days after the funeral, Margaret woke to the memory of moving to San Diego to begin her freshman year of college. That weekend, when her parents left to return home, she watched the long dormitory hall swallow them up, longing to run after them. She rushed to the window to wave goodbye, letting her tears keep pace with the raindrops spilling down the pane.

It was a pivotal time in her life—a time of letting go of old patterns and embracing new beginnings. In many respects, leaving home for the first time changed her life. Certainly choosing a college on the west coast, after always living in the heart of Dixie, presented a tremendous adjustment.

This morning, in a lonely, contemplative mood, it occurred to Margaret that her life had unfolded like chapters in a story book, page after page until her youth was over. And now, she had an opportunity to make a future chapter of her life read as well or better than those of the past. Was she up to the responsibility?

Margaret's heart ached for Tiffany and her family. She

swallowed hard just thinking of the chapter in Karla's life that had ended and the one that had also closed for Tiffany. How would Karla's family manage? How would Tiffany endure such a terrible loss? Except for the passing of time, what could possibly help lessen the heavy weight of grief? The questions piled up inside her head, while the answers floated around somewhere in space.

Oh she had heard people say good things can come out of bad situations. Or something positive can occur on the heels of a trial. Or her favorite—every dark cloud has a silver lining. But she did not know about all that, for she could not imagine what good could come from Karla's death

In this period of reflection, Margaret began to realize her efforts to try to help Tiffany had added a new and satisfying dimension to her life. Of course, she couldn't know how much help her presence had actually been to Tiffany, but somehow, the tragic situation had opened her more fully to the blessing of reaching out to help another.

For some reason she felt a strong motivation to move forward with her life, for her appetite of doing next to nothing had waned. It didn't altogether make sense, but suddenly, Margaret wanted to start working on the next chapter of her life.

She threw on her clothes and rushed downstairs for breakfast. Tiffany barely glanced up when she entered the room. Mrs. Birdwell greeted Margaret and invited her to sit. Right away, she passed Margaret the fruit plate filled with cantaloupe slices, strawberry halves, and banana chunks.

Margaret poured a bowl of granola and added skim milk. "This may not be the best time to tell you this, but if I'm no longer needed here, I'll make plans to return to

Costa Rica right away."

Mrs. Birdwell, whose eyes were red and puffy, pulled her gray robe close around her. "You've been a godsend, Margaret. We'll always be grateful to you for coming with Tiffany—for giving all of us your time and energy. You've been kind and patient, but now you must do what's best for you."

Tiffany looked up. "Mother's right. You've been a rock. I couldn't have made it without you. But I'm not fit company right now—can't seem to find the good in anything. Like Mom said, you need to do what's best for you."

Tiffany's despair made Margaret uncomfortable. She longed to change things for Tiffany and her family. For a moment she felt like a traitor about to jump ship. But she followed her instincts. Besides her conviction that it was time to move along with her life, she had a hunch Tiffany needed time alone with her family. "Is there anything I can do for you before I leave? Or after I return?" she asked.

"I don't know. I don't know what I should do or even what I want to do," Tiffany muttered. "Maybe I shouldn't go back to Costa Rica at all."

"I can't know how you feel, but I can imagine how hard it must be to figure out what to do next. I'm sorry it's so confusing and difficult."

Tiffany frowned. "Sometimes it feels like I'm only hanging by a thread."

"But you are hanging. And may I tell you how much your strength inspires me?" Margaret asked.

"I think you're confused," Tiffany said, offering a faint smile.

"Not a chance," Margaret said. "Now I need to book a return ticket to San Jose and make a few plans. Will you check in with me when you come upstairs, Tiffany?"

Then before Margaret left the room, she gave Tiffany a hug, hoping to convey her love and reassurance more with a heartfelt squeeze than she would have with additional words.

## CHAPTER 37

When her mom and Margaret left the kitchen, Tiffany remained at the table with a last cup of coffee to mull her future. After only a few sips, the doorbell rang. The familiar chime startled Tiffany, but it did not surprise her, for people from church and neighbors from surrounding farms had come in and out for over a week now.

Tiffany shuffled to the foyer and cracked the door a few inches. "Yes? May I help you?" she asked the attractive young woman who wore navy slacks and a matching blazer over a cream-colored shell.

The bright morning sun behind the woman shaded her face and set her red hair ablaze. "Don't you remember me, Tiffany?"

"I'm sorry. How do you know me?"

"It's me, Katy, your buddy from the swinging bridge."

Tiffany dropped her jaw as she opened the door. "Of course. I'm sorry. Please come in. But how ... Where did you come from?"

"Kansas City." Katy smiled and entered as Tiffany motioned her in. "I left early this morning."

Tiffany shook her head. "But I don't understand. What's brought you here?"

After a quick hug, Katy pulled away to catch Tiffany's eye. "I know. I know about your sister. I read an obituary for Karla Birdwell in the death notices of the Kansas City Star that listed you as the only surviving sister."

"But I thought you lived in Chicago."

"I do, but I'm on a case that required investigation work in Kansas City. I regret I couldn't make the funeral services, but I wanted to come tell you in person how sorry I am about your sister."

"But how did you find me?" Tiffany asked, as she ushered Katy to the living room and offered a beverage.

"It was easy. I'm a private investigator."

"No way! For real?"

"For real. You didn't answer your cell phone, but it didn't take much sleuthing to find you—it's what I do best—snoop and pay attention to details."

Tiffany laughed for the first time in days. "I had hoped to meet up with you again someday, but who knew it would happen so soon."

"I wish circumstances were different. I'm so sorry about your sister. Will you tell me about her and what happened?"

Tiffany opened up to Katy as freely as she had that morning on the bridge when she spoke so openly about her phobias. She talked about Karla, her life and death, and shared details about the accident and the funeral. "It is so hard to think about how much of life Karla will miss. It isn't fair."

"No, it isn't fair. And I understand, at least in part, how devastating this must be for you. It's one reason I came. Death is difficult to accept, and especially hard when someone dies as young as your sister did. I have a personal story that I'd like to share with you, if you don't mind."

"Please do," Tiffany said. "So far I've dominated the conversation."

"Well, when we met on the swinging bridge in Costa Rica earlier this summer, I mentioned traveling alone, but didn't tell you why."

"Oh?"

"I'd lost my husband a few months earlier. He died of a heart attack."

"I'm so sorry."

"I was lost without Jeff, and for a while I blamed God for his death. I had a thousand questions. Why did it happen? Why did Jeff have to die so young? How could I go on without him? Did I even want to go on without him? And on and on … Sometimes after work I went to the fitness center and exercised until my arms and legs ached. And at home, I slammed dishes into the dishwasher so roughly it's a wonder I didn't break something. Or I shoved the vacuum cleaner over the carpet as if I were trying to suck up hundreds of spiders before they could scurry away. And there were times I let it all out—shouting or moaning until exhausted."

Tiffany thought of her own sorrow and frustration, including her resentment of God. She wondered where Katy's story would go. "And why did you go to Costa Rica alone?"

"It's where Jeff and I honeymooned, so I returned looking for answers. I wanted to move forward with my life—find a new normal, but I didn't know how."

Tiffany offered a tight-lipped smile. "And have you? Have you found peace? Because I'm afraid I'll always hurt over Karla's death and resent that she died so young."

"That morning on the bridge your anxiety was

evident, at least to me," Katy said. "It was easy to pick up on your uncertainty about a number of things. I saw it in the way you moved and from the look in your eyes. But I also noticed something else that day. On occasion, I saw hope and determination in your eyes. Several times I heard the conviction in your voice that you would one day learn how to conquer your fears."

"So what are you getting at?"

"I believe the Lord planted seeds of hope in me through your words and behavior during the brief period of time we spent together. I hadn't a clue about it at the time, but one night after work, several weeks after I returned home, as I nursed a glass of wine before dinner, I had an image of you rubbing the cross you wore around your neck. After that evening, although I had not attended church for years, Sunday school lessons from my youth began to return in bits and pieces. I was reminded to put my trust in a power greater than myself for the guidance and comfort I so desperately longed for. By this point of my journey with grief, I had begun to realize I needed more than just the passing of time to help me feel better. Not long after this experience, I started attending church again—looking for comfort and a new direction for my life."

Tiffany prickled at the implication God could help her. He had let her down. "Where are you headed with all of this?" she asked.

"You said something that morning that impressed me," Katy said.

"I can't imagine what."

"You suggested we could learn something about human life through plant life. You talked about the epiphytes relying on the trees for nourishment. Then you suggested we could cling to God like the epiphytes for the soul food we need to grow and thrive.

"I said that?"

"And more. You also said the vines clinging to the trees that wind upward toward the light were an example for us to follow, for as we remain close to God, He will lead us out of the darkness and into the light. It sounded dumb at the time, but it was an interesting metaphor that gave me something concrete to ponder later on when the time was right."

Tiffany rolled her eyes. "I must have been high on the heavy mist of the rainforest."

"One day, not long after I had awakened to the presence of God in my life, Rufus and I went for a run in the park. Rufus is my cute little redheaded cocker spaniel."

"So your dog looks like you with lots of red hair?" Tiffany asked.

"Yes, except she's much cuter than I am. So anyway, at the park I admired the flower beds and focused on the lovely perennials, like daylilies and roses. I thought about how they come back year after year, regardless of the harsh Chicago winters."

Tiffany listened carefully for the point she assumed Katy intended to make.

"The perennials disappear from above ground when harsh, cold weather sets in," Katy said, "and over the next several months of winter their root systems lay dormant underground. Then in the spring they return refueled and ready to grow more prolifically and beautifully than ever. Right?"

"So what are you trying to say? It's natural for flowers to retreat during the winter and be restored to new life in the spring, but we're not flowers."

"No, but I've been doing a lot of thinking since we

met. And I ask you, who's to say that the same process isn't also natural for us? The process of perennials to live, die, and live again makes me believe that we, too, can persevere through dark times and, in due time, be restored to new beginnings. Especially as we begin to understand and come to believe that we can develop a new normal for our lives. At some point in the grieving process we can choose to regroup or refuel for another season of life—one quite different from what we once had or shared with the loved one we lost."

"I don't know about all of this." Tiffany had forgotten her comparisons between plant life and humans. Right now, she couldn't embrace what Katy had to say. She still doubted leaning on the Lord would lessen her pain or make her loss more bearable. It certainly wouldn't bring Karla back.

Katy leaned back on the sofa and crossed her legs. "Now, mind you, a miraculous change did not occur in my life overnight, but you inspired me to make observations that helped me turn a corner. I began to be hopeful that I could build a life without Jeff. Not necessarily a better life, but a good one, even though different."

"That's wonderful, but that's not where I am," Tiffany said.

"Of course you're not. And on some level I'll always grieve that Jeff is gone. I'll always miss him, but I have accepted his untimely death was no one's fault, and that I have no choice but to learn to live without him."

"So your life is okay now?"

"It's improving. I still struggle sometimes. I get lonely. And feel sad. But in general, I am on the path of trusting in the promise of a new beginning."

"My grandmother said much the same thing a couple

of days ago about her personal experience of losing a son. I know you're trying to give me hope, but my grief's too fresh."

Katy rubbed her forehead with her finger tips. "I've said too much, but you helped me in my time of need. The Lord placed you on my path that day in the rainforest to plant seeds of hope that would point the way to less suffering."

Tiffany stared at Katy. "Now I need help. I know you mean well, but…"

Katy touched Tiffany's arm. "I'm trying too hard, aren't I? That's me, always trying to fix things, whether I've gathered all the clues or not. Kind of like I do in my job as I try to unearth the truth to solve a case." Katy smiled. "Sometimes I gnaw at the evidence till my gums bleed—so to speak."

Tiffany forced a smile. "I'm still searching for some kind of truth—answers that will satisfy. I'll try to remember your insights, even though right now I'm too confused to know which end is up."

"Fair enough. So, when are you returning to Costa Rica to study?"

"I'm too upset to think about it. Teaching is out of the question for me, so what's the use of continuing to study and train."

Katy reached down and pulled a small gift bag from her oversized handbag. "You've opened the way for me to give you this gift."

With a puzzled look, Tiffany removed a book from the gift bag. She read the title and turned it over to look at the back cover. "What is this?" she asked, looking up at Katy.

"It's an inspirational book that I thought you would enjoy reading. It's written by a minister. He uses the story of Peter, one of the Lord's disciples who left the boat to walk on water at Jesus' command to illustrate that we must trust God enough to step out on faith to accomplish great things while here on earth."

Tiffany frowned. "What does this have to do with me?"

"When we visited earlier this summer you expressed a strong passion for teaching, and yet, such a phobia of public speaking. It is my hope the book will inspire you to move out of your comfort zone to discover a way to make your dream of becoming a teacher a reality.

"It would take a miracle," Tiffany said. "It's kind of you, of course, and I do appreciate your thinking of me. I promise to read it some day."

"You don't have to promise anything. I followed a nudge to come share with you. And I followed an urge to bring this book, hoping it would help you." Katy smiled as she stood to leave.

After a heartfelt goodbye, Tiffany watched Katy get in her car and drive away to catch a late afternoon flight back to Chicago. She waved a final goodbye and closed the front door in slow motion.

Then she turned, placed the book on a small table in the entry hall, and shuffled up the stairs to her bedroom, the only safe place left in the world. There, she would relish Katy's surprise visit and give thought to what it might mean for her life.

## CHAPTER 38

When Margaret disappeared through a revolving door at the Kansas City International airport to catch an early morning flight to San Jose, Tiffany waved a final goodbye. Then she turned and slid into the car with her mother. She reached for her seatbelt and lifted it up and over to click into place. "Everyone is leaving me. And I hate the way all of this makes me feel."

Mrs. Birdwell eased away from the curb. "You'll see Margaret again soon."

"I don't know. Maybe I should stay here with you and Daddy. You may even need me to stay."

Her mother maneuvered the car into the lane leading to the interstate. "I can't deny that now more than ever we'd love it if you remained with us. It's a terrible time. But it isn't about what we want or need. It's about what's best for you, Tiffany."

Tiffany stared out the window for several seconds. "But I don't know what I want anymore. What do you think I should do?"

"Let's review your reasons for going to Costa Rica to

study in the first place. What did you hope to accomplish, sweetie? I mean, what are some of your long-range dreams and plans?"

Tiffany shared her growing interest in tropical biology and how she hoped to fit it into her future plans. "But I don't know how I could ever teach school. Speaking to a group would be too frightening. Besides, it all seems so trite and unrealistic now. Losing Karla has changed everything."

"Yes sweetheart, Karla's death changed all our lives, but it needn't change everything. And it shouldn't. At times the reality of your sister's passing nearly suffocates me. My heart is broken and so is your father's, but you needn't sacrifice your plans for us. That wouldn't bring Karla back."

"I know, but I don't want to desert you and Daddy," she said, touched by her mother's brave attempt to offer help with her mind clouded by grief.

"Don't misunderstand—we'd love for you to live near us, but we wouldn't ask that of you. We love you very much and want you to stay with us for as long as you need to, but when you're able you must make plans to return to Costa Rica to resume your studies and move along with your life."

Her mother's remarks were a gift to Tiffany. She wanted to stay in Kansas with her parents, but in truth, she also wanted to carry through with her study plans. And she missed Zachary more than she would have dreamed possible.

Her mother reached over and gave her a quick pat on the knee. "Why don't you tell me about Zachary?"

"Oh Mama, I ..." Tiffany sniffed and pulled a tissue from the box her mother always kept in the car.

"I'm sure your heart is broken, as mine is, and you are

confused, but you mustn't feel guilty because you're alive and looking forward to something."

As Tiffany blew her nose, the light dawned—her mother had intuitively gotten to the heart of the matter. "You're right, I'm crying because I feel guilty that Karla's life ended and I'm talking about my future. This is sooooo hard—so unbelievable."

"I agree. You're suffering from survivor's guilt, but you'll eventually work through it. When you're able, tell me about Zachary and why he's so special."

Tiffany reminded her mother Zachary worked as a naturalist in the Monteverde Cloud Forest Reserve, and though she had not known him long, she considered him wonderful. "We've been together many times since we met that first day in the rainforest." Then she spoke of their first dinner date, even sharing an abbreviated version of a few tender moments, trying to convey to her mother an inkling of the depth of her feelings for him.

Her mother wiped away a tear. "It pleases me how animated you become when you talk about Zachary. I gather from your stories that he's kind and sensitive—a good person."

Her mother's genuine interest and loving ways brightened her mood. "Oh, he's that and so much more. He's also intelligent and as handsome as a Greek god."

"Oh, my! That handsome, huh? Well it's evident to me you have similar interests, like your love of nature. Your father and I will want to meet him someday when the time seems right."

"What did you think of my new friend Katy? And the chance meeting we had in the rainforest earlier this summer?"

"Who's to say your meeting on the hike that day was simply a coincidence? Maybe you were supposed to connect to counsel and uplift each other. A lot of people believe peoples' paths cross for a specific reason. And I happen to agree."

"Then why did I cross paths with that Lucy woman I told you was so rude to me on the bridge that first day?"

"Maybe she was planted on the bridge to help you build your endurance for fighting your battles?"

Tiffany chuckled along with her mother. "If that's it, she certainly did a good job of pushing me to be stronger and more assertive—something I need."

"So did Katy encourage you to return to Costa Rica and finish your education?"

"Yes, she did. And after I told her about dating Zachary, she pushed even harder."

With her eyes glued to the road, her mother said, "I like Katy. And I agree with her that you should return to study at the Monteverde Institute, as planned."

"Katy mentioned she had met a man that owns a restaurant near her condominium. So it sounds like she has made progress in accepting her husband's death and getting on with her life. But I don't know how you do that when life changes so drastically."

"I don't know how you do it either. I've never suffered a more devastating loss than that of losing your sister. I cannot bear to think of life without her. But I suppose the grief process is different for everyone. All I can do is trust that praying to the Lord for the strength and courage to meet each day with hope will eventually make a difference."

"Grandmother Birdwell said she had a lot of anger and resentment to wade through before she could accept her son's death."

"Yes, I've visited some with your grandmother. I have a long way to go in learning how to navigate this new path I'm … " Her mother choked back tears.

Tiffany turned her head to gaze out the window, unable to bear to think of the pain her mother must surely feel.

"Tonight over dinner, let's have a family discussion about your plans to leave," her mother said.

"Mama? Thanks for listening. I cannot begin to imagine how awful losing Karla is for you. The pain must be unbearable. "

"There aren't words to describe it. It's too much."

"I hurt for you and daddy. I hope you know how much I love you."

"And I love you more."

"No way." Tiffany said as she glanced at her mother. And the sweet smile she saw on her mother's face gave her the largest dose of hope that she had had since Karla died.

*CHAPTER 39*

Roughly three weeks after Tiffany arrived for her sister's funeral, she boarded a plane for an early morning flight to San Jose. Her family supported her decision to return to Costa Rica—even encouraged her.

When she spotted the Country Club Plaza during the plane's initial ascent, she was flooded with memories of her family's Christmas shopping trips to Kansas City. She and Karla had always responded to the brightly colored lights of the Plaza as if they had never seen them before, causing their parents to beam with pleasure.

The plane rose higher and higher, finally leveling off at a cruising altitude of thirty-two thousand feet. She usually loved to sit by the window and study the sky with its infinite scope, but today, it brought her no pleasure. As she stared into space, gut-wrenching loneliness for her family, especially for Karla, ate at her.

The tragedy had left Tiffany desperate for peace. Fighting tears, she closed her eyes and leaned back against the seat. And while the jet ripped through the massive clouds, she held her breath so long her stomach muscles began to ache.

Eventually, she thought about the night that far beneath the plane and many miles away a vehicle plowed through an intersection, taking two lives and damaging countless others. Images of what must have happened that night pierced her heart. She tried to control the ugly assumptions that leaked in about her sister's broken body, but she might as well have attempted to apply a tourniquet to a steel pipe to stop it from leaking.

As Tiffany tried to recall some of Grandmother Birdwell's wisdom on death and grief, or Katy's reflections on finding hope in dealing with loss through observing plant life, she heard someone whisper her name. "Did you speak to me?" she asked the man seated next to her.

He grunted and frowned. "Huh? Of course not. You looked like you were asleep."

Tiffany felt stupid. Maybe insanity had set in. She needed to get a grip on her crazy thoughts. She turned away to hide her embarrassment. And as she stared through the window into grey vastness, the plane roared past a strange cloud that was a rough likeness of an angel with wings stretched upward. Though it disappeared quickly from view, the angel cloud triggered a memory of her unusual dream the night Karla died. As she pulled up the details of the dream, recalling how several of her deceased female relatives came to her in the form of an angel to offer encouragement and hope when she was so bereaved, she began to relax. The more she thought about it, the more peaceful she felt. Hope to one day again experience joy—the deep abiding kind that can make an important difference—began to take shape inside her for the first time in a long while.

Later, on the flight from Atlanta to San Jose, Tiffany

pondered her loss and the decision to return to Costa Rica until at last, a swirling mix of angel messengers, fluffy clouds, and red roses lulled her to sleep.

Roughly an hour later, she woke with a start when the captain announced their initial approach into San Jose. "Flight attendants prepare the plane for landing," said a strong, smooth voice.

When the harsh reality of her sister's death rushed back in, she shuddered. The awful reality of Karla's passing was not some horrible nightmare she could simply dismiss. During the plane's rapid descent she made up her mind to find a way to do so. And soon thereafter, when the wheels of the plane kissed the tarmac, relief washed over Tiffany like a placid wave bathing the shoreline.

"I've missed you both so much," Tiffany said as she approached Zachary and Margaret at the baggage claim area in San Jose. Zachary's outstretched arms and warm smile offered a special balm for her wounded heart. His tender kiss on her cheek meant more than the passionate kisses they shared in the jungle the day Karla died. She had done the right thing to return to school and Margaret, and especially to Zachary.

After the long drive to Monteverde, and Zachary had delivered the girls to their apartment, Margaret invited Tiffany to talk about Karla. "I'd like to hear more about Karla and a little about your life together as sisters—that is if you're up to it."

"Karla was a good girl, but she pulled her share of pranks and bugged me and my friends—getting in our way and into our things. It hurts to recall how impatient I was with her during those times when she was young."

"I wouldn't know about that—I'm an only child. But I have dealt with two younger, bothersome cousins. Does that count?" Margaret laughed.

Tiffany managed a smile. "As we grew older we enjoyed shopping together at the mall. Sometimes we even took in a movie. Karla had such a fun-loving, carefree spirit. I just hope some of it rubbed off on me."

"What do you mean?"

"I'm so uptight about everything—the complete opposite of Karla. She had an easy-going way about her that I would love to have." Tiffany reached for a tissue and blew her nose. "Sorry. I'm a mess—laughing one minute and crying the next. Will I ever be okay?"

"I wish I could tell you. But I'm sure your mood swings are typical."

"We had such fun. We always shared a big box of popcorn in the movie—the size that costs more than a hamburger and fries."

Margaret snickered. "At least twice as much as it should have, huh?"

As Tiffany spoke about her sister, Margaret listened with the grace and goodness of an angel. Her warm and caring spirit helped lighten Tiffany's mood so much that her last thoughts before sleeping that night were not about Karla, but rather, they were about Margaret.

Tiffany thought about Margaret's basic good nature and her ability to listen well. Whether Margaret chaired a college campus meeting or facilitated a study group, her delivery was always smooth. She envied Margaret's ability to state her mind with confidence and speak in front of others with ease, something she doubted she could ever do.

Tonight, her envy of Margaret had turned into a deep admiration.

## CHAPTER 40

Tiffany stared at the hundreds of dust motes highlighted in the morning sunrays, realizing for the first time since Karla died that she had awakened to a feeling of anticipation rather than pain. She looked forward to the day ahead. Zachary was taking her to the Baldwins for lunch. After weeks of bobbing like a rudderless boat in a sea of swirling emotions, Nellie would help buoy her during the remainder of her stay in Costa Rica.

Tiffany rolled over and looked at the clock. She grabbed her cell phone and shot Zachary a quick text: *Can you give me an extra thirty minutes? I overslept.*

After a hurried shower, she threw on her underwear and stepped into a white denim skirt. Then as she slid a blue sapphire peasant blouse over her head, she reflected on how the Baldwins had become an important part of her life in a short period of time. Was it only a nice coincidence they had met right after she arrived? No, her mother and Nellie would say their meeting was God at work. The thought made her smile.

The extra moisture in the air reminded Tiffany she

had returned to the tropics. She gladly took extra pains with her makeup and fiddled longer with her kinky hair. But at the sound of Zachary's jeep coming through the open window, she tossed her hair pick into a small black tote and flew out the door to greet him.

Nellie and George greeted them warmly and led the way to the patio where the table was set for four. "We're having beef tacos for lunch and tres leches cake for dessert," Nellie said, filling their water glasses.

"Tres leches? What's that?" asked Tiffany.

"It's a sponge cake that's soaked in three different kinds of milk. It is the favorite dessert of most Costa Ricans. I hope you'll like it."

Soon after the pleasant lunch, Nellie led Tiffany to the corner of the yard. "Let's leave the guys to visit on the patio, while we talk alone in the arbor." And after they settled into the swing, Nellie invited Tiffany to share what had happened. "But first, tell me how you are doing?"

"I'm struggling. It's all so terrible—so sad." Tiffany pushed her foot against the floor of the arbor, moving the swing in a slow and gentle fashion. "I can't imagine life without my sister."

"No, I'm sure you can't. You'll need to take life one day at a time—sometimes just a step at a time. How are your parents holding up?"

Tiffany pressed her lips together and shook her head. "Their hearts are broken. It frightens me to see how solemn my dad is—holding it all inside, while my mother can't stop the tears."

Nellie gave Tiffany's hand a firm squeeze. "Tell me about Karla. I'm sure you loved her very much."

"She was a good girl—generous and kind. And

confident and brave. She easily laughed off frightening situations. And as far as a challenge, she had that 'if anybody can, I can' attitude."

Tiffany shared several stories about growing up with Karla and vented about the ordeal of her death and funeral. "I resent the driver. Actually, I hate him for what he did."

For some reason she hesitated to tell Nellie about her hostility toward God. Instead, she spoke about the mountain of grief left behind for so many people by one person's terrible choice to drink and drive.

"If you only knew how much I'd like to help," Nellie said, "but we can't fix things for each other. Coping with loss takes time and hard work. For the most part, grief is a lonely journey."

Something about Nellie's tone made Tiffany remember her Grandmother Birdwell once remarked that the person who has been through the "fire with the Lord" is more apt to recognize it in another. "Nellie, have you also suffered a terrible loss or dealt with a tragedy? Something that has made life sad for you?"

"You're quite perceptive, young lady."

"What happened? If you don't mind me asking?"

"It happened many years ago when George and I were quite young. We wanted a family, but I had trouble conceiving. When I did finally become pregnant, quite some time after we arrived in Costa Rica, our joy knew no bounds. George helped me make the second bedroom into a nursery. He painted the walls and made a crib. And I stitched a layette and bedding for the crib—even window curtains to match. I'm sure we bored everybody for months, talking about our baby. Well actually, twins, but we didn't know that until I delivered."

"Twins? Wow!"

"Yes, we had a boy and a girl—two precious tiny babies with round, perfect little heads and sweet, heart-shaped mouths. They both had light brown hair. Janey arrived first, but Joey was bigger. We lost both of them"

Judging by the faraway look in Nellie's eyes, Tiffany believed Nellie's scars from her tremendous loss, at least in part, still remained with her. "Oh, Nellie, I'm so sorry. How did they die?"

"They were born two months early. They needed help to survive beyond what a skilled midwife could provide, and at that time this area was quite remote and medical assistance nearly nonexistent."

"I'm so sorry for you and George, and your babies." Tiffany did not know what else to say, but imagining Nellie's pain came more easily than it once would have.

Nellie massaged her temples with firm circular motions, as though trying to exorcise painful memories from her head. "It happened a long time ago, but I can't help but wonder how they would have turned out. Would Joey have looked like George? And would Janey have been gentle-spirited like my mother? Or maybe spunky like some say I am?"

"Or kind and thoughtful like you, Nellie."

"But Tiffany, what I want you to hear in my story is that life is good and a gift to treasure." Nellie stopped the swing and turned to capture Tiffany's full attention. "And even though I never got pregnant again, and can still shed a tear to this day if I focus on my loss, I need you to know that I worked through the worst period of grief to finally reach the place I could accept what happened and move on. I've truly enjoyed my life over the many years since we lost our babies."

"You accepted it?"

"Now you must understand that accepting something

sad or difficult in your life doesn't mean you like what happened. It simply means you reach the place you no longer struggle against the truth of it or expend emotion wishing you could change the unchangeable."

Tiffany shook her head. "But now that I've lost my sister, it's hard to understand how you managed to go on."

"You need time. Your loss is so new. Reckoning with grief takes time, more for some than for others. In the beginning, I wished I'd died with my babies. I felt God had abandoned me."

Tiffany stopped swinging to look at Nellie. "That's where I am now and I don't know what to do about it."

"It took me a while to understand God never leaves us. He remains close to comfort and encourage us when we invite Him to. As I spent more and more time praying and reading scripture, life gradually got easier. With the Lord's help, I eventually stopped struggling with "what if" or "if only," and you will too."

Tiffany identified with Nellie's story of loss, and she wanted to receive her words of wisdom, but she doubted relying on the Lord would help her. She wanted to trust that in time she would feel better, but she couldn't quite believe it was possible. The pain of losing Karla was too fresh—too big.

## CHAPTER 41

Zachary nodded toward Nellie and Tiffany in the corner of the yard. "This is all so tough on Tiffany. I wish I could do something to help her deal with losing her sister, but I've never dealt with anything like this before." That was not altogether true, for he had grieved miserably when his dad left home. Maybe he still did. But Tiffany's situation was different. His dad had not died—it only felt like he had. "You have any ideas about what I can say or do to make things better for Tiffany?"

"I don't think there's much you can do," George said, "except be willing to listen to her. Just be kind and patient with her. You can't take away Tiffany's pain or change anything for her, but you can encourage her to talk about what's on her mind."

"But I want to help her in some concrete way."

George leaned forward in his chair. "I'm sure you do, and that tells me how much you care. Would you mind if I told you about my experience with loss? Hopefully, it would provide a little insight into Tiffany's grief."

At Zachary's encouragement, George began to tell his

story. "It happened a long time ago when Nellie and I were still in our twenties. We lost twin babies, a boy and a girl that came early. I watched helplessly as they died right before my eyes, first Joey and then Janey. That night when life left their little bodies something solid and sweet slipped out of me for good."

Zachary could not understand a god that let bad things happen to good people. *How could a good god let those babies die? And how could a god who is supposed to care about people allow Karla and her friend to die so young?* "That's tough stuff you and Nellie had to deal with. What did you do?"

"I clung to my faith and tried to make sense of it, not that I ever did. It took hard work to accept their deaths and let go of dreams enough to move on. But through it all, I eventually discovered God provides the greatest source of comfort we can ever receive in this life."

George's strong convictions about God didn't surprise Zachary, but he still doubted success or happiness depended on believing in something you could not see. The whole confusing subject of religion and spirituality—whatever the heck they were—was hard for him to swallow.

"So tell me, Zach, have you ever suffered a loss?"

Zachary made a fist and cracked his knuckles. "Uhhhhh … Yes, but not because someone died."

"Do you want to talk about it?"

"Well, I didn't think of it as a loss back then, but I can see now that at age fourteen I lost one of the two most important people in my life. My dad left me and my mom for another woman."

"What happened?"

"He moved out of the house and quit coming to my soccer games. He wasn't there after school to help me with homework. Dad vanished from my life. He no longer cared."

"How did that make you feel?"

"Hurt. And lonely. And angry. I wanted to lash out at something or someone for taking my dad away."

"How have you handled all those difficult feelings?"

"I try not to think about it." Then at George's urging Zachary opened up and talked about that time in his life, and how he coped with losing his dad. His words often fell like a waterfall bouncing over jagged boulders, constant but not always smoothly as he described how he turned to drugs and alcohol to escape disappointment and pain, and how overuse led to tragedy. "As you can see, I haven't really dealt with my feelings. I still resent my dad. Major regrets and guilt over my bad choices haunt me to this day."

George caught Zach's eye and held it. "It sounds like an awful time for you. And I can see it still hurts."

"But I should be used to carrying tough stuff around by now—I've done it for years."

"Do you see your dad often?"

"I can count on one hand how many times I've seen him since he left us."

"It seems to me your dad went in search of something he believed was missing from his marriage. Just remember, you're not at fault for his choices."

"Mom said something similar when Dad left. And later, when I made a mess of my life, she tried to help me get my head on straight. But it's hard to forgive him for leaving us, and hard to forgive myself for my part in that awful night."

George nodded. "Forgiveness can be tough—hard to talk about and even harder to do. But I think forgiveness is a choice like many other things in life. It opens the way for both parties to let go of pain, resentment, anger, guilt, regret, or shame—any of those negative feelings that can destroy the chance for happiness."

"But forgiving someone when you're hurting or angry is hard to do."

George leaned back in his chair and crossed his legs. "Yes, it is hard. Truth is that the act of forgiveness is never simple. But in my experience forgiveness usually results in positive changes."

Zachary shook his head. "No, I couldn't possibly forgive my dad—not that he's asked to be forgiven."

"Impossible things happen," George said as his black and brown beagle bounded onto the patio with a tennis ball in his mouth. "Hey, Bailey, look at you. Want to play catch, boy?" George tossed the ball. Bailey chased it across the lawn, leapt high off the ground, and caught it in mid-air. When Bailey padded proudly back, the ball held firmly between his teeth, George praised him and tossed it again. "Look at him! Bailey's just a natural at catching the ball that way." Then after throwing the ball a third time, George said, "I guess it's like that for people— certain things come more naturally to some people than it does to others. But I seriously doubt forgiveness comes naturally to anyone. I believe it takes a decided effort to confront forgiveness. It requires meeting face to face to sort out feelings, and listen as well as speak. I suspect most people find it challenging to deal with forgiveness, since pride and stubbornness usually play in to it."

Suddenly, Zachary had a sense of urgency to tell Tiffany the details of his lost year—the hurt, resentment, and guilt. He had never dealt with forgiveness, but for some crazy reason he failed to understand, he longed for an acquittal from Tiffany for the bad choices he had made as a kid.

CHAPTER 42

The next day in the rainforest ran long for Zachary. The afternoon tour was almost over and they still had not spotted a quetzal. It would make his day to spot one of the magnificent birds—not only for the group, but also for himself.

Zachary nodded toward his tour assistant as he informed the group that Lopez would stay behind with them while he rushed ahead a few hundred yards to scout out the area. "Hopefully, I'll spot a quetzal on my own, but either way, I won't be gone long. And to fill the time, Lopez will give you a little information about the quetzal's eating and breeding habits."

About ten minutes later, Zachary raced back shouting, unable to contain his excitement. "I spotted one! I found a quetzal perched high in a tree about a quarter of a mile around the bend! Let's hurry back, but remember—no shouting or loud talking or we might scare it off."

Trotting single file, Zachary led the tourists along the narrow, worn path that hugged the hill on one side and flirted with a steep slope on the other. They ran quickly, and without speaking, as their footsteps pounded the path.

After stopping at the general area where he had spotted the bird, Zachary scoured the dense, leafy canopy of a cluster of trees through his binoculars for several seconds. "There it is!" he said, his voice husky. "It's silhouetted against the gray light filtering through the trees! See it?" he asked, dropping his field glasses to his chest and pointing to the top of the trees. "It's way up there. Its head, back, and wings are bright green, and it has a shimmery look, so it'll blend in with the wet foliage of the cloud forest. It has a red chest, but that would be hard to spot from this distance."

As the group strained to see the bird through their binoculars, Zachary set up a telescope on a tripod. They took turns looking through it for a sharper, closer view. He even showed them how to photograph the bird through the opening of the telescope.

Over the next several minutes, digital cameras clicked like a chorus of crickets, while the sky darkened and the wind picked up. "I hate to put a stop to this, but it looks like rain," Zachary said as he scoured the patches of grey sky through the swaying trees. "We better get ready to head out. I think it's about to pour."

Seconds later, a driving rain pierced the dense overgrowth. The tourists scurried to protect their gear and flew along the path behind Lopez toward the entrance to the rainforest, leaving Zachary to dismantle his telescope and bring up the rear.

The rain-sodden group took shelter under a covered, wooden deck right outside the jungle. And as they waited for the rain to slacken, excitement continued to run high. They marveled over their good fortune to see the coveted quetzal, as they relived the exciting experience.

Although Zachary was as pumped as the tourists, he regretted Tiffany had not been along for the rare sighting. Surely they would see an exotic quetzal together someday.


That night in bed, after reliving the exciting find of the day, Zachary's thoughts drifted to Karla. He had never met her, but her death by a drunk driver had unearthed buried feelings about the time he and his buddies made a terrible choice that had taken a life. Her death had reopened wounds of guilt and shame and forced him to look at the awful truth of his past. And it had also stoked his anger toward his dad that he thought had been snuffed out.

For a long time now, he had tried to pretend his life could not be better. But even as he led group after group all over Costa Rica with great success, or happily watched monkeys romping through trees outside his bedroom window, unrest or sadness often intruded.

He needed to figure out how to handle his feelings and move on. But how? Tiffany seemed to be dealing with her grief. She referred to Nellie as her spiritual mentor—whatever that meant. And she described Margaret as the epitome of patience during their conversations.

Zachary longed for some of George and Nellie's peace of mind. He knew they relied on God for everything, but relying on an unseen power for the help he needed was absurd. How could it possibly be of any good?

Zachary's body stiffened at the memory of when his dad left their tension-riddled house for good. It still stung to look back on that night when his dad sauntered into his bedroom to say goodbye.

Pulling a chair alongside his bed, his dad blurted, "I'm leaving tonight, son. And I won't be coming back. You're a big boy now, so I know you can handle this." He told Zachary his plans and reminded him to call if he needed to. "It doesn't have to change things between us. We'll see each other often. I'll stay in touch."

After his dad's abrupt announcement and departure, Zachary had slipped from bed to retrieve Jock, a large, wooly, camel-colored monkey from a menagerie of dusty creatures nestled on the top shelf of his closet. It was his favorite stuffed animal as a young boy. He recalled the time his mom stitched Jock's rubber foot back in place after he had nearly torn it off in rough play. He especially remembered that her act of kindness made him feel loved. But the night his dad left home forever, he did not feel loved by anyone.

Thank goodness no one ever knew how he cried that night, while clutching the musty-smelling Jock to his chest. After all, at fourteen he should not have given in to tears, let alone holding dear a silly, imperfect monkey.

Now all these years later the morbid sound of the bedroom door closing and his dad's footsteps moving along the hall still echoed in Zachary's soul, rattling his bones and jarring his nerves.

For a long time, Zachary tossed and turned in bed, his mind spinning like a roulette wheel as he tried to connect the past with the present, and make sense of his frustration. But thankfully, sleep eventually rescued him from a litany of painful boyhood recollections.

## CHAPTER 43

For days Zachary wrestled with when to tell Tiffany his story or even if he should, but his need to purge his conscience outweighed a whisper that warned him it was too soon after Karla's death. He wanted Tiffany to know the details of what had happened to him, for how could he share another authentic moment with her if he did not tell her everything?

When he arrived home from his last tour of the day, he punched in Tiffany's cell phone number. Texting simply would not work this time—he wanted to hear her voice. "I've got to see you, Tiffany. There's something important I want to tell you."

"I'm exhausted. It's been a long day. Can it wait?" asked Tiffany.

"Let's talk at my apartment. I'll pick you up."

"We worked on a big project at school today. Weeding. Planting. Pruning. I'm too tired to be decent company."

"Please?" He whittled away at her until she began to relent.

"You sound desperate. What is it?"

"I need to speak to you in person." Telling her over the phone was out. He was confident she would understand if he could talk to her face to face.

Within a half hour Zachary returned with Tiffany to his apartment, kicking aside a pair of muddy tennis shoes near the front door as they entered. Then he moved a pile of wrinkled laundry from the wicker loveseat and motioned for her to sit.

When Zachary returned from the kitchen with drinks, he shoved aside a stack of magazines on the lamp table to make room for them. "I want to get this over with," he said, taking a seat in the chair adjacent to the loveseat. For a brief moment, he questioned his decision to tell her, since his terrible tale mirrored her sister's tragic death. Again, a whispered warning urged him to wait, but he ignored it and took Tiffany's hand to push on. "Several years ago something terrible happened that I need to tell you about."

Then in the midst of his untidy house, not astute to her needs or the least bit tactful in his approach, Zachary began to clear his soul of chaotic, cluttered feelings. "Dad left home right after I turned fourteen. He came to my bedroom one night to announce his plans to leave; making it clear his marriage to Mom had ended. He tried to reassure me he still loved me, but—"

"Why have you never told me this before?"

"It left a terrible void in my life. And after he disappeared on us, I started looking for something to make the pain go away."

Tiffany pulled her hand back.

"Now that I think about it, maybe I wanted to get back at him. I'm not saying it was his fault I turned to drugs and alcohol, but I resented him for a long time. Still do."

At the mention of drugs and alcohol, Tiffany sucked air and shifted to the edge of the loveseat.

Ignoring her shocked look, Zachary barreled on. "I went around with a pain in my gut, wanting to poke anybody that crossed me. I wanted the hurt and disappointment to go away. All the negative feelings numbed me till I didn't care about much of anything."

Although her mannequin eyes pierced his heart, he continued. "My homework suffered when dad left, and I started hanging out with a group of kids who seemed to be looking for trouble. And I ... I guess I was too. One night this kid, whose parents were out of town, had a party. Howie and a couple of other guys goaded me into smoking pot, telling me it would loosen me up and make me forget about my troubles. Actually, it didn't take much to convince me, since I'd lost my enthusiasm for the things I once liked to do. I'd forgotten how to be happy. Dad's surprise exit had sucked me dry."

Tiffany threw her hands in the air and spread her fingers wide apart. "I can't believe you're telling me all this. You have some nerve."

"I'm sorry, but I wanted to tell you. I need—"

"What about what I need?" Tiffany asked with moist, fire-filled eyes.

Zachary had the good sense to know he needed to wrap it up. "I'll get to the punch line. Looking back, I can see I made a mistake to take that first smoke, but that's another subject. So this one Saturday night something awful happened. A bunch of us hung out drinking beer and smoking pot for hours. So uhhhhh ... Well, we ran out of beer, and like idiots, piled into Brad's car to go buy more. Brad ran a stoplight and struck the back half of a mini-van. A fourteen year old boy in the backseat of the van died at the scene."

When Zachary saw Tiffany's horror-filled eyes and clenched teeth, he stopped and shifted in his chair. Hoping she was upset for him, rather than at him, he continued. "I'm almost through. They arrested Brad and took him to jail. The rest of us spent a night in juvenile detention and later attended classes on driving under the influence of—"

Tiffany's face had become granite-hard. "Stop right now," she yelled.

"Karla's death has brought all my guilt and regret to the surface."

At the mention of Karla's name, Tiffany bellowed as though someone rubbed salt into her deep and raw open wound. "NO … NOOO … NOOOOO! She shot from the loveseat as though an eject button had been pushed.

Stumbling, she bumped the lamp table and sent their untouched drinks to the hard linoleum floor. Liquid and shattered glass shot everywhere. When Tiffany fled the room, speckles of her blood added to the mess.

She ran like a crazed animal over the gravel drive with Zachary chasing after her, shouting, "Stop! Stop! Let me help you. Your ankle's bleeding." He grabbed her arm just as she reached the main road. She tried to shake him off, but he managed to hang on. "It's too far to walk. I'll take you home. Get in the jeep."

Shocked into silence at last, Zachary started the motor and backed out of the driveway without a notion of what to do or say next. He had known all along his story would likely upset her, and even questioned the timing of telling her so soon after her sister's death. But out of self-interest he had ignored all instincts to wait. Without doubt, he had made a bad mistake. He had gone too far.

Other than Tiffany's sniffles, they rode all the way to her apartment in silence. When they arrived, she jumped out and limped across the parking lot before he could bring the jeep to a complete stop. He flung the jeep in gear, killed the motor, and tore after her. "Tiffany, stop. Please … Please let me help you. I'm sorry. I'm so sorry."

Without looking back, she hurled her damaged heart toward him. "Stay away from me. I never want to lay eyes on you again. Never! You hear me? NEVER!"

"Tiffany? Please, Tiffany?" he begged as he caught up with her and took hold of her arm.

She jerked free of him as though something evil had touched her. "I mean it, leave me alone. I abhor the idea of being around *anyone* involved in drunk driving." She fumbled with her keys. "Don't you get it? I can't stand the sight of you."

She slammed the door in his face. And her pain-filled eyes and hurtful words left him with an unbearable ache as he slowly turned to shuffle away. Additional guilt and sorrow burrowed into his already crowded heart as he drove home on auto-pilot.

He regretted his bad behavior. He should not have dumped his story on Tiffany. Not now, and not in the manner he had. Of course at the time he had not viewed it as dumping. He wanted to share his past and stop harboring secrets.

Crawling gingerly into bed, Zachary curled into a ball of disappointment over lost opportunities and dreams. He held back the tears. After all, he was a grown man and hadn't cried since that awful night when his dad went away and left him lost and confused.

Eventually, the walls began to close in on him. He stretched out on his back and stared into the moonlit room, but frustrated and restless, he couldn't get a good breath.

Finally, he pulled himself from bed and went to the kitchen. He needed a beer, but he had to settle for a soft drink. While hunched over the kitchen table rehashing details of the evening, he eventually realized that not only did he ache with regret over hurting Tiffany, part of his pain came from that long ago time when his idyllic boyhood unraveled.

## CHAPTER 44

"I've never felt more betrayed than I did the night Zachary rambled on and on about his past," Tiffany said as she watched Margaret gather her supplies to paint.

"I cannot imagine how difficult it was to listen to all that," Margaret said.

"He was so insensitive. I tried to be patient, but I finally exploded." The entire episode of Zachary spilling his guts had played like a bad video, complete with static and rewinds in Tiffany's head for days.

Margaret adjusted the easel for her canvas. "I'm so sorry. And his confession came in the middle of working so hard to make sense of the tragedy that took Karla's life."

Tiffany cut a slice of pineapple into a several pieces, but never took a bite. "I can't seem to stop the images of Zachary drunk. I see him driving the vehicle that slammed into the van that killed a young boy. And for that matter, I see him in the truck that roared into Karla's car. She and her friend didn't have a chance."

"I hate to see you tormenting yourself this way."

"It's making me crazy. And I know it's unfair to harbor such resentment toward Zachary. He wasn't driving the vehicle that caused the boy's death, and of course, he wasn't even remotely involved in the accident that took my sister's life"

Margaret left the easel to sit across the table from Tiffany. "It's tough enough to deal with a major loss, but mixing in more anger and resentment to an already tangled web of emotions presents a real challenge, doesn't it? It makes it all the harder to separate your feelings and address each one individually."

"I have to push myself through each day. I've lost my appetite. I can't think clearly. And I haven't a clue how to feel better." Tiffany could not focus on her Grandmother Birdwell's wisdom, nor could she focus on Nellie's faith that seemed to carry her through everything. Faith certainly was not carrying her.

"Remember that I'm here to listen anytime you need to talk," Margaret said.

Tiffany glanced at her watch, and then she stood to leave. "Thanks, but I guess I've said enough for now. I'd better not run late for the first day of class. All summer I looked forward to the fall semester and my classes, but now my heart's not in it." Sighing, she picked up the keys to the jeep. "I was actually eager to meet my professors, but not anymore. I won't be able to concentrate on a word they say."

"I'm sure you'll retain enough to pass the quizzes. You're such a good student," Margaret said as she saw Tiffany out the door and waved goodbye.

A keen observer of nature in all of its facets, Tiffany seldom tired of watching the ever-changing sky. But this morning, weariness and dread blinded her to the beauty of the cloudless blue sky as she drove to class. She couldn't shake from her mind that the decision to drive drunk had resulted in the death of her precious sister and her friend, as well as that innocent young boy.

Sometimes she viewed the two accidents as one, as though the three helpless victims died at the hands of the same driver. Someone should be held accountable and made to pay a price for such irresponsible behavior, she thought. "But who? Zachary?" She had shouted the words aloud over the roar of the jeep's engine.

As she pulled into a parking space, a blurry vision of Zachary, alone and hungry in a jail cell filled her head. She could see him—a bag of bones in a bright orange jumpsuit. Startled by the dramatic images, a cold chill ran along her spine as she sat in the warm sunshine.

She could not bring herself to leave the jeep. She doubted sitting through the classes would be possible anyway. And certainly, she wouldn't be able to retain anything from the lectures.

Moments later, she wrinkled her brow in confusion and cried out, "For goodness' sake, am I losing my mind? Zachary was only fifteen when the young boy died. And he wasn't even behind the wheel."

She considered driving to the rainforest. Maybe a solo walk would clear her head that had begun to pound. But no, she couldn't do that. She had come all the way from Kansas to go to school. She grabbed her water bottle, washed down a couple of aspirin, and forced herself out of the jeep. Shuffling across the parking lot, she argued the pros and cons of continuing on or turning back.

In spite of her frustration, when she entered the hallway that led to her first lecture room, a voice whispered softly inside her head: *You can do this. Just go in and do your best. You're not alone. You can do it.*

Over the next several hours, additional whispers of

encouragement insulated her against sadness somewhat like a winter coat protects the body on a cold blustery day. *Shift your focus. Keep trying. Push on.*

She had always tried to be an above average student, so she decided to do her best in this difficult situation. With fresh determination and a handy stubborn streak, she vowed to make every effort to listen and take proper notes.

By the end of the first day of classes, a wealth of information about Costa Rica's diverse wildlife and the ecological system of the rainforests had fanned her enthusiasm for learning new and interesting things. The classes had distracted her for a time from her pain.

When the week finally ended, Tiffany was giddy with relief, for she had not only survived, but she had attended all of the classes and actually enjoyed them.

The emerging conviction that she could survive a dark time and still produce something worthwhile reminded Tiffany of Katy's reflections on how a dormant bulb survives the winter to push through the dry cold earth of springtime, refreshed with new glory and strength. She smiled at the thought of herself as a tulip— maybe a red tulip, bold and sturdy. The correlation nudged her into a more positive state of mind, not that she felt all that glorious or strong just yet. But maybe it would come.

On the drive home Tiffany decided to go alone the next morning to hike in the rainforest to search for a quetzal. Actually spotting the reclusive bird might nourish the tiny seedling of hope for better days that had begun to sprout within her over the past week.

And maybe one day the seedling of hope would break through and bloom into a full-blown determination to push on and accomplish her dreams.

## CHAPTER 45

"There, she can't miss it," Tiffany whispered aloud as she propped a note for Margaret by the coffee pot. Clad in blue jeans, a long-sleeved green T-shirt, and hiking boots, Tiffany grabbed a bottle of water, a bag of dried fruit, and two granola bars to add to her backpack. She had already packed her camera and binoculars, and a guidebook on the flora and fauna of the rainforest that included a map of trails and advice about hiking.

Twilight had come too soon, but Tiffany wanted to beat the morning tour groups to the rainforest by several hours. With her adrenaline running high, she slung her backpack over her shoulder and grabbed a water-repellent hoodie off the back of a chair. She eased the door shut behind her and ran to the jeep. Tossing her bag into the passenger seat, she jumped in and started the motor. For the next twenty minutes or so, high expectations danced happily in Tiffany's veins as she bumped along the rough road toward the Monteverde Cloud Forest Reserve.

Obsessed by a strong compulsion to find a quetzal, Tiffany ran across the empty parking lot and rushed into the jungle. But she came to a sudden halt, for only an eerie, faint glow filtered through the dense overgrowth. It barely lit the trail. Her breath caught in her throat. She had anticipated a haven for her early morning walk, but instead, she had entered a dark cave-like setting. Thoroughly spooked, cold concern collided with warm excitement.

In only a moment, her mood and demeanor had changed drastically. What was she thinking to come to this vast and deserted jungle alone? Her journey had barely begun, yet as she carefully tiptoed along the path, a smattering of goose bumps already prickled her body.

*Why am I so anxious? Is it only because it's dark? Am I afraid of being attacked by the secret life lurking in the thick vegetation? Or is someone waiting to do me harm?*

The parking lot was vacant, wasn't it? She pushed on, darting her eyes in every direction, as she struggled to breathe.

*Help me calm down. Give me courage. Please? Make me different— braver.*

The prayer sprang from her soul, as though she had forgotten her anger toward God. But she doubted turning to God would help. He was not around when Karla needed Him, so why should she expect help just because she was nervous about something she had chosen to do.

She longed to pull off her solo hike, but she needed a miraculous boost of confidence, not just for this morning, but for beyond the morning hike. She needed courage to pursue her dreams of getting to the front of a classroom. Although uncertain of what occurs first, confidence or courage, Tiffany had seen the combination work for others. People who were confident and courageous seemed to have a secret to uncovering a life of success and contentment.

"Ahhhhh, to be transformed like a beautiful butterfly," she whispered to the breeze. She had always been fascinated with the way a butterfly begins as an ugly caterpillar and transforms into a beautiful insect that flutters freely and confidently into places unknown. But she did not know how or where to begin to make such a change for herself. And certainly, for a person to transition from cowardly to courageous could not happen overnight. For her, it might take a lifetime.

Many times, she had heard someone in her youth group at church say, "let go and let God." The words meant nothing at the time, but now, as she stumbled along the lonely path, the phrase gave her pause for thought.

Could she let go of her faceless fears that so easily victimized her faith? Could she trust God to be in control of her future? Would He provide the hope and confidence she needed to make the inner changes necessary to achieve her goals?

No, it may have worked for her grandmother and Nellie, but she had lost hope that God would send answers. She would have to forge on alone.

Though apprehension had her in knots, she pushed on into the jungle, lured by the resplendent quetzal. Spotting the elusive bird was a coveted experience she did not want to miss. And although she suspected it would take a miracle to place her among the few who actually capture a picture of the bird, something beckoned her deeper into the heart of the jungle. An unseen force preempted her anxiety and nudged her along with a sense a purpose to her mission beyond finding a quetzal.

On the heels of the noble notion that she might be answering a special call on her life this morning, a loud screeching in the trees overhead caught her off guard. With a sinking feeling, she picked up her pace and raced down the trail. But after running several hundred feet, it occurred to her it was probably only a troop of spider monkeys that tend to stay high in the trees. She stopped to catch her breath. Panting, she leaned forward and rested her hands on her knees, while the wind whispered ominously in the overgrowth.

*But what if I eventually come across something more than harmless spider monkeys while searching for the silly, shy bird? Oh dear Lord above, what if I come across a bushmaster snake?*

Shivers zipped along Tiffany's spine at lightning speed as she pictured the huge snake lurking nearby in the tangled greenery, its massive fangs exposed. Almost faint with worry, Tiffany zipped her rain jacket up to her throat and tried to hold tension-riddled tears at bay by recalling good times with Karla. But fragments of sweet memories prompted a flood of tears. Her grief was still too fresh and her pain far too strong.

So in the dark recesses of towering trees, clad with delicate ferns and luscious orchids, Tiffany gave in to her sorrow. The wind picked up and the air grew moist as she wept for Karla. She wept for her parents and she wept for herself. Eventually, it occurred to her that she also wept over the loss of Zachary. She missed him so much.

As her sobbing subsided, she noticed the light filtering through the trees had further dimmed. She smelled a storm brewing. But before she could decide what to do, the trees rattled and swayed from strong shifting winds. In seconds the looming gray clouds burst open, releasing buckets of rainwater.

Without an umbrella, Tiffany hurried to take shelter under a nearby Poor Man's Umbrella plant, whose massive leaves were roughly six feet wide. As she sat wet and trembling on a small log under the plant, she wondered if a wild puma lurked in the shadows. Or if a Fer-de-lance snake, Costa Rica's deadliest, slithered nearby. She even imagined a boa constrictor coiled and waiting to squeeze the life out of her like some macabre scene in a horror movie.

*Oh Lord no ... not again. Please save me from myself. Help me stop imagining the worst.*

She needed to shift her focus and stay calm. She needed a granola bar. That would distract her—pass some time. She groped in her backpack, pulled out a bar, and ripped it open. Desperate to keep her mind off snakes and Karla, she nibbled like a nervous rat eating a piece of cheese as she listened to the driving rain pounding around her. Loneliness, stronger than she had ever known, engulfed her as she sat amidst the soaked vegetation.

While watching rivulets of rainwater stream down an incline, Tiffany thought of the divine power Nellie and her grandmother spoke of so reverently. Would God help her as He had helped them? Could she trust enough to let go of hostility and resentment toward that driver? Could her faith in God be rekindled?

As Tiffany hunkered in the forlorn darkness, Mother Nature released her fury onto the deserted jungle. She half expected the tender leaves of the umbrella plant to rip to shreds from heavy raindrops in the same way the Kansas wheat fields are damaged by hail during a spring storm.

In keeping with the rainstorm's frenetic pace, Tiffany closed her eyes and opened her heart to a faint and distant image. She lamented. She cried. She whimpered. She questioned. The wind whipped the trees as she pounded her legs with her clenched fists.

Then at last, she fell silent, rocking back and forth on the log in a posture of prayer. And somehow in the glacier-like passing of time, something had changed. The wind still blew. Rainfall continued to hurry across the earth. Wildlife still lurked. But during the time Tiffany spent emptying her soul, a sense of peace had come to her. She did not know when the change began or how it was even possible, but her tension had eased as she sat under the plant exposing her grief over losing Karla and the challenges associated with unreasonable fear.

Something ethereal and moving stirred her soul and lifted her spirits like nothing had before. Every fiber of her being bowed down to this reigning hierarchy of peace. A comforting presence had opened a window on hope.

At last, the light dawned: *I'm feeling the presence of the Holy Spirit. Grandmother Birdwell and Nellie referred to this—the awareness of the presence of God within that offers a surreal-like serenity and a blessed reassurance.*

In that moment, God was not only present with her, but she knew that in reality, He was everywhere in the world He created. He was in the visible plants and hidden creatures of the rainforest. He was in the birds of the air and mammals of the earth. She and Nellie talked about it, but now she had experienced God's presence in a personal way as she felt Him in this lonely, forbidden jungle.

She opened her eyes to look around. And with a fresh dawning, she realized every year God's rain nurtured the shafts of wheat on her daddy's farm and He sent the sunshine that fed the tulips in her mother's garden. He could be seen in the light of dawn and the dark of night. And right now, she heard Him in the wind and the rain.

But most of all, she felt Him within her heart.

It came to her that God waits for every heart to awaken and become aware of His powerful presence, just as He did with Grandmother Birdwell, Nellie, and countless others the world over throughout time. And He had waited for her—waited for her to grow aware of His presence in a meaningful way. He had waited for her to acknowledge His existence and desire to know Him.

As hope blossomed within her, she slid off the log, oblivious to the sodden ground that provided the life force for the wild green plants beneath her. Unaware of the heavy weight of her backpack, she dropped to her knees and closed her eyes. "O' Lord, I need you. Oh, how I need you. Please help me," she prayed. "I've known about you since I was a little girl, but it's like I'm meeting you for the first time."

She stopped long enough to catch her breath and sniffle, and then she continued praying aloud. "Forgive me where I've failed you, Lord, and teach me how to forgive others. Help me make peace with my fears and accept what will not change. Help me accept that my sister died."

Tiffany did not see angels from heaven dancing around or soft lights encircling overhead. She did not hear music or an actual voice, but still, an unusual peace bathed her soul. And with her head bowed, and sweet, pure joy coursing down her cheeks, the Lord's love and forgiveness lifted the chains from around her heart.

The feeling of liberation made her think of Katy's surprise visit when they discussed the correlation between plants and humans. For the most part, plant seeds that fall to the forest floor germinate and mature into healthy green plants. So perhaps some of the seeds about God planted in her soul throughout her life were beginning to germinate and would one day blossom into a lovely, steadfast faith.

While heavy rainfall forged new paths through the undergrowth, the log under the massive plant had become Tiffany's alter for worship. And the birds singing in the distance formed a chorus of celebration for her period of enlightenment. She had experienced an epiphany of one of the ways God works to comfort His people and reassure them in a time of need.

At last, a warm light broke through the canopy of the rainforest, and she crawled out from under the umbrella plant to gaze upward. A grandiose cathedral stretched above her. Shafts of silvery light highlighted the emerald green cocooning her. Showy tree orchids and graceful ferns laden with raindrops, sparkled in the glow. Off to her left, a cluster of exotic lobster claw heliconia plants caught her eye. Their bright red blooms, tipped in sunshine yellow shimmered in the light, filling her with awe over God's creative powers.

While standing amidst the tall, stalwart trees, it occurred to Tiffany that when the roots of trees and other plants are anchored deep within the soil, they are more apt to withstand the storms of nature. So maybe anchoring herself deep within the love of Christ would help prepare her for weathering the inevitable storms of life.

With this thought came the powerful conviction that she would one day accept the irreversible—Karla's death. He would help her learn how to move forward with her life, just as Katy seemed to be moving along.

Something had changed for Tiffany this morning in the rainforest—something profound and exciting. God's love for her, far sweeter and more important than any love she had ever known made her feel more alive than at any time since Karla died, or for that matter, more alive than she had ever been before.

A strong desire to be more trusting and to learn how to forgive others, as the Lord had forgiven her enlivened her senses and heightened her longing to live more fully—to be made new. These were the most meaningful moments of her life.

"Thank you," she whispered, savoring a peace too incredible to describe, and far too important to ever be without again. In the sacred space of time she had spent alone in the rainforest with God, hallowed hope had impregnated Tiffany with positive possibilities for her life.

## CHAPTER 46

*Margaret, I'm going to look for a quetzal this morning. If you're reading this, you fooled me. I assumed you'd still be asleep when I returned for lunch. And by the way, I'm going alone.*

"What? What was she thinking?" Margaret said aloud as she reached for the coffee pot. She liked Tiffany's attempt at humor, but thought it foolish of her to go hiking in the jungle alone. Besides, she had hoped to visit with Tiffany this morning about her plans to remain in Costa Rica a while longer. And she wanted to find work to help meet her expenses, but after learning jobs were not available to short term residents, volunteering at a day care center seemed a logical choice. But she needed to talk it over with someone before deciding. Her parents would listen, but they knew nothing about the area.

Then Margaret remembered Nellie had extended an invitation to visit her sometime. Banking on Tiffany's endorsement of Nellie's kind and generous spirit, she didn't hesitate to call and inquire about her plans for the morning.

An hour later, the two women carried mugs of steaming hot chocolate along the path leading to the corner of the backyard.

"What a showy flower!" Margaret exclaimed as they reached the arbor.

Nellie stopped and plucked a huge clematis blossom from the flower-laden vine covering the wooden structure. "Let's enjoy this bloom up close," she said, handing it to Margaret as she sat beside her.

Margaret gently stroked one of the blossom's velvety purple petals as they sat in the swing. "This is as big as a saucer, and so beautiful."

"Yes, flowers are wonderful. And I believe they are not only lovely, but they carry a special message."

"What do you mean?" Now she knew why Tiffany loved to visit with Nellie so much. She got right to the heart of things.

As Margaret rocked the swing in a slow, fluid motion, Nellie smiled. "For me, looking at an exquisite flower is like looking into the face of God. I see flowers as an expression of God's love, and looking at them gives me a sense of peace."

"I've never thought of flowers that way before," Margaret said, surprised at how easily Nellie spoke about God.

"Well, aren't flowers considered a universal symbol of love?" asked Nellie. "I mean, think about how we use them all the time to express love at celebrations— weddings, parties, and so on."

"And also at funerals," Margaret said, getting in to the spirit of a new concept.

"I can still see my mama's bright red climbing roses— they're my favorite flower—trained on trellises against the white picket fence in our backyard. If you ask me, they sparked up the fence the way proper jewelry perks up a woman's outfit."

"So your appreciation of flowers goes back a long way?" Margaret asked.

"Oh yes, especially to the time a friend of my mother's came to say goodbye just before George and I left to move here."

"What happened?"

"We were visiting outdoors near my mother's lavender lilacs, red roses, and orange daylilies, when the woman offhandedly remarked that the flower is a magnificent manifestation of the implausible potential of the tiny seed."

Margaret blew air to her forehead. "Goodness, I'll have to think about that one."

"It was her comment that awakened me to the possibility that the beauty of the intricate flower is intended to inspire us to reflect on the power of God in creation."

"Flowers are a wonder, all right. And you've given me a new way to think about them."

Still smiling, Nellie said, "I've even pondered the correlation between flowers and humans."

"Oh? You mean because they each begin from a seed?" Margaret asked.

"And because each has the potential to grow into something lovely and noteworthy."

Margaret reached out to lift a massive blue hydrangea blossom from one of the bushes encircling the arbor. "But you can't really compare a flower to a person, can you?"

"Well not in a literal sense, of course, but I do believe there's a basic similarity that is worth contemplating."

Margaret swept a hand toward the overflowing pots of blue hydrangeas and white impatiens flanking the arbor. "I used to help my mother plant flower seedlings—mostly impatiens. Now I enjoy painting pictures of flowers."

"Tiffany told me you like to paint. And since I like to dabble in photography, it seems we share a love of putting form to the beauty in creation as we see it around us. Do tell me a little about your hobby. What do you like to paint besides flowers?" Nellie asked.

"Painting is one of my passions," Margaret said. "And this summer, I've been inspired to capture some of Costa Rica on canvas. I just finished a painting of a coati and a sloth. But I especially want to paint a picture of a blue morpho."

"How wonderful! I'll look forward to hanging one of your pieces in my home."

"It's one reason I plan to stay longer. But I also want to do something worthwhile with my time other than pursuing my hobby."

"Such as?" asked Nellie.

"I have a degree in elementary education, so I'm thinking of volunteering at a day care center. Would you have a suggestion for someone to contact? Or would George possibly have a connection that might be able to help?"

"Wouldn't your elementary education degree qualify you to teach English as a second language in one of the nearby schools?"

"I've looked into it. An employer would need to apply for a one-year work permit, and that could take time. And since I don't know how long I'll stay, finding something that requires less of a time commitment would be best."

"I'll talk to George, and we'll make a couple of phone

calls and get back to you. So tell me, how did this change in plans come about? I understood you planned to return to Alabama soon."

Margaret never thought she would tire of being lazy, but the idea of doing something for someone had fueled her with ambition. "After much soul searching, I've decided to stay on for a while to be here for Tiffany. She's having a hard time handling her sister's death. Plus, you probably know she broke it off with Zachary."

"Yes, but surely they'll find their way back together. At any rate, it's kind of you to stay on for awhile. I'm sure Tiffany would appreciate your company."

"I'm seeing a few things differently since my accident. But in particular, Karla's death has sobered me into a new way of thinking."

"What do you mean?" Nellie asked.

"I've taken too much for granted for too long. I've been selfish and lazy. I'd like to learn to do better."

"Oh, but Margaret, we're all selfish or lazy at times. On occasion, we all take life and each other for granted."

"Another thing … I've always found it uncomfortable to talk about a higher power, but now I'm beginning to wonder."

"You have questions about God?"

"Many. But we don't have time right now. The taxi driver will be here any time. I asked him to give me an hour. I'm anxious to get back to check in with Tiffany. She left a note about going alone to the rainforest this morning to look for a quetzal."

"Alone? Oh my goodness!" Nellie walked Margaret to the living room where they could listen for the taxi. "I'm sure she's fine, but will you ask her to call me this afternoon?"

"Will do," Margaret said. "If you ask me, Tiffany

went in search of something far more important than a silly bird."

When the taxi rumbled up the driveway, Nellie saw Margaret to the front door. "You know, Margaret, I believe you have more layers to your personality than a wedding cake designed for royalty."

Margaret tossed her head back and laughed. "I take that as a compliment. Thanks for everything. I'll be in touch."

The thought that her inner work was beginning to show lightened Margaret's footsteps as she rushed down the driveway.

## CHAPTER 47

While Tiffany ambled along the path in the rainforest, she pondered a few of Nellie's comments: *The core of a faith journey is to first believe. A loving, trusting relationship with God takes time to create and a lifetime to nurture.*

"Be patient," Nellie had said. "Listen for His whispers of love that will come to you in a variety of ways and at different times throughout your life."

This morning, while frightened and alone in the jungle, she had awakened to God's powerful presence. The Holy Spirit had transformed the dark and miserable cave into a bright and desirable haven. And the profound encounter had increased Tiffany's faith in God's power to make a difference in her and in her life

Eager for change, Tiffany yearned for instant solutions for her problems and quick answers to her questions. In longing to be all God intended her to be, Tiffany wished to be like a perfect rose that buds overnight and unfolds petal by petal by morning. But her grandmother's wise remarks on patience came to mind:

*Patience is a virtue. Wait with patience on the Lord and His mysterious ways to unfold and guide you.*

Grandmother Birdwell had made it clear that her broken heart over losing Uncle Earl did not mend overnight, and the road to acceptance and healing was not easy. "But as surely as I sit here, the dear Lord saved me from a joyless life," her grandmother had said.

While in this deep fog of serious reflection, Tiffany's foot caught in the dense and tangled undergrowth. Stumbling, she looked cautiously around and discovered the jungle encircled her like a trap with its sameness. She had strayed from the beaten path. Even with patches of bright sky still peaking through the trees, the rainforest once again felt dark and forbidding.

Her breath caught in her throat when she spotted a strangler fig tree, but right away she realized it couldn't be the one she had seen on the night hike with her friends. This one grew far from the beaten path.

From years of practice her imagination started to bring the ancient and sinister-looking tree to life. She pictured ruthless, snake-like tentacles reaching out to strangle her. And in her mind's eye she saw wild jungle cats crouching low behind the tree, preparing to pounce.

"*Oh no, don't let me go there again, Lord,*" she cried aloud. "*I want to trust you. But I'm lost and scared. Please help me ... Please?*"

She had only just gained a new vision of the Lord, and already, He felt distant from her. Though frightened and on the verge of another crying jag, she realized trusting in Him would not come easily. It would require work to let go of doubt and unreasonable expectations.

She fidgeted in the thick vegetation. "*Where are you, God? I need you. Please help me. Please ...*"

When the sound of silence followed her outburst, a

cloud of doubt slid over her. Where was He? Where was she? And where were the birds? Anything? Not even a howler monkey could be heard barking in the distance. Hungry for a sound—any sound, she heard only her breath coming in short soft spurts.

Tired and confused, the life of the rainforest seemed dead. Wondering if she too would die, she easily pictured her body as dinner for ravenous wildlife hidden in the shadows.

*"Oh dear God! What am I supposed to do? How do I follow you? And how can I trust you? I'm scared out of my mind."*

Shocked at the sound of her own voice, she looked around to see if a creature had been startled into the open. Half-expecting to come face to face with a jaguar, she leaned against a tree and prayed for the wonderful peace she experienced earlier under the umbrella plant.

Wondering what was to become of her, she slowly slid her back down the tree and plopped her bottom onto the damp vines that covered the ground around her. *What am I going to do? Where are you, Lord, when I need you?*

With moisture-filled eyes, she looked around for familiar landmarks. Then in a trance, she looked up and stared at the leaves that danced overhead. The incredible words, *"fear not, for I am with you,"* slipped into her consciousness. Was this one of God's love whispers Nellie referred to? Or the still, small voice of reassurance her grandmother mentioned?

Listening for the Holy Spirit was all so new to her, but as the message rang deep in her soul, she chose to force her thoughts away from doom and gloom to embrace the words in the same way she had received them—quickly and powerfully. She would trust in the profound message. She would believe in the unseen.

Without a hint of how she would react tomorrow or the day afterward to any difficult or frightening situation that should arise, in this particular moment, as Tiffany stood and planted her feet firmly on the ground, blessed hope once again crept in to bolster her spirits.

The Lord would help her remain calm. He would lift her confusion and grant logical thinking to help her move forward. But she needed to believe He would. She needed to focus! That's what she needed to do! Focus!

Though still frozen by spurts of terror, she needed to focus on God's powerful presence and trust Him to lead her safely out of the rainforest. She needed to believe he would grant her the common sense to decide what she must do to find her way out of the jungle. Trust! Believe! Listen! Listen for the whisper of logic—the whisper of guidance.

Taking a deep breath, Tiffany turned full circle to scan her surroundings. She searched for something familiar, such as a large patch of ferns or a cluster of trees laden with colorful orchids—anything that might help her remember which direction she had come from. As she strained to reason, she spotted an ancient rotting log that resembled a bench some twenty yards or so to her left. Her heart raced, for she remembered seeing it earlier.

Stumbling over roots and vines, she retraced her steps to work her way past the long knobby log. Roughly a hundred yards later, the distinct trail of decomposing plants and insects stretched flat and beautiful before her.

With deep gratitude, she stepped onto the beaten path and shouted, "Yes!" Then she fished in her backpack for a bottle of water and the map of trails. After studying the map for a couple of minutes, she still could not make sense of it. She hardly knew which way was up, let alone which way to go on the path to find her way out of the jungle.

Anxiety slithered back in like a snake preying on a nest of goose eggs. In a matter of seconds, her brain turned to mush. She jammed the useless map into the backpack. She needed a compass. "I've got to calm down," she whispered. "I'm overreacting. Again! I need to think. Trust! I need to trust."

Tiffany took a deep breath of the cool, moist air, and then slowly released it. After repeating the process several times, she focused her energy on the power of the Almighty to deliver her from trouble.

Clamping her eyes shut, Tiffany pictured Jesus swinging on a vine and swooping through the jungle to cradle her in His arms. She felt a sweet sense of peace as she imagined winding her arms around His neck as He carried her toward the light filtering into the mouth of the rainforest where she had entered hours before.

Her sharp images of Jesus' kindness convinced her that even beyond this experience, He would carry her through dark days and light days, and the gray days in between. Grateful tears surfaced as she realized she could trust the Lord to point her in the right direction. He would be her compass, not just for today, but for a lifetime.

Swiping at her eyes with the back of her hand, she grabbed the trail map again and smoothed out the wrinkles, hoping it would now make sense. When it still did not, she made up her mind not to panic, but to trust with patience. And as she continued to stare at the stupid map that rattled in her hands, out of the corner of her eye she caught sight of a colorful bird fluttering by to perch high in the branches of a nearby tree. Was it a quetzal?

She dropped the map and grabbed her binoculars,

twisting the lens until a bird fell into perfect focus. Then she lowered her shoulders and stuck out her bottom lip, wondering if she would ever see one of the coveted creatures.

*Crunch! Crunch! Crunch!* Dried leaves and broken twigs scattered along the path snapped under the weight of heavy footsteps. As the noise grew louder, her heart raced faster. With her feet glued to the path, wild thoughts of fleeing flapped around in her head like a bird trapped in a cage. Trembling, she struggled to trust. To believe—

"Hey there, do you need help?" a strong-looking woman asked in a pleasant voice as she rounded a bend and stopped to pick up Tiffany's crumpled map. "Is this yours?"

"Yes," Tiffany squeaked. "Thank God you've come."

Tiffany had yo-yoed back and forth between doubt and trust for quite some time. But when the friendly, middle-aged woman, wearing a shirt bearing the words Monteverde Cloud Forest Reserve, Ranger Station came into view, hope came sharply into focus.

Tiffany had not spotted a quetzal this morning; instead, she made a discovery far greater. God had come near to her in a wilderness setting and pointed the way out.

Through her frightening experience, God in His infinite mercy had kindly offered her a glimpse of His Kingdom, assuring her she need never feel alone again.

## CHAPTER 48

When Tiffany rushed into the apartment, Margaret pulled her head out of the refrigerator and plopped the mustard onto the counter. "Oh, there you are. Thank God you're back. I mean, what were you thinking to go to the rainforest alone? I don't think it was a wise thing to do. I would have gone with you."

Tiffany made a beeline for the small couch under the window to unlace her hiking boots. "I'm sorry, but I needed to go alone."

Margaret cocked an eyebrow at Tiffany as she sliced an avocado for lunch. "Why? Why alone?"

Tiffany removed her boots and set them aside. Then as she peeled off her socks, she said, "Maybe I wanted to prove something to myself?"

"Oh? I'm just surprised you found the courage to go alone."

"I wanted to find a quetzal." Tiffany wiggled her weary toes. "I thought it might boost my confidence if I did it on my own."

"But was it wise to go alone? Especially so early in the

morning?" She wondered if Tiffany had snapped, for she always dealt with everything with such extreme caution.

"I wanted to beat the crowd. Which I did. But you're right—I shouldn't have gone alone. It was so dark and deserted that I got uptight—even a little crazy. And then when a storm blew in I really lost it."

"Good grief, Tiffany. What were you thinking?"

"I know. But I never considered turning back, for as crazy as it sounds I kept hearing an inner voice encouraging me to continue."

Margaret narrowed her eyes. "Inner voice? I don't follow you. All I know is that you showed an unusual level of courage or stupidity to go to the jungle by yourself."

"Stupidity?"

Margaret grinned as she assembled their sandwiches. "All right, we'll go with courage."

"Good."

"Not everybody has the courage to do what you did. I couldn't have done it, and wouldn't have wanted to."

Tiffany hobbled to the sink to wash her hands. "Who knows? Maybe stupidity *is* what drove me to go alone this morning, but not only did I survive, I lived through an incredible experience. I'll share later, but first, tell me how you spent your morning?"

"With Nellie. You're right about her; she's a marvel."

"What did you talk about?"

"My plans for the immediate future," Margaret said as she carried their plates to the table. "I want to find a job to contribute to my expenses, but that option is out since I'm not a resident."

"This sounds serious."

"It is serious. I'm not going home to Alabama—not yet anyway."

"You mean you're staying longer? Seriously?" Tiffany asked as she joined Margaret at the table.

"Yes, what did you think? Of course I'm serious. I like it here. Do you mind?"

Tiffany thrust a fist into the air. "Yes! And since you're staying a while longer, you might need to brush up on your Spanish, huh?"

"Oh? Do you know anyone who could help me?" Margaret popped an olive into her mouth, thinking Tiffany's laugh sounded less forced than it had for many weeks.

"I just might." Tiffany winked. "So what do you have in mind to do?"

"I plan to look for volunteer work," Margaret said.

"You?"

Margaret swatted Tiffany's arm. "Yes, me, and why would you question it?"

"All joking aside," Tiffany said, "I'd love it if you stayed on. I could encourage you as you have me. You've been a pillar for me this summer as my world crumbled around me. Now I want to listen to you and help in any way I can."

Margaret took a deep breath. "I wanted to do more for you when Karla died. I still want to help, if I can."

"Now, Margaret, you've helped me more than you know. One of your gifts is listening with your heart, and knowing when to speak and when to remain silent. I so appreciate that about you."

"And your way of opening up to share honest feelings is good for me." Margaret said. "I'm just glad our friendship has survived in spite of our differences."

"Differences? I believe we've gotten along quite well, overall."

"But we are quite different—you're so practical and

I'm so glib. People don't take me seriously."

"So? What's wrong with being easygoing? Your nonchalant ways have often helped me keep my anxiety in check."

"Nevertheless, I can admit to being self-centered and lazy—like tagging along with you this summer instead of finding a job and settling down."

Tiffany patted Margaret's arm. "Don't judge yourself too harshly. No one is without character flaws or bad habits. We all have work to do. I could make a list, but won't right now."

Margaret lifted her eyebrows and wagged a carrot stick at Tiffany. "Don't you dare forget, you hear?"

"Forget what?"

"To make a list of your character flaws, silly. And to share them with me!"

"Oh? Well don't hold your breath." Tiffany giggled.

Their comfortable teasing and shared laughter delighted Margaret. "So about this morning ... How did it go in the rainforest? Did you spot a quetzal?"

"No, but I met someone—someone far superior to a mere human."

"What's that supposed to mean?"

"I met God in an important way for the first time in my life. It was a surreal, but wonderful experience."

Margaret's eyebrows shot up. "Oh? Can you talk about it?"

"It's hard to put into words. But my memorable experience has inspired me take a more positive view of the future. It has given me a boost of confidence and hope that life still has meaning."

"That's good to hear," Margaret said without a trace of skepticism.

"I still have a lot to sort out. Accepting Karla's death

is so hard. But at least I'm doing well in my classes."

"And what about Zachary?" Margaret asked.

Tiffany polished off another bite of her sandwich before answering. "What about him?"

Margaret was convinced Tiffany needed a little prodding to face her feelings for Zachary. "Do you miss him?" she asked. "I mean, do you want to see him again?"

Tiffany flinched. "Yes, I miss him, but I'm not yet at the place where I want to see him. I still resent him spilling his guts when he did. Sorry. I just can't go there yet."

By the end of lunch Margaret had formulated a plan in her head for the two of them to go with Zachary and Jason on a weekend outing.

Although she was eager to mention her ideas to Tiffany, she would wait a few weeks to give her more time to heal.

## CHAPTER 49

A couple of weeks later, as soon as Tiffany arrived home from school, Margaret announced she had taken a volunteer position. "I'll be working at the day care center at the Catholic Church down the street."

"That's good news," Tiffany said, "especially since you have an elementary education degree and are so good with children."

"Hmmm ... Maybe I am at that," Margaret said. "I'll tell you more about the job later, but right now there's something else I'd like to discuss with you." She could hardly wait to present what was really at the forefront of her mind.

"Oh dear, this sounds worrisome."

"First, tell me if you've seen Zachary since that awful night."

Tiffany furrowed her eyebrows. "No, why do you ask?"

"He hasn't called you? Not even once?"

"Yes, but I don't answer."

"Why not?"

"I don't know what would happen if I did."

Margaret sat up straighter in her chair. "So what do you wish would happen between the two of you?"

Tiffany threw up her hands. "I haven't a clue."

"Do you remember that the last time his name came up in conversation you admitted you missed him?"

"I do miss him," Tiffany said, "but I'm still furious at him."

"You mean because he told you about the accident he was involved in that resulted in someone's death?"

"He shouldn't have told me his story so soon after Karla's death. It sent me over the edge."

Margaret agreed that Zachary made a mistake to purge his conscience at Tiffany's expense, but she wondered if her friend had overreacted. Surely it was time to let it go. She had a strong hunch Tiffany could use help dealing with Zachary's "crime."

She leaned forward and put her hands flat against the table top and delivered Tiffany her best penetrating look. "Listen, I agree that he behaved thoughtlessly. But suppose the two of you had an opportunity to talk it out? What could it hurt?"

"I've thought about that night many times, and on the one hand, I'm flattered he shared his personal story with me, but he should have waited. And I can't believe he had the nerve to go on and on the way he did. I don't see how he could miss seeing it bothered me."

"As I see it, Zachary owes you an apology, but he can't do it if he never has a chance."

Tiffany pursed her lips. "And just what are you inferring?"

Margaret pushed. "If you could talk to him you might feel better."

"You're asking a lot."

"Maybe, but would you give it some thought?"

"Well, forgiving Zachary is one thing, but forgiving that … That idiot who took Karla's life is another matter. That's going to take a lot of hard work and prayer."

"Yes, that's a tough one, isn't it?"

"The whole situation has my stomach tied in knots. And sometimes my brain is so jumbled I either snap at people or clam up."

"It's heavy stuff you're dealing with, and I can't imagine how I would react in your place."

"This conversation helps me see I still have a long way to go where forgiveness is concerned. Zachary's confession made me crazy. And thinking of that idiotic young man getting behind the wheel of his pickup dead drunk and killing my sister makes me want to punch a hole in the wall. Or worse."

"Do you suppose the anger Zachary has felt toward his dad for so long drove him over the edge? Or the guilt over the young boy's death?"

"What do you mean?"

"Granted, Zachary was thoughtless to tell you about his past when your feelings were still so raw, but sometimes negative emotions alter the way we think, speak, or behave."

"I get it. You want me to cut him some slack, but I don't know what to think. I understand he didn't mean to be cruel, but I need to give all of this more thought, and pray about it." Tiffany dabbed at her wet eyelashes with a tissue. "So, what was it you wanted to discuss with me?"

"Nothing much," Margaret said, for she wanted to reveal her plan at just the right moment.

"Now don't tell me you have nothing else on your mind. I saw the look in your eyes when we first started talking that told me you're sitting on a secret or a plan of some sort."

"All right, you read me like a book," Margaret said. "I want to talk about going on a float trip with Zachary and Jason next weekend."

"Oh nooooo …"

"Now Tiffany, can we talk about it?"

"Must we?"

"Please? Will you at least listen? A change of scenery would be therapeutic and exciting."

"I'm not sure I need excitement right now."

Margaret did not plan to give up without a fight. "Wouldn't it be a valuable learning experience for you as a biology student to float a river in the jungle?"

"Oh Margaret, I don't think—"

"Oh come on, the night hike went well. We could see and explore a different part of Costa Rica."

Tiffany whined, "We'll see plenty, especially since you plan to stay a while longer."

Convinced she should persist, Margaret said, "Now you know very well Zachary's a great guide and would love to take us."

"But how would we—"

"And Jason is always good company." Margaret wanted to know Jason better. She appreciated his sensitive nature. "Besides, Jason's always fun to be around."

"That isn't the point."

"A big dose of Mother Nature would do you good— do all of us good."

"What's going on, Margaret? I've never known you to be so persistent. What's with you? What's your problem?"

"I don't have a problem. I happen to believe we would have a fun, memorable time."

"Enough, already," Tiffany said. "So what do you have in mind as far as details?"

"Let's invite the guys for dinner tomorrow night and together we can work on a plan for a weekend outing."

"I give up. You lay the groundwork."

"Maybe it's another one of my many gifts—painter, procrastinator, and now, peacemaker."

"Peacemaker? You?" Tiffany chuckled. "Well it's for sure you'll have a challenge making peace in this situation."

"We can invite them to come to dinner tomorrow night. I'll make a big salad with a variety of fresh raw vegetables and toss in those little salad shrimps. And we can dress it with the great salad dressing we found last week at the market. You know the one—it tastes like the Thousand Island dressing we buy back home. Plus, we have a loaf of Nellie's great crusty bread in the freezer. But we need to check to see if we have butter and maybe some of the little—"

"Stop! Come up for air! Okay, it sounds wonderful," Tiffany said. "And shall we serve vanilla ice cream with fudge sauce for dessert? And top it with nuts and whipped cream?"

"Now that's the spirit." Then Margaret picked up her cell phone before Tiffany could change her mind.

## CHAPTER 50

*"No ... Please, not again. Take this misery from me, Lord. Please? I'll gladly give this to you,"* Tiffany groaned aloud as the reality of her loss crept in with the dawn peeking through the window curtains.

Overall, she had been happier—more relaxed and confident since the morning of her encounter with the Holy Spirit in the rainforest. But today, nagging sorrow again dampened her enthusiasm for facing a new day. Her negative attitude and reservations about going on an outing with the guys had resurrected her grief.

The minute Tiffany left the room last night, after letting Margaret talk her into doing something she had had grave doubts about, she started to worry. What had she committed to? Could she pull it off when she still felt so hostile toward Zachary? And yet, Margaret's theory that his ill-timed confession might have come from harboring heavy, dark secrets for so long made sense. So maybe she was a little rough on him. And just maybe she needed a thicker skin.

Tightly bound by grief, Tiffany had not considered anyone's feelings but her own for a long time. And in truth, Zachary's wounded expression at her door that awful night haunted her. Was she wrong to dismiss him? Had she neglected Margaret? For certain, she had ignored Jason, whose gentle and kind ways deserved more. So maybe Margaret was right that the trip would do them all a world of good.

Sorrow over her sister's death, along with the nervous dread of being around Zachary for the entire weekend proved to be too much for Tiffany. She threw back the covers and rushed to the bathroom, barely making it before she upchucked.

Holding a cold cloth to her forehead, Tiffany stumbled back to bed and relaxed her head onto the pillow. It was crazy to agree to Margaret's plan. She would have to cancel. Maybe she would be too sick to go? As Tiffany struggled with what to tell Margaret, she heard a faint whisper inside her head: *"Instead of always expecting the worst possible outcome in your situations, why don't you anticipate that this time the outcome will be the best it can possibly be."*

She leaned down to pull up the bed sheet that had gathered at her feet during the night. The furry sloth caught her eye as it moved slowly in the tree. Then she heard a rooster crowing in a nearby backyard and a howler barking somewhere distant. By the time the sound of someone singing sweet and low drifted in from the next room, she smiled. Margaret?

With signs of life unfolding around her, Tiffany realized how badly she wanted her mood to change. And when the lyrics to a catchy song the congregation sang every Sunday in the church her family attended, *"how great it is to be alive and feeling free,"* came to mind,

she had a sudden longing to truly enjoy life, instead of
only going through the motions of living. She threw back
the covers and jumped out of bed.

When she found Margaret already awake and working
on a grocery list, she asked, "Do we need to go shopping
right away? I'd like to spend time reading the Bible first,
if that's all right."

Tiffany had made up her mind to set aside the time
for a devotional every morning before a million things
sidetracked her.

"There's no hurry to go for groceries," Margaret said.
"In fact, what would you think about me joining you in
reading scripture?"

"What? Are you serious? What verse or chapter do
you want to read?"

"I don't know. How about one of the Psalms?"

"What about I read Psalm 23? Isn't that everyone's
favorite?" asked Tiffany.

When Zachary walked through the door that evening for
dinner, Tiffany was surprised that she wanted to run
throw her arms around him. She hadn't seen him for
weeks. He looked thinner. She wondered if he had been
taking care of himself. Though a few positive hopeful
thoughts for the evening crept in, she nevertheless sent
up a quick request for help with making dinner
conversation.

After Zachary opened the bottle of chardonnay he
and Jason provided, he filled the wine glasses while
Tiffany and Margaret set out hors d'oeuvres.

At first, Tiffany's tongue felt too frozen to make
small talk. But by the time Margaret mentioned the outing
it had thawed. "So where will we sleep? Is this a camping

trip, or what?" she asked.

"Wait a minute—aren't we staying in a motel?" Jason asked.

Zachary laughed. "You don't want to sleep in a bedroll out in the open under the stars?"

Jason rolled his eyes. "No way!"

"Well if it's all right with everyone," Zachary said, "we'll rent a couple of inexpensive motel rooms near the river—one for the guys and one for the girls."

"I vote for that," Tiffany said, trying to keep her relief in check.

Zachary suggested they pack light. "Four duffle bags, an ice chest of bottled water, and a bunch of food will nearly fill the jeep."

When Tiffany asked about a first aid kit, Zachary assured her that he always kept one in the jeep. "And I have maps and guide books. But don't forget to bring your own camera and binoculars."

Margaret frowned. "Wait a minute. Are you sure there will be room in the jeep for all of us?"

"Don't worry, we wouldn't leave you behind. You're in for a real treat." Zachary glanced at Tiffany. "Actually, I hope we all are."

Over dinner, Jason's tales of overly enthusiastic tourists he had led through the Butterfly Gardens kept them laughing. But Margaret's funny stories from her southern roots amused Tiffany even more. Watching Margaret host dinner with an abundance of graciousness and charm reminded her of Nellie. She enjoyed Margaret's dual personality—sometimes unflappable and at other times as scattered as autumn leaves in a breeze.

When the guys left, Margaret closed the door and leaned back against it. "How do you feel about the evening?"

"I'm glad it's over."

"Are you still nervous about the trip?"

"Yes. I can't help it. But I'll try to relax and curb my emotions while we're together."

"You'll get there," Margaret said. "I have a positive vibe about this trip."

"I'll work on my attitude. I want the weekend to go well, but when I'm around Zachary my stomach knots up."

"From anger or excitement?"

"Both," Tiffany said, still wondering where her good sense had gone to agree to the trip.

Margaret started clearing away the dishes. "Let's hope something happens to tilt you more in the direction of excitement. You never know, you could be in for a pleasant surprise."

"Maybe. … Or maybe not." Then as Tiffany carried the wine glasses to the kitchen, she remembered that her Grandmother Birdwell believed in miracles. She wasn't sure what to believe about miracles, but she decided to pray for one. After all, what could it hurt to show a little faith?

## CHAPTER 51

Margaret stuck her head into the open door of Tiffany's bedroom. "We need to pack. The guys will be here in about an hour."

Tiffany opened her eyes and stretched. "Wow! You're up first again?"

"Will you please come to my bedroom for a minute to offer an opinion on what to pack? I can't decide if four outfits will suffice for two days," Margaret said with a straight face."

"I doubt that will be enough; after all, you must be prepared for anything," Tiffany said, her eyes wide and playful as she slid out of bed.

Margaret turned to lead the way to her bedroom. "Oh no, what do you mean?"

"Well you never know when we might spot a fancy restaurant along the muddy riverbank. Or some royal family in a palace overlooking the Peñas Blancas River might invite us up for a visit."

Margaret grinned. "Zachary said the jeep would be crowded, so I suppose I should leave something behind.

But what? Maybe my fingernail polishes?" Margaret grabbed her curling iron and swung the long rod back and forth by the cord. "No way am I leaving this out. I couldn't manage without it."

"And I suppose your jewelry is a must?"

Margaret clamped her hands over her ears. "Oh my, my earlobes would be naked without earrings."

"What about wearing the same small pair of gold hoops the entire time?" Tiffany asked.

Margaret's mouth fell. "What? And look the same every day?" she asked.

"Well now *far* nobler acts of courage have probably taken place, my friend."

"Surely not, is all I have to say." Margaret retrieved her little gold hoops and slipped them in her earlobes, happy that Tiffany could play along.

"You're nuts, Margaret. You're full-blown nuts, but I love your sense of humor," Tiffany said as she turned to leave. "You're on your own. I need to pack."

Margaret felt good about packing lighter—it would be less to keep track of. And certainly, it would make her mother proud.


Margaret's excitement as they piled into the crowded jeep matched the morning sun that shone brighter than the yellow roses of summer. She hoped their weekend excursion would be a catalyst for healing and an opportunity for reconciliation, as well as strengthening relationships.

"Hey, what's on your mind?" asked Tiffany as they pulled away from the apartment. "You look like you're deep in thought."

"Well, for one thing, I want to try to understand why

the three of you love nature so much," Margaret said.

Tiffany smiled. "I don't know about Zachary and Jason, but I tend to believe nature has much to teach us about life."

Jason suddenly burst into song. Margaret laughed and joined in, quickly matching his enthusiasm as they zipped around hairpin curves on the two-lane mountain road, framed by coffee farms cascading into the green valley on one side and tall trees reaching for the sky on the other.

Soon, Tiffany joined in, and over the next half hour or so, they sang loudly over the wind blasting through the open jeep while Jason led them in singing a variety of hymns, including a few old spirituals. And once between songs, without warning, Margaret belted out a solo rendition of an old Negro spiritual, *Swing Low, Sweet Chariot* in a clear soprano voice.

With an open mouth, Tiffany stared at Margaret. "I've never heard you sing that way before."

"Way to go!" Jason hollered.

Zachary, who had not joined in the singing kept his eyes on the road. "Good job. More! More!"

Margaret laughed. "I heard that old Negro spiritual many times as a girl in Mobile. Have any of you taken time to listen to the words?"

"I thought the lyrics referred to going home to heaven," Jason said.

"No," said Margaret, "I googled the history of the song and learned that during the slave period the lyrics of that particular song, and a number of other popular spirituals were believed to be coded messages. The codes allowed fugitives of the Underground Railroad system to communicate certain events were about to occur, such as a planned escape from a plantation."

"No way," Tiffany said.

"Want me to sing it again?" Margaret asked. "You can concentrate on the lyrics this time. We'll do it in parts. I'll sing the lead line and you two can come in with the response. Ready?" They sang for miles, laughing and shouting between songs.

When the time came to make a pit stop, Margaret saw it as an opportunity to mix things up. So after taking care of business, she suggested Jason and Tiffany switch places for the next leg of the trip.

Jason jumped in the back seat, leaving Tiffany with no choice but to climb into the front with Zachary. After buckling her seatbelt, she turned large, vacant eyes to Margaret and mouthed, "I'll have your neck for this."

With a winner's smile, Margaret mouthed back, "Relax! You'll be fine."

When Zachary pulled away from the rest stop, Margaret shared with Jason how it pleased her that Tiffany had agreed to come.

"Yeah, a change of scene will be good for her. It'll be good for all of us. I look forward to seeing more of Costa Rica and trying new things."

"But you don't mind doing some of the same things over and over, do you? Like spotting a blue morpho?"

"No, and I never tire of listening to the monkeys howling at one another or watching the little leafcutters working with such purpose."

"The thought of floating a river has me on the edge of my seat. But I mean that in a good way," Margaret added. "I'm excited about the possibility of seeing wildlife. How about you?"

"Sure, but there's one thing I *don't* want to see," Jason said as he shuddered.

"What's that?"

"I'd die if we ran into a snake up close and personal."

Margaret popped her hand over her mouth. "A snake? Oh my, I hadn't even thought of such a thing. But aren't you majoring in biology?"

"Yeah, and I know it doesn't fit, but I'm afraid of snakes. Can't help it."

"Lots of people are afraid of snakes, including me. It's a hard phobia to shake."

"Yeah, except for Zachary. He doesn't seem to be afraid of anything. I'd like to have his nerve but I seem to be stuck in the larva stage of transformation in certain areas of my life."

"You sound like a biology student." Margaret laughed. "But seriously, we all have a lot of room for growth."

"I certainly do. It's hard for me to find the nerve to do what so many seem to do with ease. I have trouble measuring up. I mean, just look at Zachary—he reeks with courage and confidence."

"Now Jason, you just need a confidence booster," Margaret said. "So, back to the snakes—you've studied snakes in college, haven't you?"

"Yeah, snakes of North America, but not Central America. I did spend some time over at the serpentarium in Santa Elena this summer studying snakes, trying to learn which are common to this area and which are poisonous."

"And could you administer the basic care needed if a poisonous snake bit one of us?"

"Maybe. But let's hope it's not necessary."

"Ahhh, you'd come through."

"I doubt it. But not to worry—we've got Zachary."

"Now don't underestimate yourself, Jason."

"Whatever. Say, you've changed since the accident. If you ask me, you're mellower. Maybe even kinder?"

"Well, wouldn't you be a nicer person if you survived a close call?" she asked, grinning sideways at Jason.

Jason chuckled. "You're quite the girl. As spunky as ever, yet something has changed. You seem different."

Margaret sighed. "I've always been a confident person with an approach to life that borders on frivolous. But I've sobered up over the summer, what with falling off a horse and nearly busting my head open on a boulder."

"Yeah, you came mighty close to messing yourself up big time."

"But above all else, Karla's death has had a profound effect on me. Life's short, you know? I'm giving new thought to a number of things these days—trying to think through my values and priorities for a change."

"I've also done some thinking this summer," Jason said. "I love it here, but I miss my home and family. Several evenings have grown awfully long, but the extra time has given me a lot of time to think about my future and try to figure out how I might fit into this world."

"That's sounds deep. You should have called me. I've also had plenty of spare time on my hands."

"I considered it. But in all honesty …" Jason stopped mid-sentence and glanced away.

"Go on," she said. "Honesty is good."

Jason looked Margaret in the eye. "I didn't want to mislead you. It's nothing personal. I mean, you're bright and sensitive, and I might add, very easy on the eyes. But how can I say this? I'm just looking for a friend?"

"That's all right," Margaret said. "I am, too." She gave Jason a knowing look, hoping to convey that she loved him as a kind and thoughtful friend, regardless of his innate lack of interest in the opposite sex.

## CHAPTER 52

"Take it slow and easy going down," Zachary said as he led the way over the wooden planks forming a footpath along the bank.

"Oh my, can we do this?" Margaret asked as she looked over the steep, muddy riverbank.

"Why not?" Zachary shouted, smiling to himself over the even bigger challenges awaiting them.

"Come on Margaret, you aren't going to let a little mud stop you, are you?" asked Tiffany.

Moments later, they boarded the inflatable rubber raft to float the Peñas Blancas River. "It looks like we're in for a lazy ride today," Zachary commented as he gazed up at the bright blue sky.

As he shoved away from the bank, the girls adjusted their sun visors against the late-morning sun and lathered sunscreen over the exposed areas of their bodies. Then they settled back with their binoculars to look for wildlife, periodically scouring the dense jungle on both sides of the river as they glided through the gentle water.

After rafting steadily for about ten or fifteen minutes,

and seeing only an occasional small bird, Zachary suddenly shouted. "Look to your right. It's squirrel monkeys!"

"Where? Where?" Tiffany yelled.

Zachary stopped oaring and stabbed his forefinger in the air. "Over there! See them? There's a troop of them scampering through the branches of the trees at the edge of the right bank."

Tiffany zoomed in with her binoculars. "Now I do. What fun!"

"I don't see them!" Margaret screamed. "Where are they?"

"Okay Margaret, look in the water to your right," Zachary said. "See the massive log that looks like an alligator? Now lift your eyes straight up and a little to the left. Now do you see them?"

Zachary motioned for Jason to help row toward the riverbank for a closer look. A foot or two from the bank Zachary hollered at Jason, "Grab one of the vines to help steady the raft."

Jason leaned over and caught hold of a vine trailing low over the water. When the vine snapped loose from the tree and crumpled into the water, Jason flailed about to keep from falling overboard.

"Quick!" Zachary yelled, as the girls made a feeble attempt to keep from laughing. "Grab another vine. A stronger one."

"Yeah, whatever you say, boss." Jason spread his legs wide apart and clutched another vine. "Now tell us about these silly monkeys."

"They're agile little guys and quite entertaining. But they are now an endangered species because a lot of people bought them as exotic pets back in the late sixties and early seventies." Soon thereafter, Zachary put in an oar to head down river.

"Wait, I'm trying to get a video," Tiffany hollered.

"Good luck," Zachary said, "it's hard to capture squirrel monkeys on film. They leap through the trees at a fast rate of speed."

"I see one. I finally see one," Margaret shouted as she gripped her binoculars. "It looks close enough to reach out and touch."

Zachary loved that the girls sounded as though they had received a natural high from river rafting and watching the wild monkeys.

Desperate to clear the air with Tiffany, Zachary hoped to have an opportunity to talk with her alone tonight after dinner He would fall on bended knee, if necessary, to make amends for forcing his past on her in such a clumsy thoughtless manner. His timing was unforgiveable, but that was exactly what he wanted—forgiveness.

Several yards on down river, Zachary yelled, "Hey, guys. There's an Anhinga bird! It's about fifteen feet up ahead in the water—off to the left."

"What?" Margaret asked. "What did you call it?"

"An Anhinga bird, but it's more commonly known as a snake bird," Zachary said, determined to pull from his vast array of facts to share a little about the wildlife with his friends. "Take a good look. They're very interesting."

Tiffany looked skeptical. "A snake bird? Who ever heard of a snake bird?"

"Anhinga means devil bird or snake bird. The word comes from an old Brazilian language that is now extinct."

"Weird! It does look like a snake that's about ready to strike," Margaret said as they rowed past it. "You won't see one of those in Alabama."

They hadn't gone much further, when they rafted past iguanas almost as plentiful as the butterflies where Jason worked. Several gray green to brownish green iguanas sunned lazily in the branches of tall, stately trees along the riverbank, while many others crawled in the shady green grass below.

Again, Zachary signaled Jason to help him slow the raft for a picture stop. "Iguanas are tough creatures. They can dive safely into the water from a tree forty to fifty feet high."

Slack-jawed, Margaret stared at the iguanas. "I had no idea they could crawl up and down trees that way."

"Or that they can jump from that height," Tiffany said. "What a feat."

After about an hour or so of rafting, and almost a non-stop biology lesson fit in around their portable lunch, Zachary announced they would stop to visit a farm family who had lived in isolation along the river for many years. "I thought you would like to meet a family whose roots are buried in the Costa Rican culture, so right after we made our plans, I contacted them for permission to visit." Zachary wanted the outing to be an educational experience, as well as fun.

"How do you know them?" Jason asked.

"I met the family the summer I trained to be a naturalist. A group of us floated the river and visited them at their farm. They live in humble conditions without electricity and running water."

"May we visit with some of the family?" Tiffany asked.

"Oh yes, they welcome visitors. They're warm, gentle people who love to share their stories with those who show an interest. It'll be a treat, and I dare say you'll witness a unique group of people and a special way of life."

"Are there steps leading up the bank to the house?" Margaret asked.

"Yes. But the steps start several feet up from the waters edge," Zachary said. "And they may be a little crude by your standards, so don't rush it. Then when you get to the top of the bank, a boardwalk about forty feet long stretches a few feet above the forest floor."

Margaret looked skeptical. "Does it lead to the entrance to the house?"

"Right, and prepare yourself—the house is open to the elements. There's not even a door." Then Zachary refrained from describing it any further. They needed to see it for themselves.

"What wildlife will we see?" asked Jason.

"Chickens. They run around all over the property, but the wild howler monkeys living in the trees along the boardwalk are the main attraction."

"Oh wow! Are you kidding?" Tiffany quickly started adjusting her camera settings. "Do we have time to stop to take pictures of the monkeys?"

"Sure. The howlers are great subjects. They're quite used to people, since they live so close to the farm family. They almost pose for you from the tree limbs that stretch out over the boardwalk. And that reminds me; don't look up at them with your mouth open."

"Oh, you don't mean it," Margaret said, just as Zachary reached the spot along the riverbank where another new adventure would soon begin.

## CHAPTER 53

Tiffany jumped up before the raft had stopped rocking. "Let's go," she said, eager to see the monkeys and meet the family.

"Wait. Wait a minute." Zachary grabbed her arm. "The bank is muddy from recent rains. It'll be slick. Let Jason and Margaret go first, then I'll help you."

"I don't need your help," she said. But as she tried to shake him off, she stumbled and fell backward into his lap. Quickly, he encircled her with his long capable arms, and for a few seconds she relaxed against him.

He rested his head on top of hers. "Are you okay?"

"I'm fine, as you can see." Then she lifted his arms from her waist and stood. She turned penetrating eyes toward Zachary. "I can't do this. I've got to get out of here."

Margaret hollered from the boardwalk. "Hurry, Tiffany, you have to see this. Howler monkeys are everywhere."

"And she means *everywhere*," Jason yelled. "Man,

I've never seen anything like this. It's hard to believe."

Tiffany rushed from the raft and trudged through the mud to reach the steps leading to the boardwalk, leaving Zachary in her wake with a rocking raft to anchor.

In spite of Zachary's warning to keep their mouths closed, the three of them stared slack-jawed at the monkeys. Tiffany craned her neck, trying to take them all in at once. "This is such a thrill," she said, wondering for a split second if her mind was playing tricks on her.

Margaret's eyes darted from limb to limb. "Can you even believe this? These monkeys are in the middle of nowhere and not even caged."

Snapping his digital camera as fast as he could, Jason took multiple shots of two monkeys sitting back to back on an upper limb of one of the tallest trees. "The trees are loaded with monkeys! Loose and right over our heads, and almost at the back door of their house. This is incredible."

The brownish-black monkeys, scattered over long, sprawling limbs thick with bright green leaves, created a dream setting for the eager shutterbugs. A mother howler carrying her baby on her back rocketed through mature trees with grace and agility. Right above Tiffany on a strong limb, a couple of monkeys slept nose to nose. And to her right, at the point a major limb branched away from the main trunk, sat an old male monkey staring into space and picking at something on his chest. Fleas, Tiffany decided as she took time to snap a picture on her cell phone to forward to her parents.

"Hmmmmm …" Margaret snickered. "Some of the monkeys are staring back at us. Do you suppose they consider us as entertaining as we do them?"

"Why wouldn't they? No doubt about it, you *are* entertaining." Zachary let out a belly laugh as he ambled past them to lead the way to the house.

"Without thinking, Tiffany gaped when she entered the humble little house. It looked like a movie set created for the filming of some documentary about living in a remote area without luxuries. The house had a roof, but the side of the house facing the river was without a wall. A scarce amount of crude furniture graced the hard-packed dirt floor, and one quick glimpse through a door leading into the kitchen revealed makeshift sagging shelves instead of storage cabinets with doors.

Tiffany's heart ached for them, for she saw little evidence that they had anything beyond the basics. She considered it their unfortunate plight to have to make do with so little.

After offering coffee and snacks, the family took turns sharing stories about the many decades they had occupied their small parcel of land on the bank of the Peñas Blancas River. With animated fervor and great pride, they spun tales of eking out a living with only the bare necessities.

The old patriarch of the family, who appeared to be in his mid-nineties sat upright and silent in an unvarnished wooden rocking chair. His eyes revealed an enviable spark as he listened to his family describe their rudimentary way of life and tell how he homesteaded the farm as a young man.

"I didn't see a road anywhere. Do you come and go by boat?" Jason asked in his best Spanish.

A young man, earlier introduced as the old gentleman's grandson, said there weren't any roads. "We walk to the nearest town for supplies or go by boat."

"What do you do during a medical emergency if there are heavy rains and it's too dangerous to go by boat because the river is up?" Tiffany asked as she glanced at a little girl playing nearby, whose happy smile and dark brown eyes could have charmed snake's venom into perfume.

"If possible, we wait till the water goes down. But in a real emergency, we go to town by foot to ask for help," the grandson answered. Then he knelt, touched his grandfather's shoulder, and locked eyes with him. "Do you understand their Spanish?" he asked.

The old fellow smiled and nodded, and the rich contentment in the old patriarch's eyes reached beyond anything Tiffany had ever seen before.

"Do you grow most of your vegetables right here on your farm?" asked Margaret.

"Yes, we do. And some of our fruits and grains," answered one of the women. "And we have chickens and cows, which is where we get out eggs, milk, butter, and cream. And of course we also eat some of our chickens and cows."

Margaret looked stunned. "And do you cook every thing from scratch?"

"Almost. We spend a lot of time in the kitchen. We also sew and mend our clothes. And we help out with the farm chores and take care of the children. But we don't mind hard work. It's the way we live."

Margaret smiled and shook her head. "You amaze me."

When Zachary indicated they should leave, Tiffany knelt beside the old fellow and took his hand. Speaking in her polished Spanish, she said, "I'm honored to have met you and your family. I admire your strength and perseverance to work so hard. Thank you so much for allowing us a glimpse of your tranquil home."

The old patriarch smiled and nodded. Then in a quavering voice, he said, "Pura Vida."

Tiffany looked into his eyes and smiled. "Pura Vida to you, too, my friend."

Earlier in the summer, as they parted ways after the hike, Katy had used the expression "Pura Vida," explaining the Spanish phrase, commonly used by Costa Ricans meant pure life. "It is a wish for a good and joy-filled life," Katy had said.

As they crossed the boardwalk, Margaret remarked to Tiffany that the family appeared to not only accept simplicity, but to treasure it. "Even though they have to work terribly hard, they seem content."

"Yes, the old fellow, and probably the entire family, could teach lessons on how to enjoy the simple pleasures of life without all of the trimmings," Tiffany said.

"It makes you wonder how the family could be so happy when they have to live under such crude, humble conditions." Then Margaret took time to take one last snapshot of a howler asleep on its stomach with all four limbs dangling in the air.

"It's a way of life many people, at least where we come from, wouldn't understand. I'm guessing their apparent faith and loyalty to one another keeps them going," Tiffany said as she leaned against the rail, not quite ready to leave the memorable spot along the river.

Margaret dropped her camera into her fanny pack. "I didn't hear Grandpa and his family complain about anything the whole time we were there."

"Their powerful conviction to live in harmony with the land over so many years reminds me of the faith the Baldwins and the other Quakers demonstrated when they left the United States to build a new life in Costa Rica," Tiffany said.

Margaret slowly shook her head back and forth for several seconds. "You know, this entire experience reminds me of how greedy I've been and of how much I've always taken for granted. It's humbling."

Tiffany gave Margaret a quick hug. "I understand. Me, too. But they seem to view the land that provides them with their basic needs as something to revere. When I first stepped into their home and looked around at the living conditions, I felt so sorry for them. But not anymore."

As they continued across the boardwalk and traversed the riverbank to board the raft, euphoria blanketed Tiffany, much like times she had heard inspirational sermons at church or motivational talks in college. She hoped to have the good sense to always hang on to the compelling and thought-provoking encounter with the humble farm family.

## CHAPTER 54

"We'll be at the end of our trip in an hour or so, and then we'll go ashore to catch a ride back to the jeep," Zachary said as he pushed off. "In the meantime, let's keep an eye out for more wildlife."

For several minutes, the sound of an occasional bird cawing in the distance and the oars striking the water were the only sounds that broke into Zachary's thoughts about the farm family as they rafted down river.

Eventually, he glanced back at Tiffany and made a comment about the farm family. "Apparently, they have almost nothing in the way of material things, and yet they seem so happy. I'm not sure I get it."

"Yes, they appear quite content in spite of their humble surroundings," Tiffany said. "Their courage to persevere regardless of obvious limitations makes me think of George and Nellie. The family's evident endurance tells me they also have a strong faith in God. Apparently their contentment doesn't have so much to do with what they have as with what they believe."

"Maybe some folks are just born strong and

courageous." Zachary said, wondering why it always reverted back to some higher power as the source of all strength and courage. Couldn't a person have success or find happiness without God as a crutch to carry them through life's rough spots? What good is an invisible crutch, anyway?

Then he recalled the period of time when drugs and alcohol had been his crutch. They were supposed to help him find happiness, but substance abuse turned out to be only a temporary escape. Drugs and alcohol hadn't improved things for him.

But sometimes he still wanted a drink when things were rough, like lately, during his estrangement from Tiffany. Although vowing to never touch the stuff again, he wondered how much longer he could hold out. He needed something to help him forget his disappointment over losing Tiffany, and to help him forget the sad things from his past that played with his head and made his heart ache. But if he didn't believe God could help him in life, and drugs and alcohol hadn't made a real difference, what could help him?

He needed Tiffany. That's what he needed in his life—a good woman. From the moment she had agreed to come on the float trip, he'd been giddy with anticipation over the possibility of narrowing the gulf between them. Then he would have a chance to make her his. They would be good for each other. She would help him learn how to let go of his guilt about his past and his resentment toward his dad. And surely he could help her get over losing Karla and encourage her to let go of fear over things that held her back from doing the things in life she wanted to do.

"We're only a short distance, perhaps a hundred yards or so, from where we'll stop to leave the river," Zachary announced.

Margaret lifted a few inches off her seat and pointed to a spot to the left of the raft. "Oh my, will you look at that? It's a lazy crocodile sunning on a sandbar and just waiting for one of us to fall in."

In the split second it took for Zachary to glance at the crocodile, the raft hit an eddy and bounced up and down like popcorn kernels bursting over a fire. He dropped an oar that quickly disappeared downstream.

The raft began to spiral out of control. "Put on your lifejackets!" Zachary shouted.

"Oh man, we're losing it," Jason yelled. "What do we do now?"

The rubber raft swirled through the angry water, and in seconds, it slammed into a v-shaped area formed by the riverbank and a dead tree that had landed in the river at an angle.

"Hold on and stay seated," Zachary cried as he half-stood in the bobbing raft. Then with his feet wide apart, he strained to reach out over the raft to grab a long vine that dangled low over the river.

The instant Zachary made contact with the thick, leaf-covered vine he cried out and fell backward into the raft. He landed with a fierce thud, causing the raft to rock roughly from side to side.

The girls screamed and Jason looked on with horror as the raft thumped and squeaked against the exposed roots along the riverbank.

## CHAPTER 55

"Oh dear Lord, what's wrong with him?" Tiffany asked as she fell to her knees and stroked Zachary's face.

"A snake bit him," Margaret hollered. "I saw it."

"Yeah, me too," Jason yelled as he rushed to tie a rope around one of the limbs of the dead tree to help anchor the raft. "A snake bit him and we've got to do something fast."

"But what? What can we do?" Tiffany cried, concern quickly mounting.

Jason looked at Zachary, who thrashed about, moaning and clutching his hand. "You've got to stay still, man. I'll run for help as soon as you and the girls are situated."

Tiffany whined as she brushed Zachary's hair away from his vacant eyes. "Will he be all right? We have to do something."

"I'm trying to remember what I've read about handling poisonous snakebites," Jason hissed. "There's not much we can do before help comes, except make certain he keeps as still as possible. I need you to hold his arm down against the raft."

The gravity of Zachary's situation had pickled Tiffany's brain. She could only think of the worst possible outcome. What if she never had the chance to make amends with him? Her anger toward him suddenly felt petty.

"Tiffany, did you hear me?" Jason asked. "Grab Zachary's arm and make him hold it still while I go for help."

Margaret shook Tiffany's shoulder. "What's wrong with you? Do you feel faint? You *can* do this, you know. You're strong and brave. I've seen it. Do you hear me, Tiffany? You *can* do this."

After only silence from Tiffany, Margaret asked, "Do you need me to take over?"

Tiffany slowly nodded and reached out like a robot to apply pressure to Zachary's arm.

"That's a good girl," Jason said. "Hey Margaret, will you help me tighten the rope? I wanta make sure this raft is secure before I leave."

Turning back to Tiffany, Jason hollered, "Hold his arm still, but don't squeeze it. Try to keep him from moving his arm because any extra movement will make the venom move through the bloodstream all the faster."

"He can't die," Tiffany whispered. "We can't lose him. I …"

"Shhhhh!" Jason glared at Tiffany and then he leaned over to fetch the keys to the jeep from Zachary's pants pocket. "I'll climb up the riverbank and run find help."

Tiffany gasped. "You're going to leave us here? All alone?"

"I don't have a choice. You'll be fine," Jason said. "Just keep him calm. Then he looked down at Zachary. "Hey man, can you hear me? I know it hurts, but try to remember what you know about snakebites. Stay still and don't move your arm."

Zachary's eyes fluttered open, but Tiffany saw no sign he recognized them. The dangerous situation made her insides crawl, but somehow in that moment when she realized Zachary had lost his cool to the bold face of fear, a boost of much-needed confidence forced her to follow instructions. She turned her head to hide a tear and will away the knot in her stomach, but she was determined to focus on doing her part to help—to help all of them.

"What's happened?" yelled one of two men, who trudged through the knee high vegetation along the steep riverbank. "We heard a lot of screaming and yelling. It sounded like you might need this stretcher."

Jason gestured toward Zachary. "We think a poisonous snake bit him. We need help. And fast."

The men worked their way down the embankment to the river's edge. "We'll call for an ambulance. And if there's one in the area, it won't take them long to get here. You're less than a hundred yards from where all of the float trips end along this section of the river."

Tiffany whispered to Zachary, "You'll get the care you need, and you'll be all right." Then silently, she prayed he would as the men maneuvered Zachary onto the stretcher and struggled up the hill to hustle along the riverbank toward the nearby small settlement.

When the ambulance arrived, the attendants hurled instructions back and forth as they rendered the immediate care Zachary needed. Then after alerting a hospital in San Jose of their imminent arrival, they raced off, leaving Jason and the girls staring after them.

"Someone should have ridden with Zachary," Tiffany said as they turned to run to the van that would transport them to their jeep.

"He won't even be aware that he's alone," Jason said, hopping into the front with the driver. "They'll take good care of him. Besides, he won't beat us to the hospital by much. I'll see to that."

Margaret nudged Tiffany into the back of the van and slid in behind her. "Zachary will live through this. You've got to believe it."

Tiffany shook her head and stared out the window. "I pray you're right."

"Me too," Margaret said. "Let's pray for Zachary right now—out loud."

# CHAPTER 56

"Where am I?" asked Zachary as nurses and aides bustled about hooking a maze of wires to him.

"You're in a hospital emergency room in San Jose," answered a nurse. "A snake bit you, but you're where you'll get the help you need. Just try to relax and stay still while we take care of you."

Confused and in pain, Zachary watched in a stupor as they checked his vital signs with sober faces, talking back and forth in low monotone voices.

Then as he looked around, trying to take in the foreign scene, a man rushed in and introduced himself as the doctor in charge. "Can you describe the snake that bit you?" he asked. "There are two types of antivenom, one for coral snakes and one for the family of pit vipers. We have to know what bit you before we can administer the proper antivenom."

"I ... I don't know. I didn't see it," Zachary muttered. But though he didn't actually see the snake, he would never forget the awful moment it bit him and how much it hurt.

Jason flew into the emergency room, breathing heavily. "I think it was an Eyelash Pit Viper. I got a quick look at it when it dropped onto the side of the raft and slithered into the water."

"Can you describe it?" asked the physician, an urgent tone to his voice. "What color was it?"

"Green and yellow, and maybe a little red or pink somewhere. But I can't say for sure."

"What else can you tell us?" asked the doctor.

"It had those huge scales over its eyes that look like eyelashes. You know, like an Eyelash Pit Viper has."

"Are you sure about that?"

"Yes, sir, I'm majoring in biology back home. Plus, I've spent a fair amount of time this summer studying the poisonous snakes of Central America."

"About how long was it?"

"Probably about two feet."

"Thanks, young man. That's what we needed to know. We'll get right on it."

It comforted Zachary to see a familiar face. "I sure know how to end a party, huh?" he whispered to Jason, trying for a little humor through the pain.

Jason laughed. "And with a lot of drama, I might add."

"I hate that this happened."

"I'm sure you do, but it wasn't your fault. They'll fix you up. Your arm is already immobilized in a splint. So that's good. And they're preparing the antivenom as we speak."

Zachary rolled his eyes. "I feel so stupid. I really owe you one."

"Cut it out. Stop fretting and try to get some rest. I'll wait in the waiting room with the girls. Okay?"

"The girls? They're here too?" *Oh man, I can't cry in*

*front of Jason. I've got to hold it together.*

"Of course they're here. What did you think, you goofball? That they stayed to finish floating the river alone?"

"You mean it? Tiffany too?" He tried his best to smile as he moaned. "Are all of you staying?"

"We're not going anywhere without you. We're all pulling for you. In fact, we broke the speed limit coming here, so why would we leave now?"

"I can't believe this. It's the pits."

Jason grinned. "Pits? Not a good choice of words, if you ask me."

Zachary managed a slight grin. "Oh yeah, you said one of the pit snakes bit me."

"Now you hang in there, and if you'll do what you're told, we'll send up a special request for healing on your behalf."

Zachary grunted.

"Just trust everything will be fine. You hear?" Jason turned and left Zachary alone with his thoughts.

It helped that his friends waited just down the hall, but Zachary wished Tiffany would come see him. Maybe hospital rules kept her away. Or more likely, she was still mad at him.

Zachary couldn't remember much about what happened after he had been bitten, but he remembered Tiffany holding his arm down. He also recalled bits and pieces of being transferred onto the stretcher and the awkward trek up the riverbank. But the ambulance ride to the hospital blurred like a bad dream.

He had studied the venomous snakes of Central America in depth and received training in the protocol for handling poisonous snake bites, and yet, when he tangled with one, he overreacted. The horrific pain had taken his breath away. And when he pictured snake venom spreading rapidly through his body, panic scrambled his brain.

Moving with a keen sense of purpose, a nurse and her aide returned with an intravenous drip. "How are you feeling?" asked the nurse. Then she patted his arm and smiled as though he was a frightened, helpless child. And that was exactly how he felt—scared to death and limp from helplessness.

An optimistic person by nature, Zachary watched with a wary eye as they set up the IV to administer the recommended dosage of antivenom that would drip slowly over the next several hours. He squirmed inside at the thought that he needed trained professionals to work to save his life. In fact, it had never crossed his mind he could land in a hospital. Invincible people somehow avoided sickness and accidents. Didn't they? He flinched at his stupidity.

"Try to rest now," said the nurse. "You're going to be fine. We'll be in and out checking on your vital signs and to see if you need anything."

"My hand," he mumbled, "it hurts like crazy."

"I know. I'm so sorry. Snakebites can be very painful. The pain medication should start to bring relief soon. We plan to do everything possible to help you," she said. "In fact, would you like for us to send a priest in to see you?"

His heart lurched as he remembered that priests often come to the hospital to administer last rites to the dying. "If you think it's necessary. I mean, am I—"

"Oh, I'm sorry," she said. "I just meant that some people are comforted when a priest comes to say a prayer over them. I'll leave you to relax and someone will be in to check on you again before long."

He stared at his swollen, red hand and tried to

remember what he had read about the statistics on deaths from snakebites. Part of him wanted to believe that he would not die, but he couldn't seem to muster a positive thought that lasted. *What's the matter with me? Why do I feel so lost? And afraid?*

In that moment his vulnerability matched the time he wandered away from camp while his parents still slept soundly: That morning, he had awakened as the sun crept over the horizon. And as he watched it grew bolder and bolder, he became restless and bored. He left the tent to look for interesting rocks or feathers, but without a sense of direction, the Adirondacks soon swallowed him up. Lonely and frightened, he sat down on an old log, far from the trail. Scary thoughts made his tummy churn. What would become of him if daddy or mommy never came? What if a wolf tried to eat him or a snake tried to bite him? Elephant-sized tears spilled down his cheeks and onto his T-shirt.

Zachary didn't remember every detail, but for certain, he would never forget the moment his dad ran through a clearing in the trees and swept him up into his arms. Holding him close and rocking him back and forth, his dad whispered over and over, "Thank God, you're safe. You're safe."

Now as a grown man, alone and frightened in a hospital bed, the memory of his dad's concern and affection brought a sense of wonder to him, similar to the high he received from hiking to the top of a mountain and gazing over the valley below.

But his high quickly disappeared when a nurse entered the room to check on him. He could not trust her smiling face, and he did not believe her confident remarks that everything would be fine. He knew too much about snake bites. His life was in jeopardy. The truth of the situation reminded him of all the things he had left undone, and the many thoughts left unsaid or feelings unshared.

*There are so many things Dad and I could talk about. So many things we should have talked about a long time ago.*

As the nurse left the room, it occurred to Zachary that his mom should know about the accident and furthermore, he wanted her to know about it. In fact, he longed to hear her voice. This authentic need that emerged from a place deep within his soul came as a surprise to him. A strong and confident person most of the time, the accident had him reeling. He had trouble separating his emotions that were as tangled as vines running rampant in a jungle floor. Confused by a menacing web of apprehension, loneliness, and dread, he did not like any of it.

*Help me ... Help me calm down and trust that I'll be all right. Please?*

While he stared at the ceiling lights, trying to make sense of his confusing thoughts, he heard a light knock on the door to his room.

"Yes?"

A man wearing black pants and a black shirt with a white collar walked through the door. "Hello, I'm Father Gomez, a hospital chaplain. How are you doing, son?"

"Okay."

"Do you feel up to company?"

Zachary nodded, surprised that just looking at the compassionate face of a priest made him feel lighter in spirit. But it was short-lived as he remembered he might be dying. Zachary broke into a sweat as Father Gomez approached him and leaned over to place a hand on his shoulder.

"I'm so sorry about your accident," said Father Gomez, his ornate silver cross swinging freely from his neck. "I understand you had a run-in with a snake while rafting on a river with friends."

Zachary shook his head. "Yeah. I lost control of the raft in rough water."

"What happened?" Father asked.

Zachary's speech was labored as he briefly described the river conditions and what had occurred.

"Did anybody see the snake?"

"Jason said an Eyelash Pit Viper slithered over the raft when I fell."

"I imagine that's correct, since that snake is often found around tree limbs or twisted around vines that hang low over the water."

Zachary closed his eyes for a moment. "I should've looked before I grabbed hold of that vine."

"I'm sorry it happened. I hear they deliver a mean bite." Father Gomez pulled a chair close to Zachary's bed. "It's a good thing the ambulance got you here in plenty of time for the antivenom to be effective. Your friends apparently handled the situation well."

"I can't remember much. But I heard Jason taking charge. I'm glad he was with us."

"I understand you're a naturalist and quite familiar with this type of experience."

Zachary rolled his eyes. "But it's different when it happens to you."

"I'm sure it's hard to think straight when you're in pain."

"Yeah. Everything had gone so well. Everybody seemed happy. Then things changed in a matter of seconds. I let them down."

"I'm sure you did your best. None of us knows how

we will react in a tough situation or how we'll handle an emergency. It's different when our own life is at stake."

"Yeah, I never dreamed I'd lose my cool the way I did. If I had just—"

"Don't worry about 'what ifs' right now," said Father Gomez. "You need to concentrate on getting well."

"I better live through this."

"Trust that you will. Don't spend time and energy assuming the worst. Your job is to get better." Then Father Gomez asked for permission to pray.

Zachary quickly recalled all of the years he attended Catholic mass with his parents on Saturday nights, and how he squirmed in his seat through lengthy prayers with big words. He had not attended church since his father left home, but today, the presence of the priest calmed him so much that he welcomed prayer. "Yeah, go ahead," he muttered.

Father Gomez smiled and touched Zachary's shoulder. Then he offered up the following prayer: *Almighty God, please look upon this young man with eyes of mercy, and rest your healing hand upon him. I pray your life-giving powers will flow into his heart and soul to cleanse, purify, and restore every cell of his body that he might serve you better all the years of his life. Touch this life that you created with your hallowed hope, dear God. Please comfort and assure him in this, his time of need. Amen.*

Zachary would never be able to convey to another the peace that spread through him as Father Gomez prayed over him. It comforted him in an unfamiliar, but wonderful way.

"I'll stop back by to check on you later. Is there anything you need before I leave?"

"Your name, Gomez. ... I had a college buddy named

Adrian Gomez from San Jose."

"Did you attend the University of Florida?"

Zachary nodded. "Do you know him?"

"Adrian is my nephew. I ought your name sounded familiar. He has mentioned you. Adrian keeps busy studying to become a priest at a Catholic seminary."

"So he's not married?" Zachary's grin was lopsided as the first wave of drowsiness from the pain medication hit him.

"No, he's not married. He plans to devote his life to the priesthood. Shall I tell him about you, Zachary?"

"Will you? Thanks." Zachary smiled and fluttered his eyelids. "Tell him I'd like to see him."

"I see you're getting sleepy. You need your rest, so relax and trust you're in good hands," Father said as he left the room.

As Zachary drifted to sleep he wondered whose hands Father Gomez referred to.

## CHAPTER 57

When a nurse stuck her head in the door of the waiting room late in the afternoon, Tiffany jumped up so fast, she dropped her book onto the floor "How is he? Is he still in a lot of pain?" she asked.

"His pain has subsided and he is stable. We are still administering the antivenom, but if the doctors decide he doesn't need more, we'll release him sometime tomorrow." The nurse cautioned of the difficulty of predicting an exact timeline, stating it depended on a number of things, including the possibility of necrosis to the hand.

"Necrosis?" Margaret asked.

The nurse explained necrosis meant damaged tissue from inadequate blood flow. "Now I know that's frightening, but the doctor is confident you got him to the hospital in time, so it's not likely to become an issue."

"When can we see him?" asked Tiffany.

"You can go in now—one at a time, but don't stay long."

When Tiffany first peeked into Zachary's room her

heart flip-flopped at his pasty appearance. She grazed his arm with her fingertips, looking for signs of life. "Zachary? Zachary, it's me, Tiffany. How are you?"

Slowly, he opened his eyes. "Tiffany? Is that you?

The beeping monitors and the tubes twisting around Zachary brought a rush of reality to Tiffany. He looked so helpless that the last drop of anger left in her body. In that instant, any remaining resentment dissipated. "They tell me you've improved," she said.

"Seeing you will help more than any medicine ever could."

Tiffany narrowed her eyes. "I'm flattered, but I suggest you stay with the prescribed treatment."

"It was stupid—losing control and ruining everything."

"Say no more, Zachary, it was an accident. What's done is done." Then she told him the nurse reported his vital signs were good. "You'll heal and soon be leading tour groups again."

Zachary gave her a twisted smile. "How come you're so confident? Isn't the jury still out?"

She took his good hand and squeezed it. "I refuse to believe otherwise. And besides, a sixth sense verifies my conviction." It pulled at her heartstrings to see Zachary so vulnerable.

"I'd like to know about this sixth sense of yours," Zachary said.

"Maybe you will one day," Tiffany said. "Now I can't stay but a minute—nurse's orders. But remember, I'm not going anywhere. None of us are. Margaret and Jason send their best and said to tell you they'll see you in the morning."

Tiffany leaned over and kissed Zachary lightly on the forehead.

"Will you come again?" he asked.

"You *will* get well Zachary. You *will* be all right. You hear me? Remember, the monkeys are waiting for you," she said, stirred by his damp, dreamy eyes. Though frightened for him, she desperately needed to believe he would recover.

Alternating between doubt and hope, Tiffany left Zachary's bedside with a tight feeling in her chest. On her way to the waiting room, she saw a chapel. The pull to enter was strong and unquestionably real.

Silently, she sat in the sanctuary with unshed tears and scrambled thoughts shoving aside her words. But gradually, she shifted her focus to God and His power to help—to comfort and reassure her. Soon, she began to pray.

*Dear Lord, I'm scared. I'm afraid for Zachary. Please help him—give him the strength he needs to get well. Please keep him safe, Lord. Please?*

Longing to trade fear for trust and doubt for belief, she listened with the inner ear of her soul. A miracle did not suddenly occur, but during the ticking of seconds that turned into minutes, Tiffany slowly relaxed and let a sweet whisper of reassurance melt away her anxiety.

Left with a Holy peace, Tiffany believed the Lord was not only with her, but that He would watch over Zachary. She believed that regardless of what happened next, in the hospital or later on, the Lord would remain near to comfort and encourage her. Tears of relief fell from her heart, as a quiet conviction to trust infused her with hope.

She left the chapel and walked down the corridor toward the waiting room with a smile in her heart.

## CHAPTER 58

As morning light filtered through the half-open blinds of Zachary's hospital room, a cheery nurse bustled about performing her duties. He watched the saline drip slowly through the line, recalling nurses had checked on him several times during the night.

Once after they left the room, he posed a number of questions in his mind about spirituality and a higher power. There were no answers, but it had passed the time and taken his mind off his worries. For some reason, the process made him feel less lonely.

Evidently, he slept off and on during the night, for he recalled a strange dream that had him running for his life in a dark and oppressive jungle. Thousands of snakes with eyes like coals of fire and tongues like flaming darts, dangled from tree limbs, trying to reach him as he ran. When he tripped and fell to the ground, snarled roots grabbed his legs and held him captive. Then thick swinging vines snaked around and around him, encasing his body like a mummy wrapped in linen. Desperately, he struggled to free himself, but it wasn't until he became exhausted and ceased to struggle that the ruthless roots and vicious vines relaxed their hold on him.

As Zachary pondered his dream, he found it interesting to note that it was only at the point of surrender that he had been set free. Had the snake bite prompted the baffling dream? What would a shrink make of it? He would probably ask hard questions that would be difficult to answer. What are you running from? Is someone mad at you? Are you angry at someone? And worst of all, the shrink might ask what he was afraid of. And he wouldn't want to admit to being afraid of anything.

He assumed Tiffany, who loved to dissect her dreams for hidden messages, would suggest he stop running and face whatever bothered him, for only then could he know meaningful joy and peace. The notion made him smile, but his fuzzy head kept him from making further sense of it.

Tiffany was the best part of yesterday—a much-needed tonic. Her delicate kiss on his forehead, as soft as the brush of a butterfly wing, made him wonder long after she left the room if he had only imagined her.

A few moments later, after the nurse finally finished her morning routine, Margaret ambled in. She smiled and touched Zachary's good arm. "Excuse me, but it looks to me like some people will do anything for a little attention."

A hearty chuckle burst from Zachary. "Hey! Where have you been keeping yourself?"

"So how are you coming along? Are you about ready to spring out of here? And cut loose from all these wires and tubes?"

"They tell me I'm improving. The doctor is satisfied with my vital signs, but plans to keep an eye on me through today. He's concerned about my hand. It doesn't hurt as much—not as red and swollen this morning, but I might end up with a scar."

"Let's hope not. We'll start making plans right away to take you home," Margaret said, squeezing his good hand. "You know you scared us to death, don't you? But we might forgive you if you behave yourself."

He grinned. "You'd better."

"Now before I go, is there anything I can do for you?"

"As a matter of fact, I'd like to talk to my mom. Would you locate my cell phone? She's listed in my contacts—name is Elizabeth Caldwell. She'll want to know I'm in the hospital. And I want to make sure she knows I'll live—that is, if I will."

"Ahhh, you're too tough to let a snake take you down."

After Margaret left, Zachary wondered if his dad would also like to know about him. But he had not heard from him in years. Memories of his dad flooded in until the ache in his heart was soon worse than the pain in his hand.

# CHAPTER 59

"I met Adrian the first week of classes our freshman year in college. And it didn't take us long to discover we both loved the great outdoors," Zachary told Father Gomez, who had come to visit him on the third day of his hospital stay.

"Yes, Adrian said much the same thing when I mentioned meeting you. He said that even though you were from different cultures, you hit if off from the start as you shared similar memories of your boyhood experiences. And by the way, Adrian's out of the country right now, but he said to tell you to get well and that he'll be in touch soon."

"Did he mention anything specific I told him about my past?"

"No. Why do you ask?"

"I don't know. I just thought … Oh never mind." Zachary wanted to share his story with Father Gomez, but he hesitated.

"If there's something you'd like to talk about—a story you'd like to share, a confession, or whatever, I'd be happy to listen in the strictest confidence," said Father Gomez.

Zachary shifted to a more upright position. "I have a story, all right, but it's not an easy one to talk about."

With a kind and gentle smile, Father Gomez pulled up a chair and looked Zachary in the eye. "You can tell me anything and trust it won't leave this room. You can share what's on your mind and heart and know your secrets will be safe with me."

The tone of Father's voice and the look in his eyes convinced Zachary he could risk sharing the details of his past. He could tell Father about his disappointment when his dad left home. And he could also confess to his guilt and shame over that terrible night, and trust Father Gomez would listen without judging or condemning him.

So he opened up and began to talk about the summer he was fourteen when his parents divorced. "I'd heard them arguing off and on for months, but it shocked me when Dad left—left for another woman. It turned my life upside down and things were never the same again."

"That must have been hard on you."

"Dad didn't come around much after that. His selfishness changed my life. And I still resent him for it. I made some terrible choices after he left—got mixed up with drugs and alcohol. I'm having trouble forgiving him and moving on."

"It's hard work to let go of that much pain, isn't it? It takes time and effort."

"And there's more." Zachary cleared his throat and told Father about the night they went to buy more beer and the kid driving broadsided a van, killing a fourteen year old boy in the back seat.

"And even though you weren't driving, you're haunted by what happened?"

Zachary cut his eyes away from Father Gomez and sniffed. "I was about his age at the time—fifteen."

"I'm so sorry. You've carried around a heavy burden of guilt and shame for a long time, haven't you?" asked Father Gomez. "And it's a lot of tough stuff to deal with."

"And somehow it has made me resent my dad even more. I've had to face up to a number of things, and it's all too much—the hurt and regret."

Father Gomez rested his elbows on his knees and folded his hands as though to pray. "Negative feelings, such as you've lived with can make us miserable. They disrupt our lives and do a good job of blocking our chance for happiness."

"Mostly, I've tried to run from my past, but earlier this summer something happened that brought everything out into the open. Everything has come back to haunt me. And I can't seem to let go of it this time."

"Talking to a minister or a trained counselor, or even sharing with a trusted friend can help you sort out your feelings. Any one of these choices can benefit you, but never discount the blessing of talking to God to find relief from your heavy burdens or to hear whispers of guidance for handling your situation. He is our greatest listener—our greatest confidant."

Zachary gave Father a puzzled look.

"As we share our hearts with the Lord through prayer and meditation, He grants us peace that differs from the peace we find on our own. And He offers hope for our lives that is vital to contentment. Without hope, we only go through the motions of living."

"I've felt so awful for such a long time."

"Ultimately, we must be responsible for our bad choices, but bad choices do not mean we are bad people,"

Father Gomez said. "Zachary, would you like to pray? Would you like to unburden your heart to the Lord as you did with me? And ask Him for forgiveness and to help you learn how to forgive another?"

"I wouldn't know how."

Father Gomez prayed a brief prayer with Zachary and then prepared to leave. "Just talk as though you are talking to a trusted friend. Exactly what you say isn't as important as connecting to God to share your heart. Ask His forgiveness for your shortcomings and give thanks for all the good things about your life."

Focusing on the Lord to pray did not come easily for Zachary. His thoughts were scattered at first, but after awhile he zeroed in on Father Gomez's advice and began to silently share his heart—his shame and guilt—without holding back. He asked for forgiveness for his own shortcomings and sent up a plea to learn how to extend the same to others.

By the time a nurse interrupted to report that they would soon release him from the hospital, Zachary felt better. He couldn't remember if he had ever felt more at peace. Forgiveness was still a foreign concept, but the experience of trying to connect to God through prayer had actually opened him to a whisper of encouragement that positive changes could come about in his life. Hope for the possibility of reconciliation with his dad and Tiffany made Zachary feel like singing for the first time in a long time.

## CHAPTER 60

Less than a week later, Zachary carried coffee and one of Nellie's rich, gooey cinnamon rolls to the Baldwins' patio. The joy he felt toward the end of his hospital stay was gone. He felt disconnected from life in a way he could not identify. The structure of his life had been interrupted, and everything about his future seemed at loose ends.

He had survived the snake bite, but what now? Still estranged from his father and unsure where he stood with Tiffany, all the unfinished business made him jittery. He felt lost at a crossroads without a clue as to which way to turn.

He hoped spending quiet time meditating in the fresh morning air would help his mood. Usually, the sounds of the birds and animals relaxed him, but as he listened to a chattering squirrel monkey and a cawing toucan in the nearby trees, it only added to his restless feeling. He yearned for the special inner peace he experienced in the hospital during visits from Father Gomez, and especially that last day as he meditated with God—a connection he never expected to make. He never dreamed he could feel so at peace—like nothing could ever harm him again or that life was good on a profound level. Warm feelings and hopeful thoughts had cropped up during the experience, but now, a few days later, they were gone.

Now, his focus was on the negative aspects of his life. It happened so subtly that he wasn't sure which came first. Did the tough stuff push aside his good feelings? Or did his good feelings fade and allow the tough stuff to push through? It didn't matter. He was despondent.

While picking aimlessly at his cinnamon roll, Zachary wrestled with his newly found faith. He had never considered himself an atheist, but for a long time now he hadn't given much thought to a higher power. If the Holy Spirit had whispered encouragement to him at any point during his difficult years, he had not heard. Not until he thought he would die, did he awaken to a holy presence and begin to listen.

George's quiet steadfast faithfulness to serve the Lord had become an important blueprint for Zachary to follow over the last few years, and he did not doubt it had for many others, as well. And the input from Father Gomez had helped open him to a new awareness of God. But he had so much to learn, for his relationship with the Lord had barely budded.

George appeared on the patio and suggested he join Zachary. "You don't mind company, do you?"

"No, but I doubt I'll be good company."

"Ahhh, we'll find something to talk about. We always do. So what's on your mind this morning?"

Zachary frowned. "Before we go there, let me say how much I appreciate you and Nellie inviting me to stay in your home. The prospect of going home from the hospital alone didn't appeal to me."

"We're glad to have you. Besides, this gives Nellie a chance to bustle about like a mother or grandmother might."

Zachary smiled and leaned forward in his chair. "But I want to be sure you understand how much I appreciate having the two of you in my life. And I'll tell Nellie myself, first chance I get."

Smiling warmly, George said, "I assure you, Zach, that the blessing goes both ways."

"I'm grateful to be alive, but I've been restless since leaving the hospital. My visits from Father Gomez gave me a lot to think about. For quite some time now I've been aware that you and Nellie consider the Lord very important, and I heard plenty about God as a kid, but I've been far removed from this god thing for quite a while now."

"But this time when the Holy Spirit whispered, you listened with an open mind and a receptive heart. You heard things in a new way, didn't you?"

"Somehow I felt a special presence in my life that I'd never been aware of before."

"Would you like to tell me about it?"

"It's hard to describe. But I felt good from the moment Father Gomez walked into the room that first day. His kindness and compassion put me at ease. And when he prayed for me, I felt something new and good happening. He lifted my spirits—or something did. I felt at peace and more hopeful than I had for a long time."

George nodded. "Go on."

"Well I continued to have plenty of bouts with doubt and fear those first couple of days as I struggled with the possibility of dying. But during the last visit from Father Gomez, I had a strong longing to tell him about the hard stuff from my past. And at his encouragement, I told him everything, like I did that day with you."

"The priest's presence and his approach inspired you to open up to the Lord and receive the reassurance and encouragement you needed during a very difficult time," George said. "It sounds like Father Gomez's connection with God on your behalf helped bring a number of things into focus for you."

"Yes, and Tiffany has also influenced me a lot this summer."

"What do you mean?" asked George.

"Well when I first met Tiffany she seemed anxious about anything and everything. She wants to be a school teacher, but with a major phobia about speaking in front of others, she has convinced herself it's not going to happen. And after her sister died, she lost faith for a while. She blamed God for her loss and suffering."

"And you've watched her struggle, some days up and some days down," George said. "You've seen her go through several stages of grief, I would imagine, as she vacillated between denial and acceptance. But from my observations, she seems to have found the kind of hope that sustains and uplifts."

Zachary nodded. "Yes, and in the process she has changed."

"And how is that?" asked George.

"For one thing, she's more confident. And there seems to be a special peace about her."

George smiled. "Well it's certainly been my experience that the Lord's love and forgiveness has the power to transform us. He can restore our faith when we doubt and our hope when we think all is lost. He can make a difference in our lives when we invite Him to work with us."

"I figured you'd understand. I've known about Jesus

since I was a kid, but I've never focused on Him before. Trouble is I don't know what to expect now."

Looking thoughtful, George said, "I'm happy for you, Zach. You've become aware of Jesus' love for you—life's greatest discovery, I'd say. And I believe in time you'll learn to return that love."

"But I'm clueless what a good Christian looks like. Do you have time to guide me on how to read scripture?" Zachary asked. "I don't know where to begin."

Before George could answer, Nellie popped onto the patio. "Excuse me; someone is here to see you, Zachary."

Zachary had not seen his dad for so long that for a split second he appeared as an apparition. Although an involuntary thrill shot through him when he recognized him, suspicion soon took over. He gave his dad a stormy look. "What are you doing here?"

"It's been a long time, son."

"*Son*, you say?"

George jumped to his feet, introduced himself, and offered Mr. Caldwell a chair. Then he left Zachary alone on the patio with his dad.

"It's great to see you," his dad said.

Zachary grunted.

"I mean, you're looking good. So how are you doing?"

"How am I *doing*? Since when have you cared how I'm doing?"

"I've been so worried about you."

Zachary did not bat an eye or move a muscle as he stared at the man that called him "son."

"You know I've always cared about you."

Zachary gaped. Surely his dad didn't think he bought into such solicitous remarks.

His dad rubbed the back of his neck. "There's so

much I want to say to you. But you're not making this easy."

Dumbfounded, Zachary asked, "But why *now*? Why after all these years?"

"Your mother called to tell me a poisonous snake bit you. She said you almost died. I had to come see for myself that you're all right."

"Well as you can see, I'm fine. I survived. So what now?"

"I just want to … Well this visit is long overdue."

Zachary lifted his eyebrows. "Oh? You think so, huh?"

"Our separation has haunted me for years. I should have tried harder to see you and make you understand."

"Should have? Then why didn't you?" Zachary's stomach roiled with resentment.

"For the longest time after I left, your mom said you didn't want to see me. I kept trying to contact you but you always refused my calls."

"You're right, I refused your calls those first few weeks, but if you ask me they trailed off pretty fast." His dad had some nerve to disappear from his life, ignore him all these years, and then reappear as though he cared. Long before today, he had proven what kind of dad he was.

"Maybe I gave up too soon. I made mistakes—things I wish I hadn't done or could do over."

"Since when do we get over's? I've never gotten any."

"You're right. But can we try to right a wrong?"

Zachary looked away, his head filled with anger and his heart with self-pity.

"So when you never responded, I stopped trying to reach you. I failed to see you were the real victim." His dad grimaced as though in pain. "Not me."

Speechless, Zachary stared at his dad who exhaled as though he had been holding his breath for a long time.

His dad cracked his knuckles. "Maybe I took the route of least resistance because I didn't want to think about how much I probably hurt you."

"*Maybe* you took the route of least resistance? *Probably* hurt me?" Zachary had found his voice again. "You abandoned me," he spewed. "I couldn't sleep nights back then. I was sad for a long time, but then I got good and mad."

"Mad?"

"Yes, *mad!* Mad about everything and anything. I resented you for leaving. I resented *you*. And you're right, I did tell Mom I didn't want to see you, but only because I thought you didn't want to see me," Zachary shouted as he jumped up from his chair, knocking it over.

"You had a right to your anger. Still do. But I want you to understand that the reason I left had nothing to do with anything you did or didn't do."

"Yeah, right," Zachary said, sneaking a quick glance at his dad. It surprised him to see that he looked like someone had slugged him in the stomach.

"I've always loved you, Zach," his dad said, barely above a whisper.

"Is that right?" Then for the next several minutes sarcasm spilled like water over a dam as Zachary said all the things he had bottled up inside and thought his dad deserved to hear.

"Your mom and I lost something in our marriage that didn't involve you. In the end, we agreed to break up. Our love for each other died, but my love for you never did. I hated leaving you, Zach, but I thought you'd live with me part time."

"Well you didn't make that clear when you left me

and Mom for another woman," Zachary said between gritted teeth as he paced.

"Yes son, I left for another woman. A woman I didn't even know when your mother and I started having trouble. I left home, but I never meant to leave you."

Zachary picked up his chair and sat. There was that word "son" again. His dad sounded like he owned the word. "Hmmmm ... You don't say." Zachary had trouble swallowing the lump that had risen in his throat.

"We need to talk. We have things to sort through before we can understand each other. I've made some stupid mistakes. I've missed you and a lot of your life." His dad swiped at his watery eyes and sniffed. "I don't want to miss any more."

His dad's quiet display of emotion acted like a torch to Zachary's frozen heart, activating a memory of the Christmas Santa Claus brought the gift of his dreams: He had admired a bright red bicycle in a toy store every time they went to town that autumn. And Christmas morning, when he rushed downstairs to the living room, the beloved bicycle stood in front of the Christmas tree. He not only recalled his own joy over receiving the bicycle, but for the first time Zachary realized how pleased his dad seemed at his reaction. "I'll teach you to ride your new bike, Zach," his dad had said that morning.

And later when they took the bike outside, his dad held it steady so he could climb upon it safely. "You won't let me fall, will you, Dad? You won't let go of me?" Zachary had asked as he wobbled all over the driveway.

"No son, I'll stay close by your side," his dad had said as he held on to the back of the seat. "I won't let go. I won't leave you alone until you're ready."

Zachary understood now that his happiness over the bicycle that Christmas morning had also made his dad happy. His dad had known joy because *he* had. The childhood memory warmed his heart so much that the icy persona he projected for so long began to melt.

"Zach, did you hear me? I don't want to miss any more of your life. I love you."

Though warmth flooded Zachary's heart, he held back the tears that tried to come, and said, "For years, you had a funny way of showing it."

His dad nodded. "You're right. I did."

Then over the next half hour or so, they waded through many difficult questions and even harder answers, searching for understanding and forgiveness.

During the often strained conversation, Zachary watched his strong, yet sensitive dad with an overwhelming awareness that something good had evolved from his awful experience with the snake. His close call opened the door to reconciliation with his dad.

Later, after his dad left, promising to come again before his return flight to New York City, Zachary sat alone on the patio reviewing their time together. For the first time since his dad left home that awful night, he had a keen sense of hope that they could salvage their relationship.

Somehow, he felt a weight had been lifted from his soul or the door to a cage he was trapped in had opened wide.

For a silly, split second he almost believed he could fly like a bird.

## CHAPTER 61

Tiffany invited Margaret to have breakfast at a diner with a light and airy Caribbean décor that matched her mood. "This is my chance to tell you how much I loved the float trip on the Peñas Blancas River, except for the way it ended, of course. I've never properly thanked you for suggesting the trip or for helping me control my nerves during a very frightening time."

"And Jason came through for us, but that isn't all that helped you during that time, is it?"

Tiffany glanced through the expansive windows overlooking the main street in Santa Elena, and then she looked at Margaret and smiled. "You're right. My real help came when we were at the hospital and I finally remembered to plug into the Lord. When I unburdened my heart and tuned in to listen for His whispers of reassurance, it helped me feel more positive about the situation."

"You've worked hard this summer to confront the things that frighten you and that have kept you from moving forward, haven't you?" Margaret asked. "Like your fear of failure or rejection?"

"Yes, and our faceless fears are far more difficult to deal with. They're not as easily confronted or ignored, at least not for me. I can stay away from heights, and keep my distance from scary critters, for the most part, but it's the faceless fears that go with me wherever I go." Tiffany laughed.

"What do you mean?"

"I've always carried my fear of failure or rejection around in my soul like some sort of badge, letting it feed my inflated sense of self-doubt. But I'm beginning to see that such a choice was evidence of my lack of faith in God's ability to help me."

"But it's hard to change old habits, isn't it? And it takes time."

"Yes, but I'm working on it—a little at a time. I'm learning to trust."

"I've noticed a change in you over the last few months," Margaret said. "You're more confident and braver than you used to be."

"I'm trying. I'm trying to not being so afraid that I won't live up to my potential. I'm beginning to make peace with my intangible fears. I'm learning to trust more and doubt less. And I'll give you an example. A few weeks ago, when one of my professors invited me to speak about the flora and fauna common to the part of the United States where I grew up, my first urge was to refuse, like always. Just thinking about standing before my classmates made me want to turn and run. But through heartfelt prayer, I found the courage to commit. Then in spite of saying 'yes,' old negative thoughts plagued me from the moment I accepted. I regretted my commitment to speak publicly, and doubted I could pull it off. As old convictions of failure and inadequacy dominated my thinking, I fretted until it was finally over."

"So how did you manage to get through it?"

"I prayed night and day as I prepared my talk, and particularly the morning I gave it. Doubt kept creeping in, making a wreck of me. But I was determined to carry through with what I said I would do, and trust help would come."

"And?"

"To my amazement when I entered the classroom a holy calm came over me and I said what I wanted to say without going blank."

Margaret gave Tiffany a puzzled look. "Considering your previous attitude and experience with speaking publicly, it sounds like you experienced a miracle."

"Actually, that's exactly how I saw it. It was a miracle, for I did not succeed alone."

"And from the look on your face, I haven't a doubt you will succeed again."

"Not without praying myself to the front of the room first." Tiffany smiled.

"But it will be easier next time. You'll develop your style, and build your courage and confidence with practice."

"I have a lot of work to do, but the experience taught me that if I'll obey God when He calls me to do something specific that I think is impossible to do, He will provide what I need to make it happen. Of course, I don't mean to imply I've suddenly become a different person over these past weeks or months. Speaking in front of others will probably always intimidate me, but the point is that my recent experience tells me if I will say 'yes' to the Lord, He will provide."

"You have been walking this road for a while now, haven't you? Earlier this summer you found the courage to leave your comfort zone to study in a foreign country. I remember how frightened you were." Margaret smiled. "But I talked you into it. Or something did."

Tiffany smiled and reached out to touch Margaret. "And I can't thank you enough for your encouragement to come."

"You mean for responding to the urge to push you?" Margaret asked, and smiled.

"Yes, that is more like what happened. But it's what I needed."

"So, Tiffany, how would you describe your progress with handling your sister's death?"

"It's hard, but I'm progressing. I'm edging up on accepting what happened. Losing Karla has taught me you cannot assume tragedy will never touch your life. But I've also learned I can choose to enjoy the simple pleasure in life, regardless of lingering sorrow."

"So do you believe that on some level you'll always miss your sister?"

"I don't see how it could be any other way," Tiffany said as she recalled how sorrow sometimes still hovered to threaten her peace the way a rain-filled storm cloud lingers to thwart a farmer's progress in the wheat field. "It helps to talk with my parents every week, but certainly leaning on the Lord is my greatest comfort, for He provides a peace like none other.

"From watching you, I can see it takes time and patience to learn how to cope with a huge loss and trust life will be good again. Of course I don't mean to imply it could ever be good again in the same way as when Karla was alive."

"You've also done a lot of thinking this summer, haven't you, Margaret?"

Margaret smiled and looked at her watch. "I so enjoy

our conversations and I hate to end this one, but I'm due at the child care center in ten minutes and I want to call home before my mom leaves for the day."

"No problem. I have a date with Zachary in less than an hour."

"One more thing before I leave—about the snakes and spiders—they scare me, too," Margaret said.

Tiffany laughed. "That's just what I thought."

After Margaret left, Tiffany stayed a while to reflect on some of the great things Nellie and Grandmother Birdwell had shared with her. She especially loved to reflect on her grandmother's conviction that the Lord had turned her mourning into joyful dancing and her silent heart into a song, which she had based on her favorite scripture found in the Psalms.

And Nellie had said, "Although as humans we often revert to an unawareness of God's presence, He waits. He waits for us to reawaken and draw near to Him again."

Tiffany thought of the young man who struck Karla's car. His courage to contact her parents to ask for their forgiveness several weeks before had nudged her closer to accepting the unchangeable—the death of her sister. But she wasn't quite at the place she could forgive him.

*A journey of faith is never easy. Spiritual growth continues over a lifetime. Be patient with yourself as you seek the Lord's guidance.*

Even as she remembered these words of wisdom from Nellie, she questioned whether she could ever truly forgive the kid involved in her sister's death. She was wise enough to know forgiving the young man would likely do as much for her as it would for him, but her resentment was still quite strong. Maybe through prayer and hard work she would one day be able to forgive him but, she would think about the possibility another time. One thing she knew for certain was that she still had lots of work to do on her journey of faith.


Tiffany's broken heart had continued to mend at the same time Zachary's body healed. Earlier in the week he invited her to come to the Baldwins to visit, making it clear he had much to say that was long overdue. She accepted the invitation, for she, too, had plenty to say.

She drove toward Monteverde under a clear blue sky filled with bouffant white clouds that seemed to float heavenward to the melody of whispering breezes. With a close eye on the road and firm hands on the wheel, Tiffany accelerated around sharp curves with the knack of a race car drive. She dared to stretch herself in this small, but deliberate way as she maneuvered the jeep up the mountain.

*"Come!"* The heart of the rainforest beckoned. But the temptation lasted only a split second, for even the promise of the elusive quetzal could not lure her from seeing Zachary this morning.

Tiffany's foot grew heavy on the gas pedal as seductive images of Zachary cradling her in his arms filled her head. Her soul soared to meet the sky as she ripped up the Baldwins' driveway, turned off the motor, and jumped out. She rushed to the front door, arriving just as Nellie opened it.

Nellie pointed to the backyard. "Zachary's waiting for you outside."

"How has he been since his dad came to visit?"

"Reflective and more at peace," Nellie said. "We've had several good talks, and now, he wants very much to visit with you."

Tiffany rushed onto the patio and waved at Zachary,

who swung slowly in the wooden arbor in the far corner of the yard. She intended to meander down the path, but when he jumped up and rushed to greet her, she hurried to meet him half-way.

Zachary reached for her hand. "I'm so happy to see you. Your presence is the best therapy for what ails me." He smiled as though he had just been crowned king of some majestic province.

Tiffany returned his smiled. "You're better?"

"Yes indeed, and I've dreamed about this moment when I would see you again. You are even more beautiful than I remembered."

Pleased by his eloquent words, either from Shakespeare or divinely inspired, it did not take Tiffany long to suspect he had evidently made the same discovery she had that morning in the rainforest. He seemed different. Peace radiated from him—from his eyes and his smile. Even the sound of his voice indicated newly-found calm and assurance.

Tiffany and Zachary settled into the arbor swing to talk as they had not for weeks. She listened patiently as Zachary explained why he shared his tragic story when he did. And he listened with care to her honest negative reaction to that decision.

In turn, Tiffany opened her heart to Zachary, choosing to leave nothing important unsaid between them. She told him about her college romance with Eric, including losing her virginity to him. "I still struggle with guilt and shame that I allowed it to happen. I had intended to save myself for my husband."

Back and forth, they communicated without the urge to cajole, crying in tough moments and laughing through tender ones. Sharing a strong bond of love, they communicated about grief, mistakes, and forgiveness.

Eventually, they shared a warm kiss that held great promise for the future.

The scent of Nellie's fabulous roses filled the air as they sat with their hands intertwined. Tiffany's heart swelled at the happy look on Zachary's face as he watched an amazing little green hummingbird hover over a bright red hibiscus blossom.

Somewhere in the distance, a trebling bird reminded Tiffany of the plight of the endangered scarlet macaw. "I want to help protect the macaws someday," she said, realizing in that moment Costa Rica would become her home.

"Speaking of birds … How about looking for a quetzal again? You know I saw one this summer with one of my groups, but I'd love to see one with you. What do you say? Would Saturday morning a week from tomorrow work for you?"

Tiffany expressed her joy with a toothy grin. "What should I wear?"

"You look wonderful in anything, but wear boots and bring a jacket. I'll pick you up about the time the sun comes up—not down—I'm not up to a night hike yet." Zachary laughed.

Not long thereafter, Tiffany left to the sound of a sweet songbird singing in the branches of a nearby papaya tree. She floated through Nellie's garden with her feet scarcely meeting the pebbled pathway.

A door had opened to new possibilities, filling her with treasured hope for brighter days ahead.

## CHAPTER 62

After a week that seemed to go on forever, and before the dew had even dried on Nellie's roses, Zachary arrived to take Tiffany to the rainforest.

"Now tell me … Why are you so sure we'll find a quetzal today?" Tiffany asked as she hopped into the jeep and grabbed the seat belt. "I mean, why today?"

"Never give up on what you hope for," Zachary said. "Trust that together we will see our quetzal. I'm not saying when, but we'll see one. Just believe it!"

"Just believe, huh?" she asked, thinking Zachary sounded like he had just accessed a special crystal ball. "But that takes such a high level of faith."

"Of course it does."

"All right, I'll *try*. How's that?"

Zachary laughed. "Much better."

The cloudless, sea blue autumn sky that escorted them into the forest, fed Tiffany's spirits as they sauntered down the trail under the soft light filtering through the green boughs overhead. She did not doubt for a moment that the silver rays lighting their haven would ward off the gray clouds filled with tropical mist that always wreaked havoc with her hair. Nothing would spoil their time together.

From the beginning, the rainforest seemed different. High in the overgrowth of the jungle, birds sang softly in the trees, while in the undergrowth insects barely squeaked. Snakes ceased to slither. Monkeys stopped howling. Jaguars remained hidden. All the creatures waited and watched. And listened. Something was about to happen.

The air grew sweeter and the trees taller. The ferns plumped up. The orchids preened with prettiness. Red and pink blossom spikes of tough bromeliad plants shot upward with strength and pride. Every limb reached heavenward. Every vine sought the light. And each leaf danced gently in the breeze.

Hikers, ahead and behind them, laughed low and warm as they meandered through the rainforest, enjoying each precious moment given them.

But when Tiffany stepped onto the first swinging bridge, her mounting euphoria gave way to anxiety. "Oh my! I want to do this, but …"

"Everything will be all right. Trust me, the bridges are safe," Zachary said.

"Yes, you've said that before." Tiffany forced a smile. And although she was less afraid this time, a distinct uneasiness grabbed her gut.

As she stopped to take a deep breath, Zachary took her in his arms and held her close for several seconds. "We don't have to do this. If you—"

"Yes we do. If I crossed it once, I can do it again." Tiffany still felt uptight, but the image of a tattoo of a small blue butterfly on her right shoulder evoked a smile.

Hand in hand, they moved on along the bridge without speaking. Tiffany focused on the trees, looking at epiphytes and watching for a quetzal in an attempt to ignore how high up they walked. She was a little light-headed, but after walking several more yards her tension began to subside.

The possibility of finally seeing a quetzal thrilled Tiffany, but hiking with Zachary was icing on the cake of the richest kind. She no sooner thought this when she spotted one of the coveted birds. She squealed, "Look! It's a quetzal!"

Zachary looked where she pointed. Perched high on a branch, the bird was quite visible. "You're right! It's a quetzal, but not just any quetzal—it's our quetzal!"

They took turns studying the beautiful creature through Zachary's field glasses. Tiffany, who always had her camera with her, failed to bring it along. But she used her smart phone to snap countless images, determined to thoroughly document the beautiful bird so she could email pictures to Margaret and Jason, and of course, her parents.

They watched for several minutes before the amazing bird lifted from the branch and glided elegantly through the canopy of the trees, its magnificent colors a blur. Zachary leaned toward Tiffany. "I told you we would see our quetzal." Then he kissed her, sealing the special viewing with a kiss that lasted almost as long as the sighting.

"I believe we've just been given a special gift," Tiffany said when the kiss finally ended. And then these words crossed her mind: *After all, when we believe in what we cannot see with steadfast faith, and trust in God to make it real, we are rewarded.* Did Nellie say that? Or was it Grandmother Baldwin? She smiled from the inside out.

Zachary took Tiffany's hand as they ambled on along the bridge. "Would you mind crossing one more bridge, even though we've spotted our quetzal?"

"Sure, why not," she said, though secretly ready to turn back and leave the bridges behind.

As they approached the middle of the third bridge, Zachary slowed his gait and put his hand on her arm. At that exact moment a small group of hikers entered the bridge, causing it to sway excessively. Tiffany swallowed her cry of concern, grabbed the guardrail, and hung her head.

"Are you all right?" he asked.

"How much further?" she asked as she let go of the guardrail and slowly turned toward him.

"Not far. Let's rest a few minutes," Zachary suggested. Then in the center of the bridge with several people looking on, he dropped to one knee and reached for her hand. He smiled and held her eyes with his. "Tiffany Faith Birdwell, I love you far more than words can say, but I want to try. May I?"

"Please do," she whispered, her heart skipping a beat over what she presumed was his intention.

Zachary swallowed hard. "I love you, Tiffany, more than camping in the Adirondacks or hiking in the rainforests of Costa Rica. I love you more than listening to the songbirds of springtime warbling back and forth or watching the colorful leaves of autumn drifting to the ground. In fact, I love you more than watching a soft summer rain shower or a lovely winter snowstorm. Indeed, my love for you flows deeper than any ocean and spreads wider than the earth." Then he paused for air.

She stifled a giggle at his beautiful declarations and flowery words, for she suspected they had been written with great care, and quite likely rehearsed. But she wanted to hear more. "You didn't need to go to such extremes just to distract me from my fear of heights. But do go on. Please?"

"I love you so much, Tiffany, that I ask you before God and a large sampling of His wonderful creations here in the rainforest, including these nice people gathered around us, to be my wife. Will you marry me, Tiffany Faith? Will you be my wife? Will you say 'yes' and make me the happiest man on earth?"

Enraptured by his eloquent words, a dream proposal, she looked at him with a sincere smile that mirrored his, and in keeping with his technique, she said, "I will, Zachary Joseph Caldwell. I will because my love for you outshines the moon and the stars. Yes, I will marry you, for I love you far more than rafting on a river or hiking in a jungle. There could be no greater thrill than marrying you, not even spotting every quetzal in the jungle or floating amidst a blanket of flowers on gentle sea waves. You are my soul mate, and it is I who should be on my knees."

After laughing briefly together over their deliberate drama, Zachary asked, "Well then, won't you please kneel and kiss me?"

And she did.

As they sealed their intent to marry with a tender kiss, a happy howler barked approval from the bowels of the rainforest. And after the kiss ended, a toucan cawed joyfully somewhere in the distance. Then one of the onlookers shouted, "Pura Vida!"

Tiffany's smile turned to laughter as she recalled Costa Ricans use the phrase to express perseverance and gratitude for good fortune, whether large or small.

Zachary slipped a slim platinum ring on Tiffany's

finger. The delicate band held a single stone the size of a tiny teardrop similar to the one that settled in the corner of her eye. Then he kissed her again—this time with a soulful kiss like none she had ever known before. Profound contentment filled her as he pulled back and ran his hand through her hair. "I love everything about you, Tiffany, including your sweet curls."

"Kinky, not curly—but I'm glad you like my frizzy hair," she said, marveling at still yet another miracle.

A healthy dose of confidence surged through her as she glanced at the diamond, brighter than crystal clear water sparkling in brilliant sunshine. The stone matched her heart that glistened with hope.

With a wondrous smile, Zachary stood and opened his arms. "May I hold you again, my love?"

Surrounded by the mystique of the exotic rainforest, Tiffany's heart burst with love as she stood and stepped into Zachary's embrace. Her joy knew no bounds, making her feel lighter than a snowflake and higher than the stars.

Made in the USA
Charleston, SC
17 December 2013